Drug Smuggler's Guide
to Dating

Drug Smuggler's Guide to Dating

by

Mal Stevens

JEBWizard Publishing
Books with Character

Copyright

JEBWizard Publishing
37 Park Forest Rd,
Cranston, RI 02920

www.jebwizardpublishing.com

JEBWizard Publishing
Books with Character

Table of Contents

Dedication

For Laura, who always brings me home.

1   The Cheese

We were crowded into the side room, which always smelled of moldy feet. I think it was supposed to be a walk-in closet, but Derek had been using it as his office lately. The closeness of the walls probably appealed to him, being fresh in from the pokey and all.

He was leaned up in the doorway, shoulder on the frame, flexing his arms in his wife-beater t-shirt. His .357 rested casually in the back pocket of his jeans – "the drug dealer carry," Boyd called it. His feet were clad only in socks, the closest this bastard ever got to shoes, it seemed.

"Why me?" I had asked, glancing up from the pill I was leaning over and intently working on.

He let me use the little desk he kept in there to make it feel more like an office, but I was still struggling to prep the oxy. Once you got the coating off, it was usually smooth sailing, but this pill did not want to crush up well. I squirted a little more water in the spoon and gave a little stir.

"Boyd's so much better at this shit."

"I know he is, man, but you know how high strung he is. He's liable to flip out on these Mexican pricks."

He lowered his voice a little,

"I believe he's a little bit racist, brother."

I had been talking about cooking pills, but I knew Derek was right. Boyd was a much better bodyguard guard than me when it came down to it, but he was a little racist. Derek, on the other hand, was not racist. Not even a little bit, which in eastern Kentucky is a rarity, especially among convicts. I think that's why we got along right off the bat: he could tell I wasn't really either. A lot of guys come out of the joint more radicalized than when they went in, but Derek had made a black friend in there and changed his whole world view. He had told me all about it on the last arson job.

"Sometimes, you just have to really get to know someone to walk in their shoes, man, and you find out we're not so different after all," he had said.

I didn't know if mixed-race room mating in the clink was the answer to racial harmony, but it had made a difference for Derek anyway.

I was more of an equal opportunity hater, and whites were on my shit list, too, along with every other shade. My general worldview was that all people suck, especially when they are in homogenous groupings. And a group of homogenous whites was just about the worst group you'd ever encounter.

Derek was still talking while I worked on the pill and ignored the smell of cheese feet.

"This is a big deal, man, and I need someone with a cool head that I can trust."

It was a big deal for small-time hoods like us, anyway. This was narcotics smuggling. Across the border from Mexico. And not just as the mules, because Derek was putting in on the run and stood to make a decent return on his investment.

All I knew about Mexico was that the cartels apparently ran everything, and there was corruption everywhere. Don't drink the water and wear a rubber. Maybe two rubbers.

At least that's what people always said. Like I mentioned, I had never been there. Not even to Mexico's resort parts where well-educated young white men such as myself are supposed to go on spring break vacations and enjoy debauchery filled weeks of revelry.

I didn't know shit about Mexico.

Truth be told, I had dropped out of college before I even made it to spring break. Full scholarship, free ride, bright future in whatever field I had wanted to go into, I walked out on it all. I thought I had discovered my true calling in life: the needle and a spoon.

People will say, "But you're too smart to get mixed up in drugs," or, "You've got such a good upbringing, such a loving, Christian home life," or, "You know better, quit screwing around, you're wasting your God-given talent!"

3

I didn't care about any of that shit. I was tired of hearing about how great things were going to be when I graduated from college, Summa Cum Laude, of course. And I was tired of hearing how great it would be once I went on to graduate school where I would excel, of course, and find a rewarding career, doing something noble, of course. I would get married and have 2.5 children, a house and a car, and barbecues on weekends with my professional colleagues, living the American Dream.

I was tired of hearing about and planning for my bright future as an all-American boy. I didn't know if I wanted any of that shit at all. I didn't know much, except that I wasn't interested in the American collegiate dream anymore. All I knew for sure was that I was having the time of my life. I was living without a care in the world, always on the hunt for the next high. I didn't give a shit about anything.

And I knew I didn't know shit about Mexico

The flame had cooked up my concoction, dissolving the oxy in the water. I placed the tiny ball of cigarette filter in the liquid, and Derek handed me his rig first. I guess it was his pill, although I thought it would have been better protocol to offer me the first shot. He was asking me for a favor, after all.

"And I need you to keep your eye on her. Not that I don't trust her, it's not like that. She's not gonna rip me off. But ten grand is a lot of money, and that bastard that's going with her I don't really know. He's highly recommended by people I trust, but I don't know him. And I can't send her and Boyd off to Mexico with $10,000 of my money. C'mon, man."

He gave me a stern look shaking his head at the very idea.

That's when I knew that Derek knew about Mel and Boyd while he was in prison. I figured he probably didn't know about Mel and Boyd last week while he and I were on the arson job. Wouldn't be so cool about it right now if he knew about last week and the weekend before that. But he knew about their shenanigans while he was in prison.

"She's a grown woman. Got needs same as me. I was away a long time."

It was true. He had been gone a long time. Boyd had been banging Mel for a couple of years before Derek showed back up. She'd had a thing for Boyd from the first day we met her. Stevie 3 Finger had brought us over to her place where Mel was selling joints. She took a shine to Boyd right away.

We planned to get 3 for $10, Boyd, Randy, Stevie, and me, and smoke one joint with Stevie for the hookup. That would leave us two for the road, which would work out alright if we found some other party favor to go with it.

But when Mel saw Boyd, she told us to sit right down on the couch in the living room while she lit up a couple of joints and passed them around. She turned out to be a pretty cool chick. About ten years older than us, but still a looker for a dopehead. And she just kept smoking weed with us, joint after joint, one after another.

As other customers came to the door, she would conduct her business and send them on their way. She never offered to let any of them join us, and she never offered to sell us anything. She just kept lighting joints, talking to Randy about music, laughing easily, and smiling quickly. She was fun to hang with, really.

Stevie hung on forever, waiting for us to actually buy something so we could maintain our deal to smoke a joint with him for introducing us to his dealer. Finally, he just came out and asked if we were still gonna buy three for ten and split one.

We all stared silently at him for a full minute. It had been four hours, and Mel had smoked countless joints with us; I lost count at eight, but that was hours ago before dark even.

Mel broke the silence: "Jesus, Stevie. You didn't have to hang out all this time if all you wanted was a joint. Here, take this one and head on home. See you tomorrow, baby."

She smiled, handed him a joint, and ushered him to the door. He beamed from ear to ear, stuck out his hand to receive his bounty, and bid us all adieu.

"Were y'all trying to buy some weed? I forgot to ask.'"

Mel laughed and winked at Boyd as she locked the door behind Stevie 3 Finger and turned off the porch light. I guess business was done for the evening.

"That was the plan," I offered.

Mel took Boyd by the hand and said, "Well, Boyd, walk back here with me, and I'll get you some out of the good bag."

Randy and I looked at Boyd, and he looked at us. Wearing a big shit-eating grin, he said, "Yes, Ma'am," and followed her back to the bedroom.

Randy watched them with a look of disgust on his face until the door closed.

"You think that bag is any better than this shit out here?" he asked.

"Based on the amount of little kid toddler shit around here, I'd say that old bag is at least operational," I said as I lit up a smoke.

Randy found the television remote. We worked on evaluating her cable package, focusing on what that said about her parenting style and her overall life and business plans. At some point, we both must have passed out because I awoke to Boyd shaking my shoulder and hissing, "We gotta go, man. Her kids will be up soon."

"Her kids are *here*? Have they been here this whole time?"

7

"Apparently. I think she keeps them locked up in their room. Anyway, she said we should go."

"We've been here for hours! She keeps them locked up for hours?"

"What about the weed?" Randy spoke without opening his eyes or moving. I hadn't realized he was awake.

"She gave me some, don't worry, asshole," Boyd muttered.

"It didn't sound like that was all she gave you," Randy, the ball breaker, countered.

When we got outside to my 1985 Buick Regal, affectionately called "the Beast," Randy stretched out in the backseat, and Boyd took shotgun.

"Well, spill," I said as I fired that bastard up, after having added the prerequisite half bottle of power steering fluid.

There was a bad leak in there somewhere. I was thinking of switching to transmission fluid since it was cheaper. It was just gonna leak out of the power steering system daily anyway. Lube is lube, I'd heard from a crackhead one time.

"Jesus Christ, she can fuck. Shit, I've only seen it on tv. I thought Andromeda knew her way around a blowjob, but Jesus Christ, Mel puts her to shame!"

Andromeda was one of the other older women Boyd fooled with. Andromeda had been a substitute teacher at the high school, back when Boyd, Randy, and me were still in middle school; until she got in trouble.

Turns out, she had a thing for high school boys and got caught in a compromising position with four of the starters on the football team and the whole basketball starting five. Pictures were everywhere. This was before the internet, so you had to know somebody with the Polaroids. And those Polaroids made the rounds, eventually ending up in front of the Superintendent of Schools.

Andromeda never worked at the school again, but nothing else ever became of it. Small town sweeping it under the rug, I guess. Same as when the football coach knocked up a cheerleader, and the basketball coach left his wife and married one of the other cheerleaders on her 18th birthday. I guess it was a common sort of thing for the teachers to fuck the students around there.

Anyway, nowadays, Andromeda cruises the tristate area's deserted backroads looking for young male hitchhikers in the mood for a good time. And according to Boyd, it's a pretty good time.

"So, you fucked her then?" I asked.

"Yeah, I fucked her! I fucked her four times, how you like that, Randy!"

Randy opened one eye, glared at Boyd, and rolled over.

"Well, we'll never hear the end of that shit either, will we, Jack?" Randy called out; his face buried inside the crevice where the seat base meets the seatback.

I laughed, but Randy was right. We never did really ever hear the end of it. We became fixtures at Mel's house. Not every day, but most, at least for a quickie. She always sold us good weed at good prices when she sold it to us.

Mostly she just gave it to us, or Boyd worked it off in trade. Randy and I would smoke while they fucked, then we'd all smoke, then they'd go fuck again, and so forth.

Randy and I thought it was a great system. And even though Boyd pissed and moaned about us pimpin' him for pot, he enjoyed himself. Mel was a cool chick, and Boyd always talked about how good in bed she was. He always talked about how good in bed older women were, in general. Boyd had a thing for cougars, especially if they came with dope.

This went on for years. We were with her when she moved the operation to Ferndale. And when she moved across the border to Tennessee. And when she moved up into Frakes. A successful drug dealing operation has to be slightly mobile. Your loyal customers will find the new spot, and the narcs will be in the dark for a few months.

Randy left us and joined the Marines. Actually, we all joined, but the military has this policy about drug use, so they sent Boyd and me home after a few months. Neither of us could seem to kick the habit, so he and Mel just picked up where they left off.

So, with no Randy, I had to smoke by myself sometimes during the sexcapades. It wasn't bad unless the kids were loose. They were little terrors, as all children are.

The big one always spoke for the little one.

"My brother wants some cheese," she'd say.

"Far out," I'd say. "Go for it."

"He puts it in his diaper," she'd say.

It was true; I had seen the little fucker do it.

"What's your mom say?" I'd ask, and she'd run off to get the cheese, which little brother would promptly stick down his diaper.

He'd find it later when he changed it, I figured.

He changed his own diapers; the poor bastard was four or five years old, at least. Probably should have been in school or daycare or something.

It was easier when they stayed in their room. There was a baby gate that still befuddled them, poor little idiots. The girl was six or seven and should have been able to work a baby gate. But alas, they were morons. Comes from upbringing and shitty genes, my mother always said.

And then one day, Boyd and I went over to Mel's, knocked on the door, and Derek answered. He smiled all

11

big and said, "It's so great to finally meet you guys. Mel's told me so much about you!"

We neglected to tell *him* she had neglected to tell *us* about *him*.

We got no free weed that day, which was a bummer, 'cause that was all the budget would afford that day. We got along great with Derek, though. He apparently viewed us as Mel's two good friends that hung out sometimes. Since we were closer in age to her sister Tracey, who we were also friends with, Mel played it off that we came around with Tracey quite a bit.

It turns out, Derek and Mel had been together forever. He was the father of the older kid and alleged father of the younger kid, although I didn't think the math worked out on that one. He had been in the big house for armed robbery, of course, and I wasn't sure they had a conjugal visit program at Big Sandy.

Boyd and Mel laid low, but we still went there to buy pot because they were the best deal going. And besides the Xanax that Mel had started to peddle, Derek brought oxycontin into the mix. And even though Mel couldn't fuck Boyd wide open anymore, she still snuck us pills and joints when Derek wasn't looking, and Boyd snuck her the cod on occasion.

I did side jobs with Derek. His parolee job was through his dad's painting company, and I sometimes went with him to help. He only worked once a month, so he could have a paystub, and his dad would send him to small bullshit jobs he didn't want to fuck with himself. Derek would throw me $20 and some pills, and we'd roll out some walls.

Derek also did more lucrative side work, and I helped him out with that, too. If it was something big, Boyd would go as well, but he didn't like working with Derek.

So, for small shit, burglaries, targeted vandalism for intimidation purposes, dope runs, and insurance jobs, I would go with Derek alone. Which meant Boyd and Mel were alone. Well, not really alone. There were two kids who might be Derek's, a dog, two cats, a parakeet, and the goldfish, but they were alone enough to do the deed, I guess. Boyd kept showing up with hickeys.

Boyd was a hickey wearing motherfucker, always. He must tell them bitches to bite him or something, 'cause I never seen nothing like it. He had a whole system worked out with frozen spoons. He would massage and work on the hickeys with the frozen spoons, and he swore the hickeys would go away. I guess it worked, but I never knew how long a hickey would last without spoon treatments. I didn't have a horny drug dealer regularly biting the shit out of me, so I was a little in the dark.

All I knew for sure was that all the spoons were freezer spoons or dope spoons at our house, so cereal was a real bitch.

13

And now, on this day, in the walk-in closet turned criminal mastermind lair, Derek was telling me he knew Boyd and Mel were fucking while he was in prison. I decided not to bring up that many times Boyd didn't even really want to. We just were broke junkies. I didn't think that psychological nugget would help.

"I understand, I'm not mad," Derek was saying, eyes closed, body slumping down, down the doorway, finally resting on the floor, in a heap, needle dropping from his powerless hand, belt slipping down his bicep.

I could tell that greedy fucker had made his shot too big. His pill, I guess.

The sensation rushed in with the downward plunge, and I could feel my eyes rolling back, back, into my head, where they could see the wondrous things. I leaned back in the cheap desk chair, back, and back, and back, until I was floating up to the sky.

"Will you do it, man? For me?"

Derek was still talking somehow. How, I don't know. He was slumped all the way over, head resting on the floor. I could barely hear him as I passed up and up and up, higher and higher, past the trees and through the clouds.

"What the fuck, why not?" I heard myself say. "I've never been to Mexico…"

I beamed my message back down to Derek, down through the clouds, down through the trees, back into the house, and way down there to the floor.

Derek lay there, on the floor, halfway between the closet-office and the hallway. I realized, through the haze, he was obstructing the path of his maybe-baby. The pudgy preschooler lifted one leg, then the other over the comatose body in the hallway, slice of cheese grasped firmly in his little fist. He tore off a corner, placed it next to Derek's needle, and stuck the rest down the back of his diaper. Then he patted Derek on the head and wandered off toward the kitchen, no doubt in search of a slice of cheese for the other cheek.

"I'll be damned," I thought, as my consciousness exhaled its last breath. "the little mute bastard has figured out the baby gate. How long has that been going on?"

2 Fucking Boyfriend Day

B oyd dug in the closet for the black gym bag, his face awash with annoyance.

"What do you mean you don't need luggage?" You have to have some kind of luggage to make a vacation look like a vacation. Jesus."

I was waiting an hour before I told him I didn't need the bag. He had looked all over the trailer and had accidentally straightened the place up. You had to trick Boyd into cleaning, of course. In its natural state, the trailer and its inhabitants were just a step above hazmat status. We littered the place with beer cans and cigarette butts, fast food wrappers and used water bottles. We mostly used the water for cooking pills. Still, I suppose we drank the occasional bottle when the cotton mouth became unbearable.

"They said don't bring anything; they had it covered," I finally tried to explain.

"That's gonna look really fucking clever; they search you and find someone else's clothes in your bag. Real smooth. Jesus."

Boyd was waist-deep under the bed, his voice slightly muffled. Two baseball bats and brass knuckles had emerged from under the bed, a happy byproduct of the

16

suitcase search. Boyd had also made an obscenely large pile of used condoms, plucked from somewhere under there. I hoped they were bound for the trash can, but there are no guarantees in this world. They seemed to inch closer to the dirty laundry pile growing by leaps and bounds. I wondered what else might be under there in the darkness.

"What?" I yelled so his deaf ass could hear me under the bed. Not because I hadn't heard him, just to fuck with him.

Despite being half-deaf himself, and always needing things repeated to him, Boyd hated having to repeat himself.

"I said your clothes in the luggage should match the clothes on your body. So it doesn't look suspicious. What, are you gonna fill your luggage with Derek's clothes? I think he only has skinny jeans and wife beaters."

It was true; that seemed to be Derek's basic uniform. Probably had a closet full of the same outfit, like Ernest P. Worrel.

"I thought we were keeping black powder and blasting caps in it and hid it around here somewhere?" Boyd asked as he squirmed out from under the bed.

"We decided keeping the incendiary and the catalyst in the same gym bag was a bad idea. So the caps are in the fart fan, which is why it's disconnected, and you have to open the window to take a shit. I don't know where Randy hid the powder," I replied.

Boyd looked concerned by my answer.

"We have to open the window to take a shit?"

He shook his head in bewilderment.

"Who fucking knows, then," he said. "Randy was acting so weird before he left; we should have taken the powder ourselves. Shit."

Randy had been acting weird his whole life, but he acted especially weird before joining the Marines.

We had gotten pulled over a couple of months before his ship date for driving through Pineville after dark. That was all it took around there.

I hadn't been drinking, so I passed the breathalyzer no problem.

Of course, I was fucked up from popping pills and smoking weed all day, but I wasn't drunk. They gave me field sobriety tests, which I don't recall, but Boyd and Randy said I passed with flying colors. Even the fat cop was impressed with my ability to stand on one leg and touch my toes and sing the alphabet backward.

The fat cop walked me back to my car, telling me to have a safe evening, and when he gets next to the rear window, he looks down through the glass and sees Randy pulling a cigarette out of his pack.

Unfortunately, prominently displayed in the cellophane around the cigarette pack, not in the pack like a normal person, but outside the pack, held by the transparent film of the packaging, like an idiot, was a big, fat joint.

That fat cop couldn't believe what he was seeing, but he was awfully excited to be seeing it. He ordered Randy out of the car and confiscated the marijuana. He searched the car but didn't find anything else because Boyd had enough sense to hide the dope he was holding.

I had enough sense to let Boyd hold the dope while I was driving. So only Randy had to go downtown to the holding cell.

It was bullshit, one joint. What the fuck?

Randy's recruiter answered Boyd's 2:00 a.m. phone call, and he had Randy out by 10:00 a.m.; charges dropped because of Randy being about to ship out and serve his country and all that jazz.

Randy was so fucking mad at Boyd for having called the recruiter and so mad at me for getting pulled over. But his anger shifted onto the cop who had pulled us over and made this whole thing into such a big deal.

He wanted to kill the fat bastard as his final act before he 'straightened his life up' as he put it. We scoped the cop for a couple of days, mostly to pacify Randy. He was a prick, this cop, but privately, Boyd and I objected to killing him just for pulling us over and arresting Randy.

19

Maybe a reprimand or a warning or some shit like that, but to kill the bastard? It was too much.

To be honest about it, we both felt Randy should have done something better with that joint. Anything more subtle than waving it in the cop's face would have sufficed.

So, we came up with the idea of channeling his anger and rage into a more creative solution: blowing up a State Trooper's car always parked overnight at the tire shop down on Highway 92.

Randy was all for it, he liked things that went boom, so we set about getting our bombmaking materials together. It would be a simple pipe bomb with railroad ties for shrapnel.

We figured we'd set it off one night when my parents were out of town, so we could use their house to hide in. Their house was only about two miles from the target, and they were headed to Alabama to visit family for a couple of weeks anyway.

Everything was set. We did a dry run to make sure we had the escape route mapped out right and planned to carry out our domestic terrorism the next night.

After the dry run, we stayed at my parents' house, raiding their medicine cabinet for old dental surgery prescriptions. My father had bad luck with dentists but never took the good pills they always gave him. We always raided my father's dental meds when they went out of town. I figure my parents were on to us because Mom always had a ton of leftovers in the fridge and freezer when they'd leave. I know she never left the fridge full of food when we went out of town growing up. She was always worried about the power going out and everything spoiling and being a huge pain in the ass to clean up. I always figured she was leaving extra food on purpose.

So we feasted and did all the Percocet and passed out in my parents' ultra-Christian home, homemade bomb safely tucked under the couch.

I woke up the next morning to Boyd and Randy deep in conversation about not doing the job. They had both had dreams about it not going well, and they were both freaked out about it. I was a little freaked out that they were both having cold feet the morning of D-day, but I didn't press them. Randy thought he needed revenge, and Boyd came up with the bomb idea. So, if they didn't want to do it, fuck it. There wasn't any money in this job anyway. All I wanted was to get high, as per the usual. My dad was out of Percs, and it was time to hit the road.

We called the whole thing off and took the bomb apart, which was scarier than when we put the fucker together. Randy said he wanted to get dropped off at his dad's house to see his little brother for a couple of days before he left, so we took him down to Clear Creek.

Randy's dad was a student at the Bible college, where my dad worked. It was a weird little community of ultra-conservative Southern Baptists. My dad taught end of the world theology, which I suppose one might think we were living through.

Randy's dad did just enough to remain enrolled. We figured the student housing was cheap, especially the family housing. Randy's dad took advantage of the system a little bit. He didn't seem that interested in graduating. He had been preaching for years without a degree as a pastor at one of the small churches down by the creek. If he had to sign up for some courses, paid by grants and donations, in exchange for some of the cheapest rent in the area, so be it.

There was concern in my father's office about Randy's dad's lack of initiative and utter failure to matriculate in a timely fashion. They also didn't like him constantly dumping full ashtrays down the toilet, eventually clogged the entire building's plumbing. That got blamed on us, of course, but Randy's dad smoked more than the three of us combined. And drank vodka like it was his job, the drunk preacher in training. My father's office should have been worried about that shit, especially after Randy's mom killed herself to get away from the bastard.

Randy's family had a lot going on, always.

As we pulled out of the parking lot at his dad's building, Randy waved from the balcony, sort of a weird, slow wave like the Queen does.

"What the fuck is up with Randy? He's cracking up over joining the Marines, I think." I said to Boyd as we neared the highway.

"I don't know about that, but what I do know is we better be careful around him until he goes. In my dream last night, we were on the way to deliver the package. Randy was holding it in back like we talked about. As we got to the spot, he handed it up to me, but he had cut the fuse almost all the way off, and he had lit it.

"I woke up with the image of an apple with nails sticking out of it burned in my mind. I don't know exactly what it means, but I know it means we can't do this thing with Randy, or we'll die."

"Fucking hell, man. That is intense. Did you tell Randy about your dream?"

"Not exactly. He woke me up telling me he had a dream where we all died in an explosion."

Boyd looked over at me and said, "I didn't tell him any details from my dream, just that we all blew up."

"I wonder if he detonated the bomb in his dream too?" I asked. "Fucking hell, man."

Boyd had always sort of had a sixth sense about such things, a sort of clairvoyance. He just always knew shit. I knew it was because of the Room, or at least the Room had something to do with it—some sort of family thing.

Back to my luggage problems. "Do you think the bag is in the Room?"

Boyd was leaning on the hallway doorjamb, digging in his pocket for a lighter.

"Why would it be in there?" I asked, hoping there was no good reason he could think of.

"Only one reason," he replied. "To fuck with us."

That's always the worst reason.

We didn't go in the Room. Ever. For any reason. We were living in a two-bedroom single-wide trailer on the outskirts of Pineville, USA. A trailer that technically belonged to Boyd's grandmother, who lived across the park at her daughter Lindsey's.

Aunt Lindsey had a double wide that was much bigger and nicer, although you had to put up with Aunt Lindsey and Colby. Luckily, Memaw had a system for dealing with Aunt Lindsey and Colby that involved Xanax, coffee, cigarettes, and more Xanax. It was an excellent system.

Now, Memaw liked to cook, but she and Aunt Lindsey were usually too pilled up to eat. Instead, they spent their time overfeeding Lindsey's son, Colby. He was a whale of a kid, solid deuce and a half at age six. Boyd always said we had to go over there to eat Memaw and Aunt Lindsey's share because they were just going to feed Colby. And at this rate, he was gonna have a heart attack before he hit puberty.

"Do it for Baby Huey," he'd say when I objected that I wasn't hungry and didn't want to kill my buzz. "We're saving that boy, one piece of fried chicken at a time."

So, as a dutiful grandson, accompanied by his somewhat reluctant friend, we would go over to Aunt Lindsey's and kill our buzz any time Memaw called and said, "Come eat!"

She would always throw in a Xanax, or maybe two if they were the peach ones, with your plate of food. Memaw liked to share everything. And she always said how much she liked us living there and keeping the place up, although you could not tell we were keeping the place up.

 It sure didn't feel very kept up.

She would pop in periodically, kick us out for the day, straighten things up, and then have her boyfriend, Willem, over. She was in her late 70's by this point.

Boyd would complain on boyfriend day because we had to get up early and go, but we always had a good time. I liked the wake and bake and hit the road nature of boyfriend day.

"What do you think goes on in there, on boyfriend day?" I had asked one morning after she had kicked us out.

We were on the way to Pathfork to see Boyd's grandfather, Memaw's ex. Sometimes we'd go see Pepaw on boyfriend day and rile him up.

They hadn't been married for 30 years, but he'd still get jealous and try to buy Boyd's affection, to prove he was the better grandparent. The more upstanding one, the one not "still running around like a goddamn teenager," as he put it. I think it actually turned him on a little bit that Memaw was still out there getting' it.

It didn't matter anyway because he was definitely not more upstanding. He let us help him with a couple of his pot patches this year — to help Boyd get into the family business, I guess. We were excited about it and couldn't wait for spring to get here. On this particular boyfriend day, we were planning to go scout out possible sites with him. It was still too early to plant anything, but he liked to scope out a few choice spots ahead of time.

"She makes Willem dinner, and they eat it in the living room on the TV trays watching whatever movie is on the black and white station. Then she takes her teeth out and sucks his dick. He gives her a few hundred bucks, like an allowance till next time. They have dessert, and Willem goes home.

"And don't hit Totsy; she's on the move and weaving."

Boyd was right; Totsy was on the move and weaving. I had been staring at him with a dumb look on my face as he explained the particulars of boyfriend day. I swerved back into my lane, although we were still quite a way from actually hitting Totsy. Boyd had spied her shaking that thang from afar.

We were rounding the curve before the Pathfork bridge, passing the store that sometimes-had gas, and sometimes-had good cigarettes, but always had overpriced narcotics.

They were the only store around: captive audience and all that.

Totsy, the prettiest prostitute in three counties, was staggering back to the bridge from the store, dangerously close to the white line, sorta zigzagging along it. The other side of the shoulder from the white line was the guardrail and a 75-foot drop down to the Cumberland River, so I guess Totsy was picking her poison. I slowed down and stopped as we pulled up beside her.

"Morning Totsy," Boyd called out the window to her. "Rough night?"

Boyd smiled up at her as he handed a cigarette out the window. Totsy didn't appear to have her eyes open as she took the butt and stuck it in her mouth. Boyd held the lighter out the window and flicked the flame to life, sheltering it from the gentle breeze with his hand. Totsy leaned over, rested her forehead against the doorframe, and touched the end of her cigarette to the flame. She inhaled deeply.

"They're all rough nights, Boyd, you know that's how I like it," Totsy said as she slowly exhaled. "You headed up to your Pepaw's? Tell him I said 'hey' and that I might be up there later. Depends who stops down by here today."

She opened one eye enough to wink it at me as she said, "How you doin,' baby?"

I nodded at her and touched the brim of my hat with my finger.

"Always better when I get to see you, Totsy."

She already had her eyes closed again and had missed my tip of the cap. 19th Century chivalry was lost on this generation, I thought to myself.

"We can give you a ride up there if you want." Boyd offered.

"Nah, I gotta make some money before I go up there. And while it would be fun as fuck, you two broke motherfuckers can't afford my rates," Totsy said with a smile.

She was a very pretty girl if you looked past the whoring and the track marks.

"Maybe I'll see you boys later if you're still around. For now, though..."

28

She waved her hand back at us as she shook her moneymaker on down the shoulder to post up at her favorite spot on this side of the bridge.

"You have to catch 'em on this side of the river before they get up into Pathfork holler and spend all their money on dope," Totsy always said.

It was an accurate assessment of the holler.

I pulled back out onto the road and crossed the bridge leading to Pathfork, thinking about my preference for dope over whores.

"Why'd you say Memaw was sucking Willem's dick? That's fucked up to say about your own grandmother, bro."

I couldn't resist needling Boyd a little bit more about his grandmother's fellatio habit.

He looked over at me with a bewildered look.

"Because you asked, and that was what it looked like was going on when I came over there too early one time when I was eight! And fuck you for sitting here thinking about my grandmother with a cock in her mouth!"

At which point, he punched my shoulder, too hard I thought, considering he put the dicksucking Memaw image in my mind in the first place.

"You could have at least cleaned it up a little bit, cut out some of the debauchery, for my sake."

I grinned to let him know I was just fucking around.

"We are on the way to my pill-dealing grandfather's house to discuss an upcoming pot-growing enterprise; we are on a first-name basis with known prostitutes; we have two stolen handguns in the car and a little bag of coke in the glovebox, and you think my grandmother's oral sex habits are the debauchery we should be worried about?"

He shook his head. "Fuckin' Boyfriend Day."

"How much coke in a baggy in the glovebox?" I asked.

Boyd had been right that day. Memaw was sucking Willem's dick, but that was not the debauchery we should be worried about. And he was right today, too. It was all the other debauchery that had led us to this moment, looking for a gym bag with which to smuggle drugs across international borders; that was the debauchery we should worry about.

A gym bag that might contain explosives.

"Do you really think the bag is in the Room?" I asked again. "It's probably not. And they said not to bring anything anyway. Fuck going in there to look for it."

The Room had belonged to Memaw's brother way back in the day and was probably the real reason she didn't live in the trailer anymore. Her brother, Mat, was part Indian, part white, part Mexican, and all evil. He had been a voodoo witch doctor of sorts, at least that is what everybody said.

This was before my time with the family.

The stories were that he was a practitioner of the black arts, always putting hexes and spells and curses on people and places. He had allegedly killed six men, and the family had many stories about him, fucked up stories that would make your hair stand up.

His room had little in it: a twin bed, bedside table with a lamp, and an electric alarm clock that blinked 6:00 a.m. all the time no matter how often you set it or how often you unplugged it.

A weird cuckoo clock-looking church thing hung on the wall, little stain glass windows shining in the little bit of sunlight that the small dirty window let in.

When we had moved into the trailer, Boyd had said I could stay in that room if I wanted to. But he was recommending the couch. I went to sleep on the couch the first night, and around 2 am, I woke up to take a piss. I decided to see what was up with the Room. I could hear Boyd snoring down the hall as I stood in front of the Room's door, gathering my courage. Finally, I opened the door and peered inside.

The first thing to hit me was the heat; it was at least 100 degrees in there. The room was bathed in red light, although it was not apparent where the light was coming from.

The alarm clock blinked 6:00 a.m.

The only other movement was the weird cuckoo church thing, spinning around and around at an alarming rate. I stepped back, slammed the door, and heard Boyd call out, "I fucking told you! Let me know if it comes out of the Room."

Because of that first night, I slept on the couch from then on. Uncle Mat can have his fucking room. And any gym bags full of explosives that might be in there.

3 My Sister's Damn Coochie

When we arrived at Mel's, with no luggage, of course, they were already loading the car. Mike, the team member none of us really knew, had a clean Saturn we would use. He was clean-cut too, Polo shirt, little mustache, mirrored sunglasses.

"He looks like a cop; what the fuck?" I said to Derek when I cornered him in the house. He had gone in to look for a gym bag for me.

"He's Wolf's guy, from up Lexington, I guess. Doesn't really come around here except for these runs. Wolf is a snakey fuck, but I don't think he is gonna send $30k with just anybody. If he trusts this guy, I guess we can too."

Derek continued, "Besides, we are too small-time to be the mark if it's a setup. The Feds could just violate my parole if that was what this was about. We have a goddam arsenal in here. Speaking of…"

Derek reached in his back pocket and pulled out a snub-nosed .38, which he handed to me.

"Just in case, brother. Don't want you rolling out here naked. Just play it cool, follow Mike's lead, and stay close to Mel. Everything's under control," he said with a weak smile that did not fill me with confidence.

33

I think he was trying to convince himself that everything was under control, but he wasn't fooling me. I had my doubts.

Tracy had arrived, Mel's little sister, driven by her boyfriend, Glenn. They were in his hoopty. Glenn always kept a nice car: rims, a loud stereo, plenty of chrome, the whole nine.

"What's up, my brotha from anotha motha?" Glenn greeted me, giving me a high five and a fist bump. "What's happenin', Boyd?"

We all loved Glenn, easily the coolest black guy any of us knew.

"Glad we not sendin' Casanova here off with our women, right Big D?" Glenn winked at Boyd. Gotta love Glenn.

"Jack will keep his eye on 'em for us, right bro?" he said with another wink and a grin.

Mike slammed the trunk and called out, "Let's hit the road, travelers. We'll let you know when we are on the way back."

Mike had an easy confidence about him that made you believe he might actually pull this off. He was Wolf's guy, after all.

Wolf had been selling dope since they invented dope. Owned a couple of gas stations in the county he sold out of. Big, fat, nasty son of a bitch. He had killed a few they knew about, a couple right in his gas station in town.

But they never could pin anything on him. Hung juries and lack of evidence seemed to rule the day with Wolf.

I had to admit, I was feeling better about having this level of professionalism leading this expedition. Mike laid out the rules as we drove out of Frakes holler in our little blue Saturn. He told us it was about twenty hours of driving, and he and Mel would split it between them. We would stop every four hours for bathroom breaks, always at busy truck-stops where we would just blend in. He gave us each $50 to buy food, drinks, and sundries, a per diem he called it.

I figured when I ran out, I would tell him per diem meant per day, and since this was about a 48-hour operation, I was gonna need another $50.

He and Mel both thought I should give them the gun Derek had given me, less liability since I wasn't 21 yet. They said they would give it back when we got to Mexico, where there were no laws.

I complied with their request because I had brought my own gun anyway, a nickel-plated 357 Magnum snubby. You just can't beat a good wheel gun in a pinch. And mine was nice and heavy, all the better to beat somebody with if it came to that.

Between it and my two knives, I figured I wouldn't have gotten to Derek's little .38 special anyway.

"Now this is the important part. Mel is gonna give each of you two valiums now and two valiums later tonight. They will help with sleeping, help with your nerves, whatever. But that is it: no pot, no other pills, just these valiums from her prescription bottle. We can't have any other drugs in the car at all.

"On the way back, you can each hold one of your new prescription bottles and take a couple, but no crushing, snorting, or cooking. We can't be fucked up on dope at any point in this operation. When we arrive safe and sound, you'll each get your other bottle of oxy and the cash you worked out with Derek. Everybody got it? If you have any other dope, throw it out the window right now."

Mike sounded serious about this drug-free policy, but I knew better than to bring up the personal stash I was holding.

It sounded like a solid plan, at least for me. I stood to make $200 cash and two bottles of oxy 40, which went for a dollar a milligram in those days. So, in theory, they could be turned into $2,400. Of course, Boyd and I would do about half of them, at least, but I still figured to walk away with around a grand and a bunch of dope. Not bad for riding in a car for a couple of days.

Boyd had brought up that everybody else involved, except maybe Tracey, stood to make a great deal more than me, but I figured that was okay. I'm sure Mike was getting paid well. Mel, Derek, and Wolf put in 40 grand between them up-front to purchase the dope. Takes money to make money I figured.

The scam was simple. The four of us would walk into Mexico, see a doctor, and receive prescriptions for 90-day supplies of oxy 80, Oxy 40, Oxy 20, Percocet 10, Lortab 7.5, blue valium, and blue Xanax. We would then take these prescriptions to several pharmacies, having them filled over and over until we ran out of money.

Then, we walk through customs where Mike's guy would stamp one complete set of prescriptions for each of us. We'd conceal the rest of the unstamped prescriptions in the trunk of the car, with our luggage containing the stamped prescriptions right on top. The drug dogs would smell us at the checkpoint, but we had all the stamped, legal medications right on top. Mike's *other* guy at the driving checkpoint could legitimately conclude those legal scripts were what the dogs were smelling. It sounded like a solid plan, and Mike said he had done it hundreds of times with these guys at the border. I thought it would definitely work.

The trip down was fairly uneventful. I dutifully ate my two valiums, hung out with Tracey, endured Mike and

Mel's country music, and caught up on my sleep. At least we could smoke in the car, and I had plenty of cigarettes.

I smoked my joint I had brought at a truck stop somewhere in Mississippi. I snuck off while Mel was getting food and Mike was taking a shit and checking in with Wolf. I walked out past the parked semis and discovered Tracey smoking a joint too.

"I can't ride in a car this long with no pot; this is ridiculous," she said.

I agreed, and we got high under the moonlight with the sound of the interstate roaring by, talking about how Mel seemed to be into Mike. When we got back to the Saturn, Mel knew what was up, but she just smiled and put her hand over on Mike's leg as he pulled out of the truck stop and back onto the interstate.

"I was just telling Mike we should stop somewhere so we can freshen up before we cross, Motel 6 or something."

Tracey poked me and gave a knowing nod as Mel made her suggestion. I had to look away to not laugh.

We stopped at a shitty little motel somewhere in Texas, not as nice as the Motel 6, but nice enough for our purposes, I guess. Mike paid for the room, and we all took turns in the shower.

Tracey went first, and I claimed second. I hurried outside to look for her, hoping she had another joint. Also, Mel gave me the high sign to get the fuck out of the way and quit cockblocking her.

Luckily, Tracey was more prepared than me and had a joint ready when we sat down at the little picnic tables that occupied the grass between the parking lot and the rooms.

"Sort of a dump," Tracey observed as she hit the joint. "The Magnolia Inn. I don't see any fucking magnolias around here. Just as well, they smell like shit anyway."

Never one to argue with a beautiful woman holding the weed, I kept my affinity for magnolia trees to myself and took the joint when she handed it to me.

Mel and Mike emerged after about an hour, freshly showered, and glowing that glow you can only get from cheating on your spouse in a cheap motel.

I hoped Derek wasn't gonna dock my pay because of his wife being slutty. Tracey must've read my mind because she said, "And D was worried about sending Boyd with us. He doesn't know my sister at all. She was gonna fuck whoever came on this trip. Lucky it's not you, Jack. You don't want to get caught up in my sister's damn coochie."

"Oh Tracey, you're the sister I'm after anyway," I said.

We both laughed, knowing she would never cheat on Glenn, and I wouldn't fuck Glenn's girl. Friends don't do that.

"Come on, you two, stop talking shit about me and get in the car," Mel called mischievously as Mike loaded the luggage back in the car.

I wondered if he got an hourly rate or had to pay for the whole night at the ole Magnolia Inn. We headed back out onto the road for the last few miles of the journey.

The smile on Mike's face seemed to suggest he was happy with whatever rate he'd had to pay for the room. Tracey was right, though. It was better not to get caught up in her sister's damn coochie. There was enough of a love triangle going on in there already.

4 Smooth Sailing

We got into Mexico, no problem. Apparently, they don't give a fuck what you bring into their country. Mel took a thousand pictures to make it look like a vacation, she said. Tracey and I bought a couple of blankets and some touristy trinkets to make it look good, then we hit the doctor's office.

I guess you could call it an office. It had a desk at least, and a waiting room, with those crappy plastic waiting room chairs. They brought us right in as if they were expecting us.

We gave our IDs to the 'doctor,' who busily began filling out prescriptions for us as his assistant counted the pile of money Mike gave him. The assistant seemed satisfied with the count and left through the back with the money. The doctor finished filling out our prescriptions, gave us a gold-toothed smile, and walked us back out through the waiting room and into the bright Mexican sunlight. Jesus, it was bright down here.

We then went from Pharmacia to Pharmacia, filling and refilling the gold-toothed doctor's prescriptions until Mike's bag of money became two suitcases full of prescription narcotics. I was wired and paranoid as fuck because I had hit my coke when we left the doctor's office.

It turned out Tracey had the same idea, 'cause after the fourth Pharmacia, she gave me a little bump out of her coke stash too.

I was surprised that no one seemed to follow the gringos turning a bag of money into a bag of dope, but I guess our tourist cover must have been good enough for the local hoodlums. Mike looked square enough, like a manager of a Footlocker or some other shitty mall store, down in sunny Mexico with his strung-out girlfriend. OK, OK -- Mel sort of hurt his cover. But Tracey and me walking arm in arm, laughing and joking like we didn't have a care in the world probably carried the overall performance. Cocaine is a hell of a drug.

I was nervous as we walked back across the bridge with two suitcases of dope, but Mike's guy stamped us through. He asked the prerequisite questions about why we were visiting Mexico and carefully stamped the prescriptions we handed him while ignoring all the rest in the luggage. He saw everything, of course, but he just kept the line moving. Mike did have shit organized.

When we got back to the car, Mike pulled us around behind a self-storage place and repacked everything in the trunk. He gave us each a bottle of oxy, hid all the unstamped pills, and placed each person's stamped scripts in their luggage.

Mel slipped Tracey and me each a valium to help us come down off the coke before we got to the checkpoint. You don't want to be too wired around those damn drug dogs, nerve-wracking furry bastards that they are. Tracey immediately popped open her oxy, peeled the coating off one like you do when you cook it, and tossed it in her mouth. I could hear her chewing it up to make it work faster.

I didn't take any oxy before the checkpoint, I wanted a clear head, and I wasn't ready to switch to downers yet.

The checkpoint went just like Mike said it would. The dogs barked, we pulled to the side, and they had us sit on the curb while Mike's guy 'searched' the car. He found the stamped prescriptions, compared them to each of our id's, and sent us on our way. Easy.

I immediately popped two oxys and woke up in Tennessee, just outside Knoxville.

Everybody was high, in high spirits, and singing Rocky Top. Fucking SEC. My road trip companions had apparently had fun for the past 14 hours while I slept. We stopped and got a little bottle of bourbon to celebrate when we got off the highway, and by the time we were back in the Bluegrass, I was lit.

We made it up to Frakes, where Derek and Glenn were waiting for us. Boyd had not yet arrived with my car, so I went inside while they divided the loot; Mike quickly left with Wolf's share. Glenn and Tracey hung out for a little while, did a pill, and then headed home to bang one out.

I hung out staring blankly at the TV blue screen, high and waiting for Boyd. Derek and Mel were back in the bedroom, counting up their pills. As soon as Derek emerged, I knew something was up.

"Hey man, thanks for doing this. I felt better knowing you were keeping an eye on things for me."

I felt a little dishonest when I told him everything seemed to go smoothly.

"Listen," he said. "Here's the thing. We didn't make out as well as we hoped. Still pretty good, but Mike hit us for some expenses. So, I was wondering if I could buy back one of your pill bottles at cost?"

I wondered if the Magnolia Inn was one of the expenses Derek got hit with.

But I had been thinking something like this could come up, so I had a counter offer ready. "How about the $200 in cash, one oxy 40 bottle and one oxy 20 bottle?" I knew I was losing money, but Boyd and I didn't have enough sense to actually sell the dope off and make the $2,400 anyway. I would have ended up selling them back to Derek either way, to keep us from shooting all the pills and overdosing.

Derek scratched his chin.

"OK," he said. "but how about instead of the oxy 20 bottle, I give you another $200 in cash?"

I liked Derek, and I did just stand idly by while Mike fucked his old lady, and I wasn't going to tell him about it. So, we settled on an extra $300 instead of the oxy 20. We shook on it, and there was a knock at the door.

"That's probably Boyd. Let him in while I go get your money."

Boyd looked a little drunk, so we didn't stay long, and I drove us home.

"How'd we make out?" Boyd mumbled, lighting a smoke as we hit the main road.

"Bottle of oxy 40, $500 cash, and the bottle of 20s from the ride home they forgot about. Plus, I kept the second $50 per diem. Not bad for two days in the car."

Boyd agreed, but the Oxy I gave him to crush up for the ride home could have swayed his judgment a bit.

5   Pizza Rolls

We decided to lay low for a while to preserve our stash. Nothing worse than all your junkie acquaintances finding out you're holding. We needed pot, but we didn't want to go back to Mel's for a while; better to let shit cool off and settle out over there too.

Instead, we paid a visit to Trey, who had better dope anyway. We usually couldn't afford to shop there since he only wanted to sell ounces and up, and we never had any money. But today, we were flush. And an ounce of good pot would go great with all those oxys. We grabbed a couple of them for our second stop, the Fredro beer run, and headed up Brownie's Creek.

Boyd had grown up on the Creek, and he knew just about everybody. He always said it had changed an awful lot since he was a kid, though. The single-lane blacktop ran all the way from Hwy. 119, where the Creek met the River, to the bottom of Pathfork Mountain. It was a good distance, snaking back and forth, following the creek bed through the hollers. You could connect up with other single lane roads, following other creek branches, and make your way almost to Tennessee and Virginia. There were old logging roads, and mining roads, and other dirt roads that could take you anywhere and everywhere you wanted to go, if you knew them. We mostly stuck to the paved road, except for around Brownie's Creek.

I never knew exactly how much of a sense of community they had back in the old days, but school consolidation killed it. Driving down through there, you realized having the elementary school at the fork in the creek was the only communal draw they had. When it closed, the community died just a little bit.

After the school closed, all they had was the on-again-off-again bodega that sold crappy pot and a few snake-handling churches without the school. That was it on that whole road for miles and miles and miles. Broken-down shacks and shanties hidden off the road in the trees, interspersed here and there with trailers of varying sizes and in varying states of repair.

Just houses and trailers on the sides of the hills, little dirt driveways disappearing into the woods, burned-out foundations of homes that used to be. Hundreds of people living in isolation all around each other.

Still, I guess it beats living in town.

When we got to Trey's, we had to wait for him to finish up a chicken sale. Besides pot, Trey also sold gamecocks. According to him, they were the best around. I took his word for it, as I didn't have money to waste on sports betting. Boyd claimed they were not all that impressive compared to the ones he used to see when Hippy John would bring him to the fights. But really, back when Hippy John still went to the fights, Boyd was young, and I'm sure Hippy John was getting him fucked up. Hippy John had given him cocaine when he was 10. What else would a loving father do?

Calvin was there, at Trey's, and they were haggling over the price of a gamecock. After exchanging salutations with us, they kept haggling for over five more minutes without ever saying a number.

"How about what you charged me fer Rocko?"

"No, no, no, this is a superior type of bird. A Rocko and a half, at least."

"But you charged my cousin Billy Rocko-prices, almost Bucky type prices, just the other day for this bird's brother!"

"Well, that was because I still owed Billy for that shit with the one that was blind in one eye."

This went on for some time, with me looking to Boyd for clarification. Half the time he didn't look like he knew what the fuck they were talking about either. They finally came to some arrangement and walked into the barn to sort things out.

"Isn't it more complicated to keep track of what all these bird names stand for about compensation? Why not just learn numbers?"

I always liked to give Boyd a hard time about the ignorance of his people.

"I don't know. Cal never was no good at arithmetic." Boyd had known Calvin his whole life. "Never wore shoes either."

Trey and Calvin emerged from the barn, Calvin carrying a cage with a towel draped over it. He pulled the edge back a little, so we could see his prize rooster. Boyd let out a whistle.

"Good lookin' bastard, ain't he Cal?"

"You bet yer ass he is!" Calvin exclaimed, clearly very excited about his purchase. "Taking him over the mountain up Pathfork to win some money. Gonna call him 'War Pig!"

"Well, that sounds like a good time, old buddy, but we have business in the other direction. He's a good-looking bird, though. War Pig, I like it."

Boyd was leading Calvin over to his truck, careful to avoid the mud puddles.

Calvin was, of course, barefoot. I don't think he would have cared about mud puddles, a little late in the game for that, judging by the condition of his feet. Calvin placed the cage on the bench seat, riding bitch, and climbed up into the driver's seat.

"Wish me luck, boys!"

And with that, he peeled around the driveway turnabout, slung some gravel just before he hit the pavement, and headed off to make his fortune.

"Was one leg bigger than the other on that there bird, Trey?" I asked innocently.

"Why you motherfucker..." Trey started to argue, then a sly smile crept over his face.

"Maybe," he said. "Depends on which side you look at, I guess. But Lord God, that motherfucker's too sorry to put shoes on, so what does anybody expect?"

Trey turned and walked up the hill to the house.

"Come on up, boys, I got a favor to ask, and I know you boys need a smoke," he called back to us.

"You know, this motherfucker don't wear shoes half the time either," I said to Boyd as we followed Trey up the hill.

"No, he don't, but he's got the pot and he's good at math. Apparently, shoes don't mean shit, you elitist prick."

Trey's favor was an easy one: rough up this guy who had a threesome with Trey's teenage sister and had filmed it.

"There's a little bit of a timetable with this here, boys. It's already right at a little atter a month, but I'm just now finding out about it. I know who he is, but I don't really know the sumbitch. Don't know where he lays his head,

50

but I'll find out. And when I do, you'll go straighten 'em out. Make him pay…pain that lasts."

"Sure," Boyd said. "Same as before?"

"Yeah, and there's a $50 finding fee if somebody gives the little motherfucker up. So, what did you boys come down here for, besides to break my balls over my sales techniques?"

We ended up getting the ounce for almost half off after Boyd used our leverage on the chicken leg and because we were gonna help out with the sister's boyfriend thing, and because Trey liked us. Everybody liked us, it seemed, or at least tried to pretend they liked us and liked to pretend to be nice to us.

We left Trey's and headed up the holler for our second stop, the Fredro beer run.

"Don't tell him we got this pot," Boyd advised needlessly. "We'll do the pill with him, go buy the booze, and drop his ass off. We don't have any more pills, we don't want any more pills, we can't get any more pills. You're trying to take that old flame from high school out, and we gotta go."

"I know, I know. I'm not an idiot, Boyd."

I knew the standard operating procedure for the Fredro beer run.

Not being 21, beer variety was scarce. The bootlegger I had been using since I was 16 only had Bud in cans, which was standard for all bootleggers. You could find Bud Light sometimes. And for liquor, my guy carried Canadian Mist and Tvairsky Vodka. You could hunt down Jim Beam or some Jack Daniels, but that was about all you could ever find at a bootlegger's.

Grown folks that cared would head over to Tennessee or Virginia since we were in a "dry" region of the state, county after county with no liquor store. To truly celebrate you had to drive an hour and a half one way into Kentucky on the main road or take an hour roundtrip to the TN/VA border on the backroads. We preferred backroads when we were high, so we always traveled the backroads because we were always high.

Fredro was an old junky friend of Boyd's dad. Hippy John had some fucked-up friends, himself being a junky alcoholic. It was always best to avoid Hippy John if you could, but Fredro could be managed.

Our usual practice was to give Fredro a ride, buy him a half-pint of Blackberry Brandy, or do a pill with him in exchange for him buying our alcohol. He always needed a ride anyway, so he could pick up a couple 30 packs of Milwaukee's Best. A professional alcoholic such as Fredro couldn't survive on bootlegger prices.

To maintain his body's requisite alcohol level in his blood, he would have had to switch to moonshine. It was relatively cheap and very effective, but it came with its own set of drawbacks.

Bad moonshine has been known to make a motherfucker go blind, and it has killed a few, and it will get you drunker than you've ever been. Which, for some of us, leads to God knows what. So, we helped old Fredro by giving him rides to get cheap beer, potentially saving his life.

The worst part about Fredro's was enduring the Price is Right. This was back in the Bob Barker days, with all the ladies in the shimmery dresses. Fredro loved the Price is Right. And he was fuckin good at it. For somebody that didn't own shit, and didn't buy shit, that motherfucker knew the price of everything.

We thought about trying to clean him up and get him on the show but figured he probably wouldn't be able to do it clean and sober. Fredro was definitely a drunken savant.

And he wouldn't let you leave until after the Showcase Showdown. So, you couldn't get there too early, 'cause you'd have to watch the whole show, and you'd be fucked up because Fredro was making you drink with him. And you couldn't get there too late, 'cause immediately after, Fredro would do a big shot of Oxy, or sometimes morphine that he got from his crazy 'Nam Vet brother-in-law, and he wouldn't be able to function for a while.

And if it was morphine he stole from the brother-in-law, you didn't want to be around when the brother-in-law showed up looking for it. 'cause Fredro's brother-in-law Jasper truly was crazy and really would kill you as soon as look at you. The war had fucked him up for real.

Nope, the best thing to do was get there about a quarter 'til, watch the showdown with him, learn all kinds of interesting facts about the price of all the goods and services available in the showcase, and how it compares to the one from yesterday, do a pill, and then leave immediately. You had to do the pill before you got him in the car, or he'd talk your ear off the whole way.

However, there was something about changing his environment after he was already high that could shut Fredro up. We definitely had our system down for the Fredro beer run.

Luckily, on this day, we had a pill with his name all over it. Trey had put us behind a little bit, but we were still pulling up his driveway just as the show was ending.

"Better hurry, Jack, before his mind starts making plans. Hope he doesn't have any coke today."

Coke days with Fredro were fun, but they were long and a little dangerous. Fredro liked to shoot his .40 cal. in the house on Coke days. He was working himself up to shoot himself with it, I believed.

Fredro had this crazy notion that it was a sign of how tough and crazy you were if you could shoot yourself. He shot himself once with a .357, twice with a 9mm, once with a .38, three times with a .22, once with a .25, mostly in the arms and legs. He had tried with a .45, but it misfired.

Fredro took it as a sign from God when the .45 misfired. He cleaned up and quit drinking for two weeks, went to church, and rolled holy. But he got snake bit at the Holiness Church and, when he got out of the ER, he was back to normal. We had actually been a little worried about him, being mostly sober all that time. He wasn't even watching the Price is Right during those two weeks.

Fredro hadn't shot himself in over two years, and we all did our part to convince him he was plenty tough and crazy enough and didn't have to prove it by shooting himself while we were there. Coke days still got hairy, though.

He was glad to see us that day because he was out of everything but cigarettes and coffee. It had probably been a pretty intense Showcase Showdown, Fredro watching it with no booze.

He offered us coffee while he prepped his pill.

"Got a couple of clean pins back there too if you need 'em. Cleaned and repackaged 'em myself."

"No, we're good," Boyd did most of the talking for us, especially with Fredro.

"Just gonna line ours out right here," he motioned to Fredro's pill plate sitting on the coffee table. "Jack's gotta drive."

"Suit yourself," Fredro stated matter of factly as he tied off. "Glad you boys got here when you did. This way we can get over and back before your dad gets here, Boyd, with the coke."

I glanced at Boyd, hoping he was considering spending some quality time with his father, who apparently had coke and was coming over to share it. You didn't have to worry as much about Fredro when Hippy John was there. It was more likely that *he* would shoot Fredro if they were doing coke together.

I could tell from Boyd's scowl he was not entertaining the notion. If I wanted coke, we were gonna have to get it elsewhere.

"Yeah, we gotta get back to the house, Fredro. Jack is trying to bang this girl he knew in high school later tonight."

I nodded in agreement, wishing I actually still knew a girl from high school. Genius prick turned asshole junky did not pull as many ladies as you might think. But I didn't sweat it that often. If I had drugs, I didn't give a shit about anything else. And we usually had drugs.

56

We made it to the beer store and stocked up on Tanqueray and Wild Turkey with a case of Bud in bottles, so much more fun to shoot at when they were empty than cans. We dropped off Fredro and we headed for home. Would've made it too, except for Pizza Rolls.

Happy Mart on the corner by the 119 bridge had the absolute best pizza rolls on the market: greasy, cheesy, meaty, and greasy. But living the frugal lifestyle to which we'd grown accustomed, we rarely splurged on things like pizza rolls and their golden gooey goodness.

Usually, a trip to Happy Mart meant cigarettes and Mountain Dew, and then walking over to Long John Silver's, which occupied the prime spot in the Happy Mart food court area. If our old buddy Kenny was working, he would always toss us the old chicken strips and fries destined for the dumpster. Real good guy, Kenny. If he wasn't working, we just smoked more and made a better plan for the next day while we counted up enough change for two items from the McDonald's dollar menu.

But today we were flush, today we were living the high life, today we were splurging on Pizza Rolls.

We roared into Happy Mart in our old jalopy, smoke and steam and fluids hissing out of it, kicked open those big, heavy, American made steel doors that creaked and groaned under the weight and lack of lubricants, and rolled out with a cloud of pot and stale cigarette smoke trailing behind us.

We sauntered up to the automatic doors which whisked open with a whoosh to reveal...Stevie 3 Fingers holding a bag of ice and a two-liter of Shasta cola. He had three fingers on one hand, including the thumb, the result of an ill-advised attempt to get injured on the job at the furniture factory, draw a disability, and win a settlement from the insurance company. Stuck his hand right into the saw. Turned out he was high, so he failed the insurance company's required drug test, and received nothing. He still qualified for partial disability, but Boyd always said he probably could have qualified for that out of general stupidity. If they had a test for it, we were sure Stevie would fail, or pass, depending on how you looked at it. He was too stupid to do much of anything, let alone work for a living.

Stevie raised both his arms when he saw us and exclaimed, "Thank God you boys is here, good news, good news," and stepped toward us as if he would wrap both of us up in a big hug.

Boyd and I both sidestepped him, on either side, attempting to keep from being impeded in our quest for Pizza Rolls. But Stevie tried to corral us both with outstretched arms, ice in one hand and the soda dangling precariously in the 3-finger hand.

Boyd was having none of it, though, and spun under Stevie's arm while simultaneously flipping open his favorite cold steel blade with the tanto tip he kept razor sharp and slicing a seam down Stevie's bag of ice. The ice exploded through the opening and spilled all over the floor, while Boyd kept walking without a backward glance, the knife already back in his pocket.

Stevie was stammering, "Wha, wha, what?" and the Happy Mart clerk was looking over at all the ice all over the floor, so I pulled his arms down, and gently led him outside. I was explaining that I would get him more ice, but that he had to remember not to grab Boyd in the future as Boyd was always a little wound up and jumpy.

Even though I had seen Boyd do similarly unnerving shit before, (he was always showing off how fast and accurate he was with a blade or a gun), it was always trippy for people the first time they saw it. And frankly, it still scared me. Glad he was on my side, I guess.

"Now Stevie, what's this big news you got?" I asked as I led him out of the doorway, trying to calm him down.

"Great news, great news," Stevie began, his fears and discomfort giving way to excitement as he talked about his great news. "There is gonna be a big party at the cabins tonight and we," he paused for dramatic effect, "are invited."

The cabins at the Shilaleh Village were some misguided fool's attempt to bring the "cabin in the woods" resort experience to our neck of the woods. The problem was there were no tourists to stay in them. We were pretty far off the beaten path for people looking for a cabin in the woods vacation. And these were not the type of hills you would go to for a nice cabin in the woods vacation. Our hills have eyes.

"WE, us, are invited? Who invited us?" I asked out of politeness.

No one would invite us to a party through 3 Finger Stevie, and sensible folks with a credit card with which to procure a cabin rental would not invite us at all.

"Well, not us, exactly. Meatballs heard about it and all we need is ice, a mixer, and a ride."

"Who invited us where?" Boyd emerged from Happy Mart with a bag of ice and no Pizza Rolls.

"Shilaleh Village, some girl Meatballs knows," Stevie answered.

"What, no Pizza Rolls?" I asked Boyd as we turned toward the car.

"No money Bro. Barely had enough for smokes. Stevie, your ice, my good man," Boyd said as he handed the ice to Stevie3Fingers.

Rather harshly shoved it into his chest, I thought, but I realized he was right. Better not flash too much money in front of Stevie. He'd want to go look for a pill on the way to the party, if we decided to go, and we definitely couldn't let him know we were holding. His junky Spidey sense would likely figure it out anyway. Junkies always seemed to just know that kind of shit.

"Shilaleh, eh? Sounds like fun. Haven't been up there since Jeffrey shot that party up. Hop in back, Stevie, you're with us."

I realized we had decided to go to the party, and wondered about picking up Meatballs, and what all that might entail.

Boyd continued, "No room for Meatballs, though. Sorry."

Stevie3fingers looked at the empty backseat with a dubious expression on his face. Like he didn't believe that he and Meatballs could not both fit back there.

"Truth is, Stevie, I like you," Boyd said as he opened the door for him and ushered him into the back seat. "Despite your lack of awareness and comprehension of the concept of personal space, and your dubious lineage and questionable hygiene, I really do enjoy your company."

Only Boyd could insult the shit out of you and make you feel kinda good about it, like you were glad and honored that he liked you despite yourself. Boyd pushed the seat back into position after Stevie climbed in and shut the door.

"I like you, Stevie, but I can't take Meatballs on as a passenger. At this I draw the line."

 I was glad Boyd was drawing the line for who could ride in my car or not, especially since it was the correct line.

"Understood," Stevie said smartly, although his face said he obviously did not understand.

I thought he might have figured out we already had dope, since dope was about the only reason anybody brought Meatballs anywhere, including Stevie who was his best friend. Meatballs was a weird and annoying guy.

But Stevie is the guy who stuck his hand in the machine without realizing they would probably drug test him at the hospital, so he probably didn't put too much thought into any of it.

Instead, he leaned back in the seat as I pulled out of the parking lot and Boyd got the music right, and said," Boys, I hear the whole damn Middlesboro cheerleading team is gonna be there."

Boyd raised his eyebrows as he looked over at me, hopeful for cheerleaders. I remained skeptical but, glancing around at Stevie looking wistfully out the window, I said, "Stevie, you simple bastard, you should have just led with that."

 Despite having no Pizza Rolls, I realized we were in for a good time.

6 You'll Shoot Your Eye Out

Shilaleh Village parties were always a little strange. You always ended up with an odd cross-cultural mix of people from around the tristate area. Different schools, different neighborhoods, different hollers. Word would spread, and before you knew it there were a hundred people there. Coming out of the hills and woodwork.

There was always a fight brewing, and there was always somebody trying to move some dope to all the partygoers. The best acid party I ever went to was at one of the cabins. Some city kid named Thad was walking around selling it, constantly drumming his fingers in time to the beat blasting through his oversized headphones. Never seen him before or since, nor had anyone else that I could find. And when I asked him what he was listening to, he pulled one headphone off his ear, swiveled it to me so I could hear the white noise static blasting through his brain. Like a TV when the antenna is out.

It was good acid.

"Oh," I had said.

Thad had nodded wisely and sagely, put the noise back over his ear to achieve complete surround sound, and drummed off into the night. That was the last time I had been to Shilaleh.

I knew we were in trouble when we walked up to the cabin.

"What's up, my Brothers!" Glenn called to us from the porch railing he was sitting on. Tracey was leaned up against him, lazily smoking a cigarette.

"Welcome to the party, boys!"

"Surely this is not your party, is it?" I asked as I shook Glenn's hand.

"Hell no. I don't know who's it is. We was just about to leave anyway. Some prick is in there trying to charge us $10 a cup for the keg, while he's charging everybody else $5." Glenn's voice dropped an octave, and he glanced over his shoulder, feigning nervousness," I think he's racist."

"No way, not around these here parts, you don't reckon, do you Glenn? These white hillbillies? Racist?" I joked. "That sounds crazy to me."

"Come on, baby, let's just go," Tracey pulled on his arm. "We don't need any beer anyway. You don't even like beer."

"But we do love fuckin with crackerass white trash, don't we Glenn?" I said. "Which prick is it?"

"Damn, you're one funny fuckin crazy white boy. Always wantin' to start some shit!" Glenn laughed. "Are you sure you're not black?"

"Only on the inside. Where is this white supremacist cup bearer?"

"Here we go, you motherfucker," Tracey muttered. "Jackie, you fucking asshole, I told you just the other day I didn't want Glenn getting in anymore trouble. Stop egging it on!"

And she punched me hard in the shoulder.

"Look, goddammit, don't think just because y'all is road trip buddies you can sit around and talk about me like I'm not here."

Glenn shot us a dirty look.

"C'mon Glenn, let's redirect that anger to its appropriate target," Boyd coaxed him over to the window. "Which prick are we talking about?"

"It's the one they call the Butcher…" Glenn motioned toward a scrawny white kid in a cutoff Metallica t-shirt, dirty jeans, and dirtier Caterpillar boots. He had an awful looking tattoo that was supposed to be barbwire wrapped around his left bicep and the word "Butcher" tattooed down his right forearm.

"Jesus Christ, you get all kinds up here, I reckon." Boyd said, trying his best to maintain a straight face, but then we both burst out laughing. We laughed so hard for a minute straight that Tracey and Glenn both looked at us like we were nuts.

"I'm sorry, I'm sorry," Boyd said in between laughs. "I'm sure he's racist, but he is just about completely harmless. He thinks he's a badass, tries to be one. But he's not. That tattoo used to say Bitch, after he beat up the littlest Gilbert kid, the teenage one, and the other brothers held him down and ChaChe Gilbert tattooed it on him. He had it changed into Butcher, and now he makes up different stories on why people call him that. What's his story for today?"

I couldn't stop laughing, and it only got worse when Tracey told us the Butcher story for today.

"Says his dick is so big, when he fucks bitches they always bleed, so people call him the Butcher."

I was laughing so hard snot was coming out.

"That's marvelous," I managed to choke out.

Glenn was smiling a little too, but he still nodded seriously toward the window.

"He's got a piece on him too. Keeps flashing the butt stuck in his pants so you can see it."

"Probably a fucking BB gun, my man," Boyd laughed. "Don't worry, my friends, tonight our beer cups cost zero dollars."

Turning on his heel toward the door, he bellowed,

"The door, good sir!" at which point I hopped across the porch and held the door for the three of them, slightly bowing at the waist like any good doorman would do, and Boyd led us into what appeared to be the Butcher's party.

The radio was blaring "The devil went down to Georgia," by Charlie Daniels, and as we made our way across the room and into Butcher's line of sight, his face dropped. He knew the devil may have gone down to Georgia, but now his henchmen were here, and we knew who he really was.

And he knew damn well we didn't carry BB guns.

"Butcher!" Boyd commanded from halfway across the room. "Four of your finest beers! Good to see you again, as always!"

Butcher stammered and stuttered, but lucky for him, the actual keg owner poked his fat head around the corner.

"Boyd, that's my keg, not Butcher's."

Big Joe's fat torso slimed its way around the corner, following the head. "Cups are $5."

"JoJo, when'd they let you out? You've dropped at least a dress size you big bastard. Anyway, welcome home. Five dollars for everybody? Sounds good."

Boyd had known Big Joe for years too, before he got sent up for slinging out of the pool hall. Must have just made parole, or more probably, overcrowding leading to early release.

"Nobody calls me JoJo anymore, Boyd. And yeah, for you, everybody costs $5."

Big Joe glared at Tracey and Glenn from under his fat furrowed brow. Did it look more furrowed because it was fat, or more fat because it was furrowed? Either way, it wasn't a good look.

"Of course, they don't JoJo, of course they don't," Boyd was saying," but you and I go way back, and I like you. Damn, it's good to see you Joe. Tracey, pay the man."

Butcher was filling beer cups as fast as he could, and I handed Tracey a $10, which she put with her own $10 and handed to Glenn. Always best to make a white supremacist handle money from a black man. We took our beers and turned back towards the room.

"I think you might be right, Glenn. They might be racists," I said, as we made our way back across the room. "But that... is a BB gun."

Glenn laughed, "Well thanks anyway, man. C'mon Baby, let's go smoke that joint outside. Y'all want in?"

I took them up on it, but Boyd stayed inside searching for loose women. As we settled in to our high, we observed more people coming up for the party. The word was getting out. More of the Pineville crew, Butcher and Joe's people, showed up. And the Brownie's Creek crew stumbled in, Calvin and his brother Gilrod, Mikey and his sister, Boney Monie and her sister.

Things were going well, the keg was flowing, the weed was burning, the barbiturates were taking effect. Then one of the Brownie's Creek kids, probably Cal if I was guessing, puked in the ice cooler. Stevie and everybody else that brought ice had put it in a big cooler being used for mixed drinks and frozen cocktails.

Butcher talked loud and stupid about motherfucker this and motherfucker that and pacing back and forth. I was scanning the room looking for Boyd to see what his take on the situation was, but he was nowhere to be seen.

I was thinking that Calvin would be in trouble if Butcher jumped on him because Cal was shitfaced and couldn't fight anyway. Even though Butcher was quite the pussy and definitely not as tough as he wanted to be, he might be hard enough to beat up an incapacitated Calvin.

Since Mikey was rolling with Calvin that night, I knew Butcher would end up in trouble. Because Mikey was a genuine badass.

As Butcher marched back and forth, raising all manner of hell about assholes not holding their liquor, he walked too close to Glenn. Glenn reached out and snatched the gun right out of Butcher's waistband. He then hopped back behind the kitchen island, while Butcher let out a welp and hopped two steps away from the island into the living room.

By this point, Glenn was reading the gun barrel.

"Uses .177 BB's only. Air Rifle USA, Inc. is this a fucking BB gun? It is! It is a fucking BB gun! You'll shoot your eye out!"

People in the room, initially shocked that someone had drawn a gun, snickered, then chuckled, then laughed out loud as they came back from wherever they had attempted to take cover.

"You'll shoot your eye out, you'll shoot your eye out" echoed from all corners of the room.

Butcher, mortified, ran down the hall, right past Big Joe and Boyd, who were emerging from the back room.

Glenn was standing on top of the counter now, putting the BB gun on top of the upper cabinets.

"For safe keeping, so the little feller don't get hurt," he said, which brought raucous laughter from the room.

"Butcher, the BB Bandit!"

It was really getting good to him now, and Tracey was laughing but gently pulling him down off the counter, and towards the door. Everybody was laughing, but they were still rednecks, and Glenn was still black, and the host, Big Joe, wasn't laughing.

It was time to hit the road.

"We should get out of here too," I told Boyd as we reconvened on the porch. Glenn and Tracey had bid us farewell on their way to the car.

"Yeah, we're leaving too. Gotta get Cal and these girls home," Gilrod clapped Boyd on the back as he half carried Calvin to the truck. "Take it easy, boys!"

"What was up with Joe and you back there," I asked Boyd as we watched Gilrod and Mikey throw Cal over the side and into the truck bed like a sack of potatoes, then gingerly place some unidentified passed out girl in the truck bed next to him. Mikey and his sister jumped in the back of the truck with them, while Gilrod, Boney Monie, and the rest climbed in the front.

"He wanted us to do something for him, but I said no. Then he went on his skinhead propaganda spiel. Prison has not been good for that guy."

"Well, was it anything good he wanted? Maybe we go to the source to get paid, bypass JoJo altogether?"

Before he could answer me, a rock whizzed by our heads and hit somebody in the back of the truck with a soft thud, just as Gilrod slung gravel back at us as he goosed the engine.

He immediately slammed on the brakes as Mikey yelled out, "What the fuck!?!" and jumped out of the back of the truck. I saw Butcher duck around the side of the porch as people spilled out of the house.

"Who threw that fucking rock!" Mikey was shouting over and over, as he stormed back up the driveway on foot. "Who threw that fucking rock!"

I could hear people behind me, asking what rock, what's going on, who is that; the usual murmurings you always heard when shit went down.

Then, Devin stepped forward. Pineville High School's star running back, for a minute, back in the day. He was still a big motherfucker though, even now, several years removed from his glory days. He was the token JoJo's crew ran with so the sensitive ones could feel like they weren't all the way racist.

Devin stepped forward to claim responsibility, to tell these Brownie's Creek douchebags what's what, to take credit for throwing a rock I was sure he didn't throw. Wars, I thought, are started over shit smaller than this, with even less clear motivations.

Devin got out, "I did."

At which point Mikey tagged him square in the jaw with a right cross, clearly knocking him out. And before you could blink, before Devin's eyes had fully closed really, Mikey hit him two more times on the way down. The left hook landed almost immediately after the right cross, knocking Devin's newly bobbled head one way, and a sweeping right hook came in at about midsection level, which happened to be where Devin's head was in the process of passing on its way to the ground. His head snapped back the other way, and Devin's body fell to the ground, completely unconscious.

Mikey was good at what he did. He and Boyd went way back, they had been neighbors when they were kids. Mikey's dad drank, a lot, like everybody, I guess. Anyway, the dad would tie one on and start to beating on Mikey's mom, and then work his way around to the kids. Mikey always fought back, but usually to no avail.

He did learn to fight though, and Boyd learned how to be a functional cut man, fixing Mikey back up and sending him back into the ring the next night. Mikey's little sister had finally done the old man in. At least that was the rumor.

He turned up shot in the face one morning, apparent suicide the sheriff said. Never recovered the weapon, determined vagabonds must have come in and stole it out of the dead man's hand, before the family found the body. Must have been pretty fast vagabonds since everybody was in the house when Boyd and everybody else heard the shot. Holler justice, I guess.

Anyway, one of our favorite scams was taking a client's $100 to beat somebody up and paying Mikey $50 to do it for us. He enjoyed doing it, so everybody made out well. Plus, Mikey didn't have to talk to the customers, which was not his strong suit.

His strong suit was fucking motherfuckers up, which he was doing at his leisure as the stunned crowd looked on. People always think there will be some yelling, and some shoving, and then somebody will throw a punch, and somebody else will retaliate and there will be some grappling and wrestling and eventually the fight will get broken up, with minimal injury to all parties involved. People are never ready for the way Mikey handles his business, and when they realize that Mikey is not there to push and shove and wrestle, that Mikey is there to fuck a motherfucker up, they get nervous and try that much harder to break the fight up.

I stepped in front of a couple of Pineville boys moving in to stop it, yelling over my shoulder, "Get you some Mikey, Get you some!"

They stopped short, which was surprising since we were outnumbered about 23 to 5, if you counted Calvin, who was still passed out in the truck. The crowd was pressing in, and more cries of outrage rang out.

Apparently, mine was the minority view, that you shouldn't pick a fight with Mikey, and if you did, you did so at your peril. Sometimes you have to own your fuckups. And right now, Devin had fucked up and was getting fucked up. Mikey was straddling him alternating hands, relentlessly punching him in the face. Shouldn't have said he threw that rock.

Fucking Butcher, the weaselly little prick.

They were getting close now, and suddenly, Big Joe led the charge to grab us and save their token black friend, even though they had been giving my black friend a hard time just a few minutes earlier. Which is kinda shitty if you think about it, for both Devin and Glenn.

Boyd jumped forward into Joe's path and shoved his pistol in Big Joe's big belly. The belly fat engulfed the barrel of the Browning 9mm, but JoJo stopped on a dime, hands shooting up in the air, eyes wide and scared.

I heard Boyd hiss, "I'll shoot you in your fat belly, and you'll bleed out before the paramedics get here."

It was a stretch, of course, it can take some time to die from being gut shot, and we weren't that far in the wilderness, but Joe believed him.

"JoJo, we're leaving," Boyd said, and to punctuate it, he raised his pistol and let off two quick shots next to Joe's left ear. I took this as my cue to fire, and like any good wingman, I opened up.

I didn't shoot at anyone in particular, mostly into the side of the cabin as they all ran for cover, aiming too high to actually hit anyone. The crowd dispersed screaming and running, everybody but Devin, who remained a bloody pulp on the ground. Shouldn't have said he threw that rock.

"We gotta go." I called to Boyd as I backed down the hill, reloading. "Think they got anything bigger than that fucking BB gun?"

"Let's not find out!" Boyd and I turned and ran to the car, popped the trunk, threw the guns inside a bag, and slammed the trunk shut. We jumped in the car, and discovered Stevie3Fingers, who I had not seen since we got here.

"We gotta get outta here boys, they're up there shooting!" he exclaimed.

We both stared at him for a second, looked at each other, and shrugged. As I peeled out of the parking space, Boyd said,

"We are aware, Stevie, we are aware."

It was enough for ole Stevie to realize he was in the wrong car, and he started squalling and screaming about just wanting to go home and not wanting to die and please just let him live and woe is me, but it was too late. He was in it with us now.

We were speeding down the gravel road, heading for the entrance to the Village, when we saw all the lights. Blue lights. Two cops running up to the car, guns drawn, flashlights shining, orders barking. Other cops fanning out into the woods, cop cars parked with lights shining in the woods looking for the gunmen.

"Hands where I can see them!" the cop was yelling at me as I stopped the car. I put the car in park, and Stevie's screaming only got louder, about not wanting to be there, and please, someone just save him. Suddenly, Boyd blurted out, in a high-pitched whiny voice that matched and complimented Stevie's hysteria,

"Oh God, oh God, officer they're up there shooting! I don't wanna die, we just want to leave!"

It was the perfect storm of Stevie's honest hysteria, and Boyd's well-timed acting skills, and the officer's own nerves, and he made a judgement call. He lowered his gun and shouted,

"Get out of here boys, just go! Get out of here!" and he spun to join his fellow brothers in arms in their pursuit of the gunmen in the woods. The police cars drove around us and proceeded up the hill toward the cabins, leaving us alone in the road with only Stevie3Fingers still screaming.

Boyd and I looked at each other as I sped us down the road toward home, a little confused, a little bewildered, but mostly relieved. A smile spread across my face as I realized we might just pull this crazy shit off.

"Shut the fuck up Stevie," we said in unison.

"I really will shoot you," Boyd said a minute later even as Stevie had lowered his screaming to a dull whimper.

"Relax, relax. The guns are in the trunk, man. Jesus, calm down," I tried consoling him as I swerved around each hairpin turn, tight corner after tight corner. We practiced this road a lot, for just such an occasion, and we were making good time.

Boyd shot me a dirty look for telling Stevie the guns were in the back. But his yelling was making it hard to drive, and something had to be done.

"Look boys," Stevie was stammering now. "just drop me at my house, I won't say anything."

"Nope," was all Boyd said. I was intently watching the road but glanced up to see Stevie's expression in the rearview. I couldn't see him; he must be slumped over in the back seat.

"Well just drop me anywhere near town and I can walk. That way you don't have to go into town."

There was no way we were going anywhere near town.

"Nope," Boyd repeated. He took out his favorite knife, that obscenely long and wickedly sharp Knifemakers he had sewn into the inside of his camo jacket. His cousin had sent him the jacket while he was in the Air Force. The cousin ended up being gay, but that never bothered Boyd or the rest of his family, as far as I could tell. And Boyd loved that jacket. Had several knives sewn in it.

I always thought it was too conspicuous for our line of work. I just knew the description would always be a white guy in a camouflage jacket, and another nondescript white guy. I always figured it would be better if it was two nondescript white guys, but I didn't press the issue too much.

Boyd cleaned his nails with the tip of his knife. Seemed like overkill for nail cleaning, but just about right for intimidating the witness.

"Well maybe just drop me off here, or anywhere? How 'bout it fellas, just anywhere that's convenient for you."

"Stevie, it's like this," Boyd was staring at him in the rearview mirror, having commandeered its angling to suit his purposes; driver be damned. "You've seen too much to be out here running your mouth ... at-at-at!" he interjected to cut off Stevie's protestations the way Memaw would scold the cat when he tried to jump on the counter.

"You've seen too much for tonight, about tonight, and since I don't really trust you..." Boyd's voice trailed off as Stevie's eyes got wider and wider. Boyd spun around in his seat and gestured at Stevie with that giant fucking knife. "Since I don't fully trust you, for tonight, you'll be staying with us. We'll bring you back when this blows over, one way or another."

Depending on how the kidnapping goes, I thought. Sometimes kidnapping was sticky, I'd heard, and I wasn't sure that we should be topping off our shootout with taking a hostage. I thought we could have at least picked a prettier one if we're taking hostages. Stockholm was no good with this one.

Boyd interrupted my train of thought, "Slow down, Jack."

He was right Stevie knew too much. And he did have a big mouth.

And I was driving too fast. Even had they figured it out by now and were in hot pursuit, I was going too fast. And so, as I careened around a recommended 35mph curve, according to the sign, at 70 mph according to the speedometer, the tires screeched as they did their best to hold onto the road and Boyd buckled his safety belt.

That was always a bad sign, I figured, since Boyd hated seatbelts As I came out of the curve, a deer darted out into the road. I swerved around him, cut it back too far, tried to correct, and fishtailed. Stevie screamed at a higher pitch than the tires.

I could see Boyd out of the corner of my eye, grinning a sick grin and lighting a smoke, saying, "I got this, I got this."

I was fighting like hell to keep the damn thing in the road, and losing, when suddenly, Boyd grabbed the emergency brake handle and jerked it up. It locked the wheels and sent us into a 360-degree spin that finally ended with us sitting crossways in the middle of the road, tires smoking. The engine shuddered and died.

Stevie was deep in prayerful negotiation with the Almighty in the backseat. I looked over at Boyd. He took a long slow draw on his cigarette, grinned, and said slowly,

"I told you, you was going too fast. Now if you please, let's get this fucking car off the road."

I fired the Beast back up, swung us around, and headed on down the mountain. At some point, Stevie stopped praying and passed out. I suppose that could have been the answer to his prayer.

In any case, it made the rest of the ride home pretty quiet. When we made it to the trailer, we parked at the back of our lot, almost all the way behind the trailer, and threw a tarp over the car. Boyd gently helped Stevie inside. We put him in the recliner, where he slept peacefully till morning.

Besides the near-death experiences, I felt we were courteous and kind kidnappers. He seemed comfortable, anyway.

Boyd and I had a powwow in the kitchen, to figure out what to do.

"Think anyone will talk?" I asked.

"Well, JoJo is probably on probation or parole, so he probably didn't stick around. The Brownie's Creek crew is solid. Devin was unconscious. A lot of those Pineville fucks would be too scared to say anything. Even if they did, it's their word against ours, it was dark, do they really know we were the shooters, beyond a shadow of a doubt? I don't think so. Plus, Tootie would have to admit he let us flee the scene."

I laughed out loud. It hadn't registered with me who the cop was. It had been Tootie, big blockheaded football jock, douchebag Tootie. Always hated dopeheads like us. This news almost made the whole thing worth it.

"And the Oscar goes to Boyd Johnson, for 'oh God, oh God, officer they're shootin,'" I laughed thinking of Deputy Dipshit letting the perps escape in the most action he'd probably ever seen in his young career as a lawman. I laughed, thinking about all those cops storming the cabins, pointing guns at everybody, demanding to know where the shooters were, only to be told that they had just now let the bastards go.

We laughed till our sides hurt, but we knew we had to get out of town. Tootie's famous temper had not abated since high school, and everybody said he had killed this junky

Bill last year. Killed him in cold blood and got away with it, 'cause who believes a junky's people?

"Let's head up to Paulding Michigan," Boyd said. "I used to hunt up there with Pepaw back in the day, before Uncle Barry shot that guy and everything went to shit."

Boyd's Pepaw and Pepaw's brother, Barry, had owned a coal company at one time, until Uncle Barry got drunk and shot his mistress's husband. The bullet, 44 Magnum, had blown the husband's arm clean off, and kept going through the wood paneling from the living room to the sitting room and struck the mistress. She ended up paralyzed, with a one-armed husband and a crazy boyfriend in jail.

Understandably, she broke things off with Barry, went back to the husband, and together they sued the shit out of ole Barry. They took everything, including the coal company. Barry only served a couple of years, since nobody died, I guess, and Pepaw moved on to dope dealing. But they never went hunting in Michigan again. C'est la vie.

"It's gonna be cold up there but fuck it. Better get packed."

At least we had travel money to get out of town with.

7   New Car and New Destination

By the time we got done packing, which didn't take long since we didn't have much of anything, Stevie 3 finger was awake and nervously smoking a cigarette. I was throwing duct tape, a roll of garbage bags, and an old bottle of Vodka in a milk crate to carry out to the car, when I noticed him nervously edging toward the door.

"Settle down," I told him as I brought him a cup of coffee. "We're gonna drop you off on our way out of town. Gonna lamb it for a while."

I grabbed my milk crate.

"This ain't for you," I tossed over my shoulder as I walked out to the car, laughing a little at inadvertently scaring poor Stevie.

He shouldn't have gotten in our car, I guess. Probably a good life lesson for him.

When I got back inside Boyd had emerged from the back and was sitting comfortably on the kitchen counter, listening to Stevie gush about how glad he was and how we had nothing to worry about. Said he had a mouth like a steel trap, poor thing. We were probably never really gonna kill Stevie, but it was good for him to think it, I suppose.

"This is good coffee, Jack!" Stevie said too loudly as I walked through the door.

Probably should give him a pill to calm him down, but I knew how Boyd felt about needlessly sharing drugs. He didn't believe in using our own stash to medicate and treat other motherfuckers.

"We're not savages, Stevie. Damn straight, it's good coffee."

Boyd raised his cup in a toast, then took a giant gulp. He hopped down off the counter.

"Let's get this over with, while the pigs are still focused on donuts!" he exclaimed, slamming his cup down on the counter and marching out the door. I smiled at Stevie and ushered him out the door behind Boyd.

"Aren't pigs always focused on donuts?" I asked rhetorically as we drove Aunt Lindsey's car back over the bridge after dropping off Stevie3fingers, still in possession of as many digits as he started with the night before. "And do you think it's possible Stevie might have been awake while we discussed Michigan last night?"

"Yes to both," Boyd answered confidently. "Which is why we can't go to Michigan. We need a new car and a new destination.

"I vote somewhere warm, and I know a guy that's always trying to unload one shitbox or another."

We used Lindsey's car to hit a couple of junky hangouts over in Middlesboro and unload about half our oxy. Then we bought a used car from Pork Chop out at the garage in Pathfork for $850 cash. 1996 Corsica, nothing fancy, 150,000 miles on it, but Pork Chop had tuned up the engine and it ran good.

We liked shopping there 'cause it was easy and you could usually pay with pills if you had to. You were better off using cash, 'cause he gave a shit price on pills, but in a pinch, it would do. And his cars always ran, at least for a while.

Now the tricky part, registering the plates so we could feel confident in driving cross country.

"Into the lion's den," I muttered as I walked up the steps into the clerk's office.

The clerk's office was across from the courthouse, which was next to the jail. The police station was on the corner, and the sheriff's office was in the building with the clerk's office. I was surrounded on all sides by some of the finest law enforcement agencies in the land, but I wasn't worried.

Luckily, I had a great disguise to use with government officials. Normally, I wore my hair long and carried a slightly scruffy beard. I wore boots, jeans, sweatshirt, and jacket. Dirty ballcap most days, or a sock hat when it was cold. And I wore contacts mostly.

But when I had to deal with the white man's governmental system in any capacity, I wore khaki pants, a collared polo shirt, windbreaker, sneakers, and a clean, blue, UK Wildcats ball cap. I would shave and wear my glasses, and I looked like a different person, especially if I had my hair up under my hat like I had it on this day. I looked just like any other upwardly mobile college age white boy, here to fill out some paperwork.

I even walked right by Tootie, who was leaned heavily over the desk of the receptionist at the Sheriff's office as I passed by in the corridor. Never even looked my way.

By the time I made it to the clerk's office, with that damn Elvis impersonator motherfucker that ran the place, I was confident in my disguise. Maybe not as confident as the Elvis impersonator was in his, but he was the king, after all.

I emerged back out onto the street, stuck the paperwork in the glovebox and headed for home where I had left Boyd. He couldn't pull off a disguise; he was too nervous.

"How about going to see Clint in New Orleans again?" I suggested. "It was hot as fuck last time."

It had come to me in the clerk's office, while I was wondering what all kind of places an Elvis impersonator could find work these days. I figured Memphis and Vegas, and probably New Orleans. I had thought of all the crazy shit we had seen going on in New Orleans when we went.

"Good idea," Boyd beamed. "Mardi Gras is coming up, maybe that's just what the doctor ordered."

I often wondered what a doctor would order up, a real doctor, if I ever went to the doctor. Maybe I should see a doctor, I thought. Things had been pretty fucked up lately. Existential crisis of sorts. The point when a young man starts to think about what he's doing with his life. And if he has managed to stay ahead of the STD's.

We were already down a man. Randy had stayed in the Marines. We had all joined, but Boyd and I were kicked out about a year in on drug charges. In my case it was to be expected. I had failed the entrance drug test four times, twice for pot and twice for cocaine.

"Jesus, son, we only test for two things and you've popped on both of them twice each!" the recruiter had screamed at me. "How can you ace the ASVAB test but still be such a dumbass?!"

I didn't get into how that test was passable by an average chimp, a well-trained one could probably ace it too.

And I didn't get into how I failed the first test for pot 'cause I have a slow metabolism and it apparently takes forever for pot to get out of my system. And the second test I popped for cocaine because I had not been smoking pot and I had to maintain my daily buzz somehow. And the third test I popped for pot 'cause the recruiter had surprised me two days after the second test and I had smoked a joint since I figured it would be another month before the retest. And, of course, I failed the fourth one because I'm a junky and what else am I gonna do?

What I said was, "if you would have told me y'all was only testing for pot and coke I would have switched to barbiturates months ago," which he did not find amusing.

Anyway, we had all gone in together, done basic training, which is the only time I would have actually had clean pee. If that was important to them, they should have tested mine then. But instead, they tested it at the duty station where I was assigned, in Washington, D.C.

Apparently, the Marine Corps Silent Drill Platoon had just all tested positive for Ecstasy, so the base was on high alert for drug activity. I was a paper pusher in the Separations department. I thought it was a fitting assignment, really.

My room was at the corner of a breezeway in the barracks. They had these long breezeways like cheap motels have, with all the room doors in a row. It gave a good spot to smoke, and one breezeway leading from my corner room was full of smokers. It was the breezeway for everyone getting booted, so they weren't limiting themselves to smoking tobacco.

The other breezeway from my room was all regular law-abiding mean green Marines. I knew more of the guys getting kicked out, since I was processing their paperwork in the Separations department. I was watching them come in to meet with the Staff Sergeant who coached them on their reentry to society. I never saw a happier group of people as the ones leaving military service.

Of course, I smoked pot with these guys. What else am I gonna do? It was just a matter of time before I failed a test.

Boyd, who was stationed in Virginia, also failed a drug test, even before I did. We got discharged on the same day, though. I bought a bag of pot from one of my Marine buddies and drove down to Virginia to pick him up for the car ride back to the Bluegrass. It was a good trip back, although we were a little melancholy that our Three Amigos had become a Dynamic duo.

The three of us had been through a lot together; Randy's mom had committed suicide, Boyd's dad had tried to kill him, and my parents had kicked me out as part of the tough love initiative. The three of us had been inseparable, even moving in together for their senior year of high school in a shitty little apartment over in Middlesboro. We had made our own little tribe. There were others that passed in and out, but it had always been us three at the core. Now we were down to two.

91

We had spent the winter with Boyd's parents when we first got out, until Hippy John clocked Boyd upside the head with the butt of his 10mm 1911 model. From behind I might add, in a most cowardly fashion. As Boyd crumpled to the floor, Hippy John stood over him and cocked the hammer.

"This has been a long time coming, you son of a bitch," he said as he brought the pistol to bear on Boyd's unconscious body.

Cocaine and moonshine will motherfuck you every time.

I was midway through my fight or flight response, and my gun was across the room with my hat and coat and boots. I had not counted on needing a gun to retrieve a beer from the kitchen, which was what I was doing when this all went down.

I had just decided on flight, when Big Carolyn, Boyd's mother, came flying around the corner from the hallway. She was swinging a shovel that she proceeded to use to beat Hippy John's brains out. He went down like a sack of potatoes, and my jaw dropped to the floor. This was the most amazing sequence of violent events I had ever seen.

Big Carolyn glanced over at me. "Don't look so surprised, Jack, he called me a bitch after all."

Then she got that nurturing, loving, look all mothers break out on you, and said, "Oh honey, I'm sorry you had to see that. Here, help me get Boyd up and in the car. Y'all should go stay with Mom and Lindsey for a couple of days. I'll clean all this blood up."

Never one to argue with a woman holding a shovel, I loaded Boyd into the car. Boyd came around about halfway to Lindsey's. I told him what had happened, and he let out a low whistle while rubbing his head and trying to light a cigarette.

"Guess he was madder than I thought. Fucking junky."

"Mad about what?" I had asked. "You were just standing there, not even doing anything."

Boyd dug in his pocket, and eventually produced a little baggy with about a gram of coke in it.

"This, for starters," he said, giving the baggy a little shake. "Plus, I pinched a big ole bud out of his private stash."

Carolyn called Hippy John's homegrown "Crazy Weed." Maybe she was right. Hippy John smoked the shit out of it and was crazy as fuck.

"If I'd have known that I wouldn't have stolen his Wild Turkey he got for Christmas!"

I laughed as I reached into the backseat to retrieve the bottle. "I figured you might need it for the pain."

"Fuck him," we said in unison, which necessitated a laughing fit, until Boyd said his head was hurting and took a big swig out of the bottle.

We had lived at Memaw's ever since. We hatched a plan to get some grow lights and start seedlings, but we had our main investor back out. And we were planning on starting a few outdoor patches with Boyd's grandfather, but shit with his family was always so fucked up. Who knew what would happen by spring?

I had tried to get my old job back, driving Bubbles the dope dealing entrepreneur around for his business ventures, but he was still sore about my having bested him in a drinking contest. I felt he had no right to be mad, it had been his idea in the first place, it had been him who tried to cheat using cocaine as a PED, and it had been him who tried to not pay when he lost.

I suppose it had been me that talked all manner of crazy to him while I was drunk, and me who left him stranded down at crazy Darla's after he finally got me my ounce of pot winnings. And it was me who told him to "Suck my balls, Fat Man," but I figured he should let bygones be bygones.

It had been well over a year since all that happened, and he was still crying about it.

We scrapped some metal and copper periodically, and occasionally made money with muscle work, and did some mild midlevel drug dealing here and there, but we really had nothing going. This score from Mexico was the first honest work we'd had in months, and it would not be a regular thing. We were small time hoods, not international drug smugglers.

A road trip was just what we needed, a change of scenery and a chance to come up for some air. Things were feeling a little tight lately.

We decided Boyd should call Clint, to set things up, even though Clint was my childhood friend. He was still pissed at me from the last time we went down there.

We had gone down two summers ago, which is a shit time to visit the low country. It was one of the last things we did, all three of us together. Clint was in the ten-year multiple degree program at Tulane University, with ambitions of stretching it to twelve. He was working on his second master's degree, something about film study.

He got mad at me for suggesting that studying the patterns and frequencies of various sexual positions in American film sounded, a little, like an excuse to watch a lot of porn. I mean, shit, that's all he had been doing for three years. I didn't mean it like a bad thing, more like 'good for you working the system,' but he took offense anyway.

Then I got drunk, picked a fight with Boyd, and Clint made me walk back to his dorm by myself. I got lost, and found my way to a strip club, because, let's face it, I am into porn too. I was a little jealous that I hadn't thought of studying porn as an art form in college myself. I might have made it if I had.

I spent the next two days on good behavior, pot and Xanax, light dose of beer, no liquor. This was a tried and true formula to keep me from getting too loose. I had been officially banned from hard liquor for quite some time, but too much beer could have the same effect. I'm a bad drunk, which Clint knew already, but I think he was a little unnerved with our prescription medication regimen.

Luckily, Boyd smoothed things out with him. They went to the library and looked up ancient Asian weaponry, and spent a couple days making and utilizing slings, bows, and spears. I don't know what the other coeds thought about the weird Asian porno kid out in the commons hunting squirrels with his new redneck friend. But Randy and I had a blast smoking dope and narrating from the balcony.

They are used to seeing some crazy shit in New Orleans, 'cause nobody even called campus security. Clint had a great time, invited us to come back whenever we could. And so now, Boyd was calling to cash in.

8 New Set of Glasses

The half of the phone call I could hear sounded quite positive and just like that, we were on the way. We stopped by Mel's and traded her the title to the Beast for an 8Ball.

We told her we were on the way to Indiana to the riverboats for our 21st birthdays. I had just celebrated mine, and Boyd's was the following week, so we told her we were gonna make a weekend out of it. She agreed to pick the Beast up in a few days, since we said Lindsey was still using it. In reality, we just didn't want that car on the road until we were out of the state.

We embarked on our escape with a decent amount of supplies. We had the 8 ball, 19 oxy 40's, 22 Oxy 20's, about 25 Xanax, almost an ounce of pot, a case of beer, 2 pints of Tanqueray for Boyd, and a carton of cigarettes. We could get more pot when we got there from Clint's guy on campus, and you could find anything you wanted out on the street at Mardi Gras. New Orleans is just that sort of city.

I was driving, which kept me from drinking. I was supposed to lay off the sauce this trip, and the coke was key for my driving style. Cocaine, coffee, and cigarettes, and I can drive to the moon and back in one sitting.

Once we were through Tennessee, with a state between us and Deputy Tootie, we relaxed. At least as much as you can relax in the throes of a coke binge. We talked at great length about where we were headed, what plans we could come up with for the future. The future endeavors looked bleak, so we found solace in reminiscing about past capers and exploits.

We laughed about the last time we had gotten out of Dodge, several months ago. We had broken into our buddy Jeffrey's grandmother's house, to steal his guns back for him. Church let out early, and we had to bail without all the guns.

There was no time to cover up the evidence of our being there. I had even left a footprint from my Converse sneaker. When we saw the paper's coverage of the "Converse Bandits," who were apparently terrorizing the neighborhood during Sunday church, we decided we better hit the road.

As luck would have it, we had run into an old acquaintance from our church youth group, who had finally gotten with the party culture and no longer found me repulsive. She had been quite the churchy prude back in the day, looking down her nose at dopeheads like us. But when we saw her, she was already drunk and invited us to a party at EKU in Richmond. It was a two-hour drive, but we needed to get out of town anyway, so we took her up on it.

Turned out to be quite a party; I drank too much, hooked up with the former prude, got into the pure grain and passed out in their living room for 38 hours. We didn't know anyone, so Boyd sat right there in the living room with me for a day and a half, playing their Xbox and cleaning his gun whenever anyone who lived there came around.

For all their bravado, none of those frat boys wanted to ask the rabid redneck who's cleaning his pistol in the living room how long he and his comatose friend are planning on staying.

When I finally woke up, they gave us a hundred bucks to get bus tickets back to Bell County since the church girl had ditched us days ago. We didn't mention that our car was parked around the corner. We took their money and went to Waffle House for breakfast.

We had pulled a lot of stupid shit, Boyd and me, shit that should have gotten us pinched one way or another. We always made it through unscathed, but how long could this go on? We were good, but shit, I felt like our luck had to run out at some point.

At least I felt that way when I was alone and being honest with myself. I knew that it was possible for us to continue to make it. Some people lived this way their whole life, but the more common outcomes were death or prison.

I wasn't scared of either one, I knew I could handle prison if I had to, and I figured I wouldn't see death coming until it was too late anyway.

Like all junkies, I knew *I* couldn't OD.

Some of our spheres of influence were more dangerous than others, but I always felt like Boyd and I could handle anything that came up. I figured if we really fucked something up, or really stole form the wrong motherfucker we might get killed. But I also knew the assassins would have a rough fucking time of it. Boyd was a deadly motherfucker, and he was on my side.

But I had been thinking, of late, about what else might be out there. I had been thinking about if I was planning on hustling forever. Already it was harder to make a living than it had been just a few years before. You couldn't fleece the same people the same way every time; you couldn't break in the same house over and over; you couldn't run the same scams all the time; you couldn't even count on your dope dealers anymore.

People were getting busted, and paranoid, and turning each other in. You used to be able to count on the drug dealer not setting you up, at least you generally had more dirt on him than he had on you.

But people were getting crazy during this opioid epidemic, as the newspapers were calling it. It seemed like anybody was liable to turn on you. Everybody was a potential rat. You didn't know who you could trust.

It just felt like things were changing.

We were in the actual middle of Mississippi, which is the actual middle of nowhere, when we got pulled over. For being from out of state, I think, but I knew the drugs, alcohol, and guns would be a bigger problem than out of state plates.

I hadn't been drinking, but he pulled me out of the car for some sobriety tests. I performed the most extensive set of sobriety tests ever devised by the State of Mississippi, the likes of which would have been the envy of any Chinese acrobat troupe. I stuck the landing by reciting the alphabet backwards, which impressed the trooper immensely. He seemed a little disappointed when he had to cut us loose. As they say, cocaine is a hell of a drug.

We hit New Orleans wide open, figuring there was no better way to experience Mardi Gras than with a full slate of illicit substances coursing through our systems.

I quickly realized I didn't remember shit from the first trip. Or maybe the city had undergone a transformation or something, but Clint kept bringing us places "again" and I didn't recognize any of them.

We spent most of the first night at his favorite strip joint; still into porno.

When I woke up back in the dorm, Boyd and Clint were nowhere to be found, so I rolled a couple of joints, grabbed my gear, and hit the streets. I grabbed a 40 oz from the bodega and wondered down the boulevard toward the French Quarter. There were people everywhere, of all shades and persuasions, getting down to party.

I smoked a joint with two old guys on a park bench, admiring the Spanish moss hanging from the trees. The old guys told me all about how one of 'em had been a blues guitarist before the arthritis fucked his hands up. He had played in all the joints up and down the French Quarter. The other guy had made a living installing handrails on people's balconies, especially just after Mardi Gras every year when the tourists had been up there drunk and leaning on them, pulling them loose form their moorings. The musician gave me his top five list of blues joints to visit while I was in town, but I was too high to remember it. Probably a good list.

As I wandered down toward Bourbon Street, I took a couple of shots of some kind of awful liquor with a half-naked dude spray painted silver. He was running down the street passing them out. I was hoping it had acid in it, this guy being spray painted silver and all, but I think it was just cheap booze.

I found beads in the bushes when I went to take a piss, and immediately gave them to some blonde chick that walked up, flashed her tits, and took them from around my neck.

I knew I needed to find more beads. Saw all kinds of topless women that day, beads and booze creating some magic spell that made women crazy, and topless.

I finally wandered back to the room to find they had finished off the rest of the coke. I wasn't mad, since I had taken a good couple of lines with my coffee. By this point I was pretty fucked up anyway. I did an oxy while Clint explained that he had run into his neighbor, who was also having people visit for Mardi Gras, and she had suggested we all hang out. I nodded along. Sure, chill with the neighbor chick, etc., etc.

I was knee deep in the oxy by now, but still hanging in the conversation. Boyd was outlining the drug situation and giving me dirty looks, talking about how there wasn't enough to share, except maybe pot, but probably not pot either, and I was nodding along with him. Yes, yes, don't share the drugs.

We should ration the drugs, being lacking in the impulse control department. I knew how Boyd got at the tail end of benders, when the drugs were finally gone and the sickness set in. I didn't want to run out while we were away from home, without Memaw's Xanax cocktail to help him sleep it off.

To alleviate our fears, we took out two Oxy's for the night, a couple of Xanax apiece, and rolled three joints. We figured we would get some booze enroute and headed back out to the French Quarter. We were bound and determined to make it to Bourbon Street, which I used to lobby for permission to drink bourbon.

I knew the pills were kicking in when Boyd nodded along with my proposal, and by the time Clint raised objections based on my previous performances under the duress of hard drink, I was at the counter buying some Jim Beam.

I'm told we didn't make it to Bourbon Street, because of my liquor purchase and subsequent consumption. Apparently, I picked a fight with some lovely black ladies sitting on the stoop of their house enjoying the warm weather, the good music, the lively atmosphere of Mardi Gras, and a bucket of KFC.

It was not clear to the women if I was picking a fight, or drunk, or just a crazy white boy. I had launched into a dissertation of sorts, on reparations due to all African Americans for slavery, that somehow circled around to how these women should give me some of their chicken since I was from Kentucky and had invented fried chicken.

They eventually gave me a chicken wing to shut me up and get me to go away, but not before Boyd recommended that they piss on it first, since I was being such a dick. It is unclear whether they actually pissed on it or not, with Clint saying they did and Boyd abstaining from the conversation.

The next morning Clint filled me in since Boyd and I were apparently not on speaking terms. After polishing off my ill-gotten chicken wing and the rest of the bourbon, I headed into a liquor bodega and tried to buy crack off a bewildered Pakistani. He sold me a liter of rum instead.

This led to me composing a song about being a pirate that I sang endlessly and at high volume as we walked down the street, Boyd and Clint trying their best to distance themselves from me. They came rushing back, though, when I got jumped by a group of Brazilians who I had accused of being Mexicans, although the word I apparently used was "wetback."

The Brazilians were not amused and the biggest one punched me in the face, hard, which seemed to have pissed me off. I beat him with my rum bottle about the head and face. His two friends grabbed my arms, but the one I bit only held on for a second, Clint said. The other one let go when Boyd smashed him in the side of the head with an elbow.

Clint bullrushed the fourth friend who had tarried too long evaluating his fight or flight response. Clint was choking him out before he had made a firm decision as to his role in the melee.

He let him go when he tapped out, which apparently enraged me further and I kicked and stomped the Brazilian before he could get up. I was screaming at him and at Clint, who luckily had rolled to safety.

Boyd explained to him, "Don't ever let 'em go, Bud. Choke 'em till they're unconscious, then beat them at your leisure. This ain't the fuckin UFC."

Boyd then turned to me, pulling me away from the battered Brazilian, and nodding to a cop who was leaned up on his car watching the whole thing.

"We better go, you drunk bastard. You sure can take a lick though. I think that kid broke his hand on your face," he smiled as he tried to steer me down the street. "Always starting shit, though."

According to Clint, I flew off the handle again, turning on Boyd and calling him everything but a white man. I demanded that he stop treating me like an idiot and acting like he could kick my ass all the time.

"It was weird," Clint was telling me as I squinted at him in the bright midday sun pouring through his room's open door. "He tried to give you a compliment and you just freaked out on him. Started bringing up old shit and talking about not being happy. It was like watching some weird breakup or something. Are you guys dating? It's okay if you are."

I hadn't thought of it in those terms before. I suppose we were more like heterosexual life-mates, but I could see Clint's point. Boyd and I spent an awful lot of time together, and things had been strained lately. Like any couple, we were struggling with questions of our future; where we were going, how will we budget, should one of us look for a job.

Jesus, it did sound like dating.

"We're not dating. Just friends."

Fuck, that sounded like something someone caught in a relationship they were unsure of would say. It's not serious, I can leave any time. We're just having fun.

I had to change the subject.

"Where are my glasses?"

"Ahhh, that is a good one. Nobody knows," Clint said with a slight smile.

It turns out that in the midst of my verbal abuse of my heterosexual life-mate, he ended the argument by punching me in the face and knocking me out. Clint said he stayed with me until I regained consciousness, but Boyd stomped off into the crowd.

Clint had tried to drag me home, but I refused because since it was Mardi Gras, I deserved to see more titties first. So, he let me spend what little money I had at the strip club and trade my Xanax for a lap dance. He finally convinced me to accompany him back to the dorm by assuring me that all the Tulane girls would be topless when we got there, which turned out to be a lie.

"About a mile out, you said you needed to piss, so we stopped beside a church and you went to relieve yourself in their holy bushes. You emerged from the bushes, with no glasses, burning with anger, cursing God and man for blinding you so you couldn't look at naked titties anymore. I dragged you back here, screaming the whole way, all manner of blasphemy about God blinding you. I gave you one of your oxys once we got here and you passed out after puking in the sink." Clint shook his head. "I think you owe Boyd an apology. And me too if we're being honest. And probably God and organized religion too."

"And half the population of the southeast United States, apparently. Jesus, man, I'm sorry. Gotta lay off the sauce. Now, come walk me to the car so I can find my spare glasses."

I told Boyd I would talk to him when we got back, and he grunted something incoherent. He was still asleep on the couch. After retrieving the glasses, we arrived back at the dorm, fresh set of eyes on, Po Boys and a 12-pack in hand, I glanced into the neighbor's room as we passed by.

I saw something that changed my life forever. Sitting on the edge of the bed in Clint's neighbor's room was the most beautiful girl I have ever seen.

9 Dibs!

She had long, dark curly hair, flowing gently down her back, one lone curl hanging down the side of her face, gently brushing her cheekbone as she laughed at something that was obviously very funny. She had piercing blue eyes, big and beautiful, even as she squinted slightly as she laughed. Her smile was captivating as she said something in response to the funny thing she had just heard, something that made her smile and shake her head. A smile I wished so desperately to be a part of.

"What the fuck, man!"

Clint had crashed into the back of me. Apparently, I had stopped short in the doorway. Embarrassed, I quickly shuffled past the doorway and into Clint's room. I was awestruck, I wanted to drop everything and go back to that doorway where I could see this vision, this goddess, this guest of the neighbor.

But I didn't want her to see me in my hungover and unwashed condition. I burst into Clint's room, saw Boyd hunched over the coffee table snorting oxy, and hopped over to him. He was just coming up off a line when I grabbed him in a big hug.

"I'm sorry! I love you! I'm an asshole! And dibs!"

I let him go as he pushed me away, high and smiling. I knew he accepted my apology. He knew I was always a shitshow when I drank.

"Dibs?" he said, "What dibs?" he offered me the rolled-up dollar bill and nodded to the table, trying to share his oxy with me.

I pushed his hand away, "You'll see, motherfucker, you'll see. I gotta get a shower!" and I headed for the bathroom feeling my hangover melt away as I contemplated the girl next door.

"You're an asshole, but I forgive you!" Boyd called after me as I left. "Next time I'm not holding back when I punch you!"

My face felt like I should remember that warning the next time I drank, but there was no time to get bogged down in that now. There was only one thing I was concerned with, only one person. There was no time for oxy, no time for hangovers, no time for sore faces.

I had to find out who she was.

My disgust and discomfort at the communal nature of dorm showering was only an afterthought as I tried to scrub away the drug haze. It wasn't really working, of course. But I knew I had to try; most college girls were not that into our particular brand of drug scene.

I knew I wanted to meet this girl and I knew I needed to make a good impression. Unfortunately, one shower does not wash the junky off the junky, so I looked pretty much the same at the end of it. But I did smell like Clint's shampoo, which was a definite improvement.

I realized as I put my dirty jeans back on that I was suffering from a dearth of clean laundry. I hoped my last clean t-shirt and freshly scrubbed body would impress the object of my affection. I knew I would be walking a tightrope to drink just enough to be social, but not enough to be an asshole.

I also knew I sucked at tightropes.

Clint's neighbor Karen came over a couple of hours later, with her friend. Allison was her name, like the melody.

I had erred on the side of caution with my drinking, nervously sipping the same beer for an hour and a half, so my vocal chords were not lubed up enough for coherent conversation. Luckily, I said hello, though it was not a sweep her off her feet type of hello.

On the plus side, I was not drunk enough to act a fool, as my mother says, so I suppose the first greeting was passable.

I couldn't think of anything to say as they all discussed the excitement of Mardi Gras, the crazy shit they had seen so far, and planned to walk down to the parades as a group. My throat had an enormous lump in it, I couldn't manage the English language in the moment. I could feel my face flush and my heart pounding in my chest as I watched her like a creepy weirdo, engulfed by her radiant beauty, unable to look away.

She had the biggest, bluest eyes I had ever seen, eyes that sucked me in and let me swim around in them. Her long brown hair was pulled up in a bun, like a schoolteacher, but sexy, so fucking sexy. She had on a little t shirt with a zip code emblazoned across the chest, 02807. I knew I would never forget that zip code as I was checking her out, curves in all the right places; and she was so tan for February. She had bell bottom jeans and cute little sneakers covering what had to be cute little feet.

I was thinking about how perfect she looked, when she glanced over at me and smiled, the most beautiful and warm smile I had ever seen. It was a little joyful, a little playful, a little mischievous, but mostly kind and inviting.

In my drug addled brain, when she looked at me and smiled, I felt like she loved me as much as I thought I loved her, and I melted. Just absolutely melted into a puddle of lovey dovey mush right there on the floor.

Turns out she was smiling at me because they were saying goodbye until later when we were going to see the parades together. A goodbye smile. There had apparently been a whole conversation and plan put into place while I was lost in lovestruck bliss.

As they left Clint's room, Boyd turned to me and said, "Where's that little brunette from? Rhode Island? Yuck. She's hot, but you can have her little blue state ass. Liberal bastards, always infringing on our second amendment rights. Maybe there's still hope for Karen."

I had no idea where Rhode Island even was, but Boyd always had an opinion about those who would impinge on our right to bear arms. Not that our home state actually allowed people like us to bear the arms we bore in the manner in which we bore them. But technicalities such as that were never used to tone down the rhetoric. Gun nuts are gun nuts regardless of actual facts.

I was just happy he wasn't interested. I had called dibs, but that shit didn't always work, and I was not good at talking to girls I was actually interested in. I could woo a drunk girl at a party, someone who had no interest in me for the long haul. And I could talk to girls interested in me if I was not too terribly into them.

But if I liked a girl, really was swooning even remotely close to how Allison was making me feel, I was a drooling, babbling idiot. There was an alcohol balance that could be achieved, about 2.5 beers with a steady intake of .75 an hour, but I was shitty about maintaining the balance. I would always drink too much and talk and talk and eventually it would become crazy talk and they would be scared away. And other drugs like pot and oxy just made me clam up, worse than if I didn't drink any beer. So it was a delicate balancing act I had yet to master.

But I knew I had to figure it out if I was going to have any chance with Allison.

10 Seen Any Good Titties?

We set out from Tulane in a little group: me, Allison, Boyd, Clint, Karen, and some of her other friends. I wasn't sure how many there were because I only had eyes for Allison. She had added a sweater to her ensemble, and oh holy shit, she was even hotter than before. Fuckin' sweaters do it every time.

I nudged Boyd and nodded toward Allison in her sweater. He didn't get it. Maybe he didn't have a deep-seated fantasy involving hot chicks in Mr. Rogers style cardigans the way I did.

Or maybe when I had turned him down about doing a pill before we left, he had done my half along with his. Either way, the cardigan wasn't doing it for him.

As we walked down the tree lined boulevard, gentle breeze shaking the new leaves ever so slightly, I listened to the others talk as I watched Allison. She moved with such grace and flashed that effortless smile at me periodically, that smile that had me hanging on everything she did. I still wasn't able to contribute to the conversation, and it was getting to that weird point where it's been too long to start talking now.

Perhaps I would be better off playing the strong silent type for the foreseeable future. But it wasn't to be, because as we passed a little bar, Karen and her other friends wanted to stop in for a drink, while Clint and Boyd wanted to continue on. So, we parted ways, saying we would meet up later at the parade. I wished I was staying with the girls, but it felt like it would look too desperate. Nobody likes the overly desperate stalker type who follows you literally everywhere and never speaks. A little creepy.

When we got to the parade, it was immediately apparent there would be no meeting up with anyone. The crowd was immense, pressing in from all sides. It was slowly forcing us toward the street where a river of bodies flowed through. The mass of bodies formed a current of sorts, that made crossing the street impossible.

As we considered our situation, a surge from behind us propelled Boyd out into the street and he was swept away in the current. Clint and I fought our way back from the brink, but Boyd was lost to us. I couldn't see him anywhere in the mob. We maneuvered to the edge of a building where we could press flat against the brick and hopefully maintain position until Boyd made his way back. After a couple of cigarettes, we decided he was probably not going to find his way back, and even if he did, we might still miss him in the crowd. It was insane, and only getting more crowded as the sun set.

"Knowing Boyd, he's probably knees deep in wild naked titties by now," I commented as we pushed our way out of the crowd, working our way away from the epicenter of Bourbon Street.

We wondered back toward campus, me hoping to find Allison, Clint hoping to find cheap beer, and we compromised in to a divey little place called The Boot. We got a couple of pitchers of beer and spent some time catching up.

We had been best friends in grade school, but obviously drifted apart. And my drinking habits had not endeared me to him as of late. But we talked, as old friends do, of past exploits and future endeavors, saying things like, "I can't believe we lost touch," and "We've got to do better staying connected," the shit people always say they know won't happen.

We agreed that Boyd and I were lucky to be alive and not incarcerated by this point, and that Randy had been the smart one to stay in the military. There was nothing in Bell County but coal mining and moonshining, and both had a low survival rate.

I told him I was proud of him for sticking in school, something I hadn't done. I had lost my scholarship right away and dropped out after only two semesters. I wasn't sure what he was gonna do with a degree in porno, besides make porno, but I guess filming people fuck all day might not be so bad.

We decided that my biggest assets were my car and my lack of responsibilities, which on their own didn't seem like the best cards to be holding. But we decided that just meant I would be ready for whatever that river card was.

I knew I hoped Allison was in the mix somehow, but that seemed like a stretch. She was here on spring break from college, and I was here laying low from the shootout. Not the same worlds.

When we got back to the dorm, I could see her standing on the balcony. They had long balconies, wrought iron, with all the entrances to the rooms off of it. She was truly a vision, in a sheer orange dress, cut just right to accentuate her body. The dress blew gently in the breeze, billowing slightly behind her as she leaned over the railing to call down to us, a long curl of hair framing her lovely face.

"See any good titties?" she sang out, flashing that winning smile.

I had stopped in my tracks at the sight of her, the second time she had done that. I was staring up at her with the biggest, goofiest grin on my face. One of those smiles that just keeps growing and growing until your face feels like it can't stretch any further. A smile you know is too big, bordering on creepy, but you can't control it. Seeing her, up on the balcony, smiling down at me... at me... my heart was hers from that moment on. And I couldn't stop smiling about it.

I thought I had prepared myself, medicinally, to converse like a human. But fuck me if she hadn't thrown all that shit out the window with her amazing beauty. Fuck, she was gorgeous, was all that came to mind. And you couldn't just keep repeating that over and over. It would be way too creepy.

I don't know if I said anything to her heckling or not. I don't know if her heckling was an offer to show me her tits or not. I probably should have done more follow-up on that.

Clint pushed me forward and spoke up for us, saying something about not seeing any good ones. I couldn't in that moment remember any tits I'd ever seen that night or any other. She was consuming my everything, and I was loving it.

When she asked us, with a little toss of her head toward Karen's room, if we wanted to come up for a drink, I literally floated up the stairs and into her world. Clint merely said, "Sure, we'd love to." Clint and Karen had been neighbors for a few months now, so she filled us in on the girls' plan.

Apparently, Allison was in town for several more days, and since this was Fat Tuesday, technically the end of Mardi Gras, they wanted to head down to the beach. But they had no car, and Allison was chiding Karen for asking all the worst types of likely date rapists for a ride. All they

119

needed, she was saying, was a nice guy with a car and no responsibilities.

I couldn't believe my ears! I had two out of three covered and could probably fake the funk on the third!

"Ladies, I've got a car and no responsibilities!" I blurted out, forgetting that I was supposed to mention being a nice guy too.

Allison beamed at me, and my heart skipped a beat.

I was bewildered a little bit that I felt so good, worried a little bit that there would be some sort of crash, and sketched out a little bit that I wasn't consulting Boyd as to the nature of our vacation plans. But ultimately, I was happier than I think I had ever been. Road trip with my newfound Yankee goddess. Sounds wonderful, I thought.

Karen had a few more questions for Clint as to my character, and he gave a very nuanced testimony that accentuated my honesty and truthfulness while downplaying my problems with drugs and alcohol. Clint was good. Probably should have been in law school instead of studying porn.

In the end, they decided that since we were all friends of Clint it would be OK. If we did rape and kill them, at least the police would have somewhere to look.

I assured them this was an excellent line of logical reasoning, and also that we wouldn't rape or kill them, and ran next door to tell Boyd the good news. He was back from his solo adventure, in good spirits, and agreeable to the whole plan.

I found him in the bathroom rinsing blood off his hands, paying careful attention to under the nails. He was shirtless and had a little blood on his pants. His hat was also noticeably absent. I had forgotten he wasn't with us the whole time, and I inquired as to the nature of his obvious situation.

"While you were lining up some tail over there, two ghetto-ass motherfuckers tried to jump me. I got one of 'em pretty good, and the other one ran off. I ditched my knife and bloody shirt and headed back here. We don't have enough oxy for a prolonged road trip, but I guess we probably need to get out of here. We should just go for one day down to the beach, then head back home. We only have a couple days of dope left."

"She said she would buy all the gas and beer. Private school trust fund kid, I guess. And you can have my pills if you want, long as we get some pot or something."

I thought these were all valid points in favor of a longer road trip, but I could tell Boyd did not believe me about giving up my pills. I admit, it didn't sound like something I would do.

"Buying the beer and the gas, that's a good deal, man. What's her name again?" Boyd asked with a smile.

121

I had a brain fart. I could see her face, I could hear her voice, I could still smell that little whiff I had gotten when she brushed past me in Karen's room. But her name escaped me.

"Beautiful?" I suggested as Clint and Boyd both groaned, and Boyd threw a pillow at my head.

"Jesus, man, you're gonna have to work on that if you think you're getting into her pants. Have I taught you nothing? Jesus Christ, man, you got it bad. Clint, you coming on this escapade with us?"

"No, I have to do a project to turn in next week, and besides, I would be the fifth wheel in your little Corsica."

"He's got us there, we do drive a Corsica," Boyd said with a smile. "When do we leave?"

He appeared to be fully packed up. I wondered if there was more to his bloody knife story than he was saying in front of Clint. Probably for the best. Despite his performance with Karen and Allison as a character witness for me, Clint would fold under real police questioning. So, the less he knew the better. I knew I would get the whole story later.

Fuck, I hoped this didn't turn into one of those aiding and abetting situations. I had bigger fish to fry.

I told Boyd the girls wanted to leave in the morning, to which he replied, "Well in that case, I propose we get shitfaced!" which we did to great effect, drinking all the beer in Clint's entire dorm. As luck would have it, we didn't run into the girls again that night, so Drunk Jacko did not make an appearance and kill this whole program before it started.

We set out in the morning, four travelers who barely knew each other. Some of us were hungover, some of us were excited, some of us were obnoxious, some of us were starting to jones for heavier dope as the supplies dwindled.

I, myself, was in love as we set out on what was to become the defining road trip of my life.

11 Bon Fucking Voyage

We were headed for the beach, Boyd and me in the front and Karen and Allison in the back. They talked nonstop for the first three hours. Non. Stop. Boyd would turn the music up to drown them out, and they would just talk louder, demanding that we turn the music back down. He would roll his eyes and comply, ever the gentleman.

They complained about our smoking, Karen because she didn't smoke, and Allison because we threw the butts out the window. She was an environmentalist, decrying the destruction of our natural world one cigarette butt at a time.

She had no idea. We used to play a game called spread the filth, in which we would drive through the rich neighborhoods emptying the car of several weeks' worth of garbage. Beer cans and liquor bottles, crushed cigarette boxes and fast-food wrappers would form a trail of filth behind us, right down the middle of those rich bastards' pristine neighborhoods.

"Manicure that, motherfuckers," we would scream as we blared hate music and brandished our ignorance.

I saved my cigarette butts, to be disposed of appropriately, although I was not sure if she noticed or not. I hoped she did. Boyd smoked twice as many, to make up for me not throwing mine out the window.

They complained about Boyd's drinking so early in the day, which was absolutely necessary given the circumstances. He didn't have enough dope to deal with Karen being an animal rights activist vegetarian. She had recently been arrested for locking herself in an animal cage at the Petco, a feat she was still excited about and planning to repeat.

Boyd observed there were easier ways to get arrested if that's what you were going for, but his advice fell on deaf ears. Karen was anti-hunting, anti-guns, anti-meat, three things near and dear to Boyd's heart, so I knew part of his drinking was to help him cope with these wild-eyed liberal Yankees. He came from a long line of hunters and gun nuts.

The other impetus for his daytime drinking was to take the edge off his narcotics crash.

I myself was fond of firearms, though not on a par with Boyd and his family. And I had been rabbit hunting and deer hunting and grouse hunting and turkey hunting with them, but my favorite firearm sport was plinkin'. Boyd and I would sit for hours, shooting cans and bottles and other bits of trash, challenging each other to trick shots and practicing quick draws. It was our version of reusing and recycling.

Boyd was amazing with a sidearm and won us a lot of money over the years at the shooting matches in the hollers. You had to be careful, 'cause some of them shooting matches were rigged. And honestly, the traditional shooting match had more to do with the choke on your shotgun than on your skill at handling it.

Most of our money was made on side bets, Boyd doing trick shots with his pistol. I played the role of hype man and kept track of the money. It was a good system. There was always some redneck who couldn't believe Boyd had just shot the lid off a bottle flying through the air and would bet his coal mining paycheck he couldn't do it again.

There was a lot Allison didn't know about me yet, and that was for the best. So far, she and Karen seemed mostly interested in talking each other's ears off, which gave me time to reflect on the state of things. We had gone to Gulf Shores, Alabama, with Boyd having talked the girls down from a full-on trip to Florida. Florida was just too far, too much gas, etc. He had made a very persuasive argument, secretly based on our lack of narcotics for such a trip.

In reality, we were dangerously low on all drugs. The oxys were long gone, and Boyd had stolen the rest of the Xanax, claiming he lost it in his scrape the night before. I knew he was hoarding it, trying to ration for himself and figuring this whole side trip was my idea so I would have to suffer with no pills. I was a little surprised that I felt as good as I did, but I chalked it up to the endorphins or synapsis or whatever the fuck was being released every time I looked at Allison or heard her voice. I had it bad for this girl, and it was keeping the dope sickness at bay.

We were nearly out of pot, which was a bigger problem, and I knew Boyd's condition would only get worse as his pill supply dwindled. I knew what it looked like when we were out of dope, and it wasn't pretty.

But overall, I was in good spirits, listening to Allison talk to Karen and Karen talk to Allison, and ignoring Boyd's constant bitching. I loved every minute of it. Even when Allison insisted on playing her mix tape she had brought, and the two sang every song and it drove Boyd crazy and he started talking about ritual suicide. I could not be deterred from my infatuation. This was the most amazing woman I had ever met.

And since I was doing all the driving, it gave me the perfect excuse to refrain from true participation in the conversation. Had to watch the road after all. This was a good thing, because experience had taught me that the quickest way to a cockblock was me attempting to engage a beautiful woman in conversation. I would always fuck it up some way, and I was determined not to fuck this one up. All I had to do was drive this car, be loose and agreeable as to timetable, and shut the fuck up.

Boyd would be a problem, though. They were talking about days and days of road trip adventure, and I knew he would never make it. The situation came to a head when we rolled into Gulf Shores.

We had driven around to find a public access beach and picked up more beer. I was looking forward to watching these college coeds strip down and go swimming in their underwear, as that was the next agenda item on the itinerary. It was turning into a lovely afternoon.

But when we piled out of the car, Boyd was telling me we had to run back to the store for cigarettes, and that he was gonna buy some swim trunks. I knew something was up because I had never known Boyd to spend money on any apparel, let alone swim trunks. We were hicks, we swam in our shorts. But I climbed back in the car to see what he wanted. The girls didn't' seem to care one way or another as they ran off down the beach, leaving a trail of clothes behind them.

"You are killing me, Smalls," I sighed as I started the car, imagining the sexy ocean frolicking that was about to go on without us.

"Let's at least get out of the parking lot before we discuss it," he said as he lit up one of the smokes he apparently was not out of. I shook my head and drove about three blocks inland before pulling the car over.

"What?" I opened the negotiations.

"What," he answered. "What indeed. What the fuck are we doing here? Let's just keep driving and head back home. Fuck these Yankee bitches."

I can't say I was surprised. We were out of dope, or nearly there, and Boyd was always testy when the prospect of unplanned and unsolicited sobriety loomed on the horizon. But ditching these girls in another state? That would be low, even for us.

"We can't leave them here. That's shitty! A fucked-up thing to do to somebody. Plus, they know Clint and he will think we're assholes!"

Plus, I am in love with this girl, I thought but didn't say.

"They'll be fine. They got money. They'll hop a bus and be back to their college lives in no time. And Clint already thinks you're an asshole, and it's about time he learned that I am an asshole too. So why the fuck not? Are you really gonna fuck this Yankee broad? 'cause I am not fooling with that animal rights nutjob Jew bitch. I don't need that drama. I'm not that hard up for some pussy."

I let the thinly veiled insult regarding my love life go for the moment. He was right. Not in what he said, but in what he meant. He meant that he was going through withdrawal and probably wouldn't be able to get it up while he was dope sick. And he meant that these girls were way too country club for our trailer park asses. And it was a lot to go through just to get laid. An epically large amount of hassle, just to get some pussy.

He was right, but I wanted to stick it out. I told him how I liked this girl and wanted to give it a try. I told him how Karen had said her brother in Birmingham could get us some pot, so everything would be alright 'cause we would have weed.

"We will not be alright. It is not going to be alright in any kind of way. It's gonna suck and the car ride back to Bell County is gonna suck ass. So, you better enjoy this shit, you selfish prick."

And with that he climbed out of the car, slammed the door, and threw his cigarette down in disgust.

I shook my head, got out, and walked around the car to lean up against the passenger side with him. You had to soothe him when he got this way, feathers all ruffled up, mad and anxious. You had to pet him a little bit, like one of those weird hairless cats. I imagine those poor cats are always mad and anxious.

I didn't bring up all the times I had driven his punk ass around so he could get laid. And I didn't mention how I was beginning to think Allison might be the one. Instead, I told him how this was the kind of story we'd tell when we were old and gray. About the time we picked up these two hot Yankee chicks at Mardi Gras, of all places, and spent a week dicking them down all over the Southern

United States for our 21st birthdays. Old man barbershop type of story. Right up there with shooting up a party in the midst of a gang war, which I reminded him was a very good reason to chauffeur these two northern debutantes around for a few more days, drinking their beer, smoking their weed, and burning their gas.

And maybe, just maybe, acquiescing to bone them for our trouble.

"Dickin' 'em down all over the Southern United States?" Boyd couldn't help but laugh at my argument, and he agreed the best course of action would be to get a bucket of chicken and head back to the beach.

"I guess Karen is kind of hot. Probably looks good naked, and surely to God she doesn't talk that PETA shit while she's fucking, does she?" Boyd clapped me on the back. "You always know just what to say, Jacko."

We spent that first night on the beach, sitting around the campfire, with me feeding Boyd beer so he'd pass out. Karen quickly followed, leaving Allison and me sitting under a blanket.

We were huddled together against the cool dampness that settled in as we watched the waves crash under the moonlight. She had been telling me something about someone going somewhere, and I was hanging on every word yet not comprehending. I was a little drunk, and the melodic sound of her voice seemed right in tune with the gentle ebb and flow of the tide, rising and falling in a beautiful melody that wrapped itself around my heart.

I had it bad.

As we lay on the sand, I thought to myself, you're fucking losing it. You just met this girl. You have absolutely nothing in common. She's a rich college girl with dreams and aspirations and a good heart. You're a trailer trash dope fiend with only bad intentions in every situation. What the fuck are you doing, falling for this girl?

She had been telling me about her hometown, some island off the coast with beautiful beaches she couldn't wait to see again. It all sounded so wonderful. I was resting my head on my hand, elbow in the sand, looking down at her as the moonlight reflected off her eyes, those deep blue eyes that kept swallowing me whole.

I wondered, in the back of my mind, if she was one of those sirens of Greek mythology, sent to wreck my ship on the rocky shore, 'cause I was completely hypnotized by her beauty and charm. I decided if she was a siren, I was gonna wreck this motherfucker for sure.

"You don't say much do you?" she grinned up at me. I figured if this was how a shipwreck happened, it wasn't so bad. Bon Voyage, I thought to myself, as I leaned in to kiss her for the first time, bon fucking voyage.

12 I Brought My Webelos Shovel, Just in Case

I awoke the next morning, snuggled up with Allison, spooning comfortably under the blanket. Spooning is its own indicator of the odds for successful coupling. If you wake up spooning and it is immediately uncomfortable, get the fuck out of there. The spooning doesn't lie.

I kept my eyes closed, feeling her easy breathing, holding her tight. I thought about how amazing last night had been, even though I still had all my clothes on. We had kissed and caressed, and done some of that heavy petting they always warned us about in Sunday School. At least I figured that was what they were talking about. Baptists are sort of vague on the specifics, and I never felt comfortable enough to ask what in the hell heavy petting actually meant.

I felt a sudden wave of panic, as I thought of the possibility that last night might have been my one shot to nail Allison and I had blown it with soft sand and crashing waves lulling me to sleep.

But I thought of the way her eyes had twinkled in the moonlight when she smiled so sweetly at me and nestled her head into my chest. I thought of the way she had kissed me before rolling over and pulling me onto my side behind her to hold her tight.

I wondered who had fallen asleep first, and decided it was probably me. I could fall asleep at the drop of a hat, and I started to wonder if she had wanted me to be more aggressive from the rear spoon position. I couldn't be positive, because honestly, who knows what crazy things are in a woman's mind, but I felt pretty sure she wasn't disappointed in the way the night had gone. Nobody goes into the spoon position if they are seeking further erotic stimulation. At least I didn't think they did.

I held her tighter as we lay there, and she let out a contented sigh, reaching up and grasping my hand, pulling it to her lips and kissing it.

I didn't want the moment to end, but I knew we had to get moving. Karen wanted to drive all the way into Bumfuck Sylacauga this morning to see her aunt before making our way to Birmingham to see her brother and get some pot. And I knew we were gonna need some fucking pot.

It was gonna be a long day. I finally opened my eyes to find Boyd squatting by the fire and scowling at me. I wondered how long he had been watching us sleep. Knowing him, it could have been a while.

"Wakey, wakey dickhead. We gotta go get some smokes."

He was upset I was hooking up with this girl. And he was mad that Karen was above the IQ threshold he imposed on potential romantic partners.

Boyd had an IQ threshold for girls, and those above the threshold would never fall for his bullshit. Karen was clearly above this threshold, and she wasn't getting fucked up with us. Drugs and alcohol can help you out with threshold mediation, but that would not work in this case. Karen wasn't drinking, and we had no dope. It was killing him that Allison was clearly out of my league, yet, somehow, I appeared to be pulling it off.

"We gotta get some pot today, I'm crashing hard. Beer won't cut it, and I am not drinking liquor with you. But I need something."

Boyd spoke low and quickly, but Allison still heard him. I guess she was awake too, also keeping her eyes closed and enjoying the moment.

"Karen's brother can get some pot, calm down. Jesus, you sound like a junky. What's up with that?"

Allison rolled over away from me, and Boyd and I looked at each other. He sort of shrugged with a half apologetic look on his face and rolled his eyes. The truth hurts, I suppose.

He was right of course, as was she. We were junkies, and to his point, she would eventually figure this out. I didn't think it had to be first fucking thing in the morning, but I suppose that is how it happens sometimes.

"Let's get some coffee," I offered, changing the subject.

"And smokes," Boyd reiterated.

He was a needy fuck in the mornings. Much to his chagrin we had to break camp and pack up the environmentalist way, which took much longer. In Bell County, you just throw everything into the fire pit and leave it. But Allison insisted we leave no trace of human occupancy on this pristine natural habitat. Apparently, there are all kinds of creatures, big and small, that inhabit the ocean and the sand and the beach, and none of them like our garbage being left in their home.

I could tell from Boyd's expression he wanted to tell her that we as Appalachians didn't like northern capitalists coming into our home for the past several hundred years and stealing all our resources, replacing our trees, and coal, and natural gas with clear cut hillsides, blown apart mountains, slurry and sludge filled valleys and poisoned water. So fuck what you think about my litter, he wanted to say.

It was circular logic, I know, but the scars of the War of Northern Aggression still ran deep for some Southerners. You did sometimes feel like you were colonized a little bit. Especially when the money flowed only one way, and mineral rich areas were poverty pockets.

Eventually, the earth was saved from our litter and we made it to America's greatest monument to environmental destruction, the gas station, to get Boyd smokes before he died. He still would not give up shotgun, the whiny fucker. So we hit the road with two chatty Yankees in the back, one sullen Southerner in the front, and a lovestruck dopehead pretending not to be a junky at the wheel.

It was about a four-hour drive to Sylacauga, and Boyd slept fitfully the whole time. This suited me fine, as I just wanted to listen to Allison talk to Karen. I didn't get half of what they were talking about. College scholars and dropouts diverge after high school.

They start to actually learn things in school, as opposed to the bullshit we learn in high school. Academic things, great writers and philosophers, social theories, actual histories. While they are filling their brains with all the knowledge academia offers, we are filling our brains with how to score, how to dodge cops, how to talk your way out of a room. After a couple of years, college kids and street kids can barely communicate, let alone have anything in common.

Boyd's shrug had said it all. She would eventually find out who I really was. I could only play the mute game for so long.

Although, apparently, I had gone mute for six weeks one summer, back when Boyd, Randy, and I had shared an apartment. I had finally broken my silence by standing up from my usual spot on the couch, executing a perfect standing backflip with a perfect 10 landing, and stating emphatically, "That's how it's done, Mary Lou!"

Boyd and Randy had been stunned into their own silence for a couple of moments, before clapping me on the back, high-fiving, and telling me how great it was to have me back. They said they thought I had gone up and wasn't coming back down.

I didn't realize I had not been speaking. I thought we had been having all sorts of meaningful conversations for the past month and a half, but it had apparently all been in my head. We chalked it up to bad acid and huffing paint, both of which I now avoided.

But this self-imposed silence with Allison was different. I knew damn well why I wasn't talking; I didn't want to screw things up. She didn't need to know what a callous, douchey, self-centered prick I was, and she didn't need to know about the extent of the drugs. I had gleaned enough from her conversations with Karen to know that my strongest attribute, an incredible tolerance for substance use, was not something that would impress her.

I figured that unless it was true about opposites attracting each other, I was fucked as soon as she got to know me. Because Allison was sweet, and kind, and loving, and empathetic, and concerned for the wellbeing of the world around her. And I was none of those things. She had only kind things to say about everyone and everything. She was the nicest person I had ever met, and it made me love her all the more.

Things got hairy in Sylacauga. The plan was that we would drop Karen off at her aunt's house and the rest of us would go get something to eat while she had her visit. But the incident at the McDonalds made the situation untenable.

We had used the pissers and placed our orders. When we emerged, there was a very large black woman standing by our car.

"Ya'll Kentucky asses hit my car and scratched it!" she yelled as we approached. "See, right there, there's the scratch!"

This scratch appeared to have been there since the Reagan administration, and I told her as much as I dodged past her and opened my door.

"Get in the car," Boyd said to Allison, as I climbed in and fired up the engine. Boyd and Allison both hopped in, and I could see Boyd had his gun drawn. He was holding it down low enough for the lady to see it through the window. She backed away yelling about how her people were just inside and they weren't scared of us honkey motherfuckers and they would be right out.

I slammed the car into reverse and tore out of the parking lot, glancing in the rearview to see Allison's reaction. She looked a little rattled, and asked shakily, "What the fuck was that?"

I didn't know if she had seen Boyd's gun or not, but I offered, "these blacks down here are racist, I guess?"

I was hoping to move past it, but Boyd was having none of it.

"Sure, sure. I'll tell you what the problem is. The liberals in Washington have given 'em too much freedom and power and now they walk around here like they own the whole country. We oughta go back there and shoot that bitch in the face. This is Alabama, goddammit, you can still shoot blacks down here!"

Boyd started getting antsy, and I knew under these stressful dope-free conditions it wouldn't be long before the state was mongrelized and the Zionist expansion of power through control of banking and Hollywood speech reared *its* ugly head.

I had to act fast, so I said, "I've got an idea. Let's go see Junior and Papaw. Junior will have something for the head. Let me find a payphone."

My mother's family is from Bumfuck Alabama, near Sylacauga, over in Clay County. Mom and Dad had moved away from Alabama before I was born, so I had only ever seen my mother's family on holidays.

But I had made a trip down the previous spring with Boyd and Hippy John to go turkey hunting. Hippy John loved turkey hunting, as did my Papaw. And Junior loved to party, so we had all had a blast despite not bagging any turkeys.

We finally found a pay phone and I called my dad. I needed to call my grandparents to tell them we were coming. You can't show up in that holler unannounced. Pawpaw don't drink no more, but he's the only one of his eight brothers that don't. And they all live right there on the same dirt road, kind of Deliverance style if you're a stranger. I didn't have their phone number, so I had to call my dad.

Boyd came to the phone booth with me. Turns out it was Dad's birthday. Surprised the shit out of him 'cause I never call on his birthday.

"Hello, dad. Happy Birthday."

"Ummm, hello." Followed by silence. "Thanks. How are you?" he finally continued.

He knew I wanted something, he just had to figure out what it was and how to dodge it. I didn't have time to fuck with him, so I just came out with it.

"Great. Listen, I'm in Alabama and was thinking of dropping by the old folks' place here in Clay County as we pass through, but I don't have the number. Could you give me Mamaw's number please?"

I thought it was a great explanation, clear and concise. But Dad wanted more.

"When did you go to Alabama? Why did you go? When are you coming back? Your mother's worried, you know."

I could hear her in the background. She was always worried.

"I went to Mardi Gras. I met a girl. We are in Alabama, visiting some of her friends, and I thought it would be nice to introduce her to my grandparents. Plus, the situation in Sylacauga might escalate into a race war."

"Jesus, son." It was always good to get the Reverend to invoke the Almighty. Lets you know you had him rattled.

"And you want to bring this person to Clay County? I don't think that's a good idea, for her, but here's the number."

He rattled off the number and hung up.

Good talk, Dad. Honestly, it was probably good advice. Few cultured women could handle Clay County, and Allison was definitely a cultured woman.

"You think this is a good idea, bringing her down there?" Boyd asked as we walked back to the car where Allison patiently waited.

"Probably better to meet my extended family than yours, if we're trying to convince her we are normal folk," I answered.

Boyd laughed, "you sure about that? Remember Junior and the dog?"

I laughed too because he was right. Boyd's family might be drug dealers, but mine was moonshiners. Two sides of the same crazy coin, I guess. And Junior was a trip for sure; he had made the turkey hunting excursion memorable.

Boyd, Hippy John, and I had gone down there with the plan of camping in the woods, killing a couple of turkeys, and smoking a lot of pot. We were escaping the early spring briskness of Kentucky to experience some of that good southern hotness in Alabama.

The weather was good, but all the land around there seemed fenced off and posted up. No trespassing signs every 10 feet and No hunting signs every 20. Everything marked up with private hunt club logos and insignias.

Now we've never let a little ole sign deter us from quietly camping; but we saw early on that we couldn't wander around making turkey calls and blasting shotguns. Luckily, we had plenty of Hippy John's good pot. So, we just spent the couple of days sneaking around the hunt club's land smoking dope, enjoying nature, and staying out of sight.

Boyd and I had a bet going as to what would actually happen if we came upon another person out there. He was betting that Hippy John would play it cool if we walked up on somebody, but he would flip out if somebody walked up on us.

I was playing the odds he would flip chicken either way, slit their throat, cut their ears off for trophies and bury the body in the woods. I was so sure; I had brought my Webelo shovel for the occasion.

You just never knew about Hippy John. He killed three or four over the years before the feds finally got anything to stick. And that was only 'cause that feller didn't die and could testify.

Anyway, we saw no other people, so all I used my Webelo shovel for was to bury the firepits. We spent our last full day there hanging with Uncle Junior. He said he had the day off, but he seemed to have most days off.

We had a great time. Junior gave us the grand tour of the county, drinking and smoking all day. That night we drove down to the creek to get high; Hippy John had brought a couple of pills to cook.

"Hot damn, you boys is wild!" Junior had exclaimed when he saw the needles. "I'm off the pin right now, rehab you know, but you boys go ahead now. We come down here to party!"

He crushed his beer can and grabbed another.

"Your momma would shit if she seen you now boy. She ain't never been cool with a good time. And your preacher daddy is a stick in the mud too!"

I laughed because it was true. My mom was the oldest sibling and definitely the least fun. Her and Dad were a couple of righteous do-gooders. No fun at all.

We got hammered down by the creek, swapping stories and telling lies. But when we went to leave, the truck was stuck in the mud. They're famous for their mud down there, and according to Junior, everybody gets stuck in the mud now and then.

"I don't know why they don't just get some goddam four-wheel drive now and then," Hippy John muttered.

He was worse than Boyd when things didn't go as planned. Boyd and I always joked that we should make a reality TV show featuring Hippy John called "Awww Fuck!" where cameras follow him around on hunting and fishing expeditions capturing all the ways he flips out when shit don't go his way. And shit never goes his way, he's an unlucky fucker when it comes to things going according to plan.

Junior gave him a sour face, and said, "C'mon Y'all, it's just over yon hill," and gestured vaguely out into the night. I didn't know what yon hill meant, but I knew if we had to go just further than that we were probably in for a hike. Talk about a buzzkill.

When we finally hit the paved road, I opened my mouth to make a smartass comment about the location of yon hill, when lights appeared around the bend. They were coming toward us, headed in the opposite direction we were heading, but that didn't stop Junior from trying to hitchhike.

He did it in the most Junior way possible, standing in the road, pistol in hand, slowly waving his arms in slow arcs over his head, like he was trying to conduct a symphony orchestra that only he could see. It was a lot for a high person to take in, and I started laughing and staggering in the shoulder.

When he got to what must have been the crescendo, judging by the intensity of the arm flailing, the truck swerved around him, not slowing down. They sped off into the night. At which point Junior shot at them, screaming obscenities to punctuate the bullets.

"Don't you know who the fuck I am?!?" he yelled after them as their taillights disappeared into the darkness.

"Probably do," Hippy John said. "Probably do."

He had his gun drawn, holding it discreetly in the crook of his folded arms.

I had stopped laughing and looked over at Boyd. I caught the glint of moonlight on a gun barrel from him too. Shit, I thought, I don't wanna use my Webelo shovel to bury my uncle.

"C'mon, y'all," Junior called back to us as he staggered on down the road, oblivious to the guns drawn behind him. Or he might have not given a fuck if he did know.

"We'll stop in here at Otis's and get a snort."

Hippy John and Boyd nodded at each other, holstered their guns, and followed Junior down the road. I realized the outline of a building was emerging through the trees, down off the side of the hill.

I had never met Otis. He was one of my Papaw's brothers, and Papaw didn't fool with many of his brothers because he had got religion and the rest of them hadn't. But I figured we were with Junior, so we'd be alright.

We crept down Otis's driveway toward his doublewide trailer. It had a covered porch roughly the same size as the trailer, making for a pretty large total structure. The moon splashed some light between the leaves of the heavy canopy of trees that covered Otis's little corner of the world.

We paused by the 56 Ford pickup truck on blocks with no hood, half an engine, and broken windows. An Alabama yard restoration in progress. The pickup was not the only restoration project going on, it appeared.

"Now follow right behind me and be careful. Otis is always setting booby traps out here." Junior pointed to a trip wire running from the Ford over into a bush, attached to…something.

"People say Otis ain't right, but you just gotta know how to deal with him. And he makes the best fuckin moonshine around." Junior sounded convincing, at least as to the quality of the moonshine, so we carried on.

I was excited to meet my kin, but I was getting a little nervous as to why we were sneaking in. And why did Junior know how to sneak in?

Junior led us on a roundabout route, avoiding trip wires and two bear traps. There was a heavy dog chain staked near the porch, with no dog attached.

"Where's the dog?" Hippy John hissed through clenched teeth.

I looked at Boyd, who had his gun in his hand. I guess he wasn't planning on getting bit, should the dog make an appearance.

"They is probably asleep in there, I'll just see if he has anything in his cabinet out here on the porch. I don't want to wake him. Don't worry about the dog,"

Junior said as he put one foot on the lowest step.

Suddenly, the door burst open, temporarily bathing the porch steps in light, but only for a second. The light was almost immediately obscured by a great pot belly of a man, clad only in flowered boxer shorts, a pink silk kimono robe, and cowboy boots. In his hands he held the biggest double barrel shotgun I had ever seen, almost big enough to make me miss the rest of the outfit.

"Junior, you goddam son of a bitch! You shot my dog!" yelled the giant pot belly man.

The shotgun was being used to talk and gesture with, as he yelled at Junior.

Which meant he wasn't planning on using it, I assumed, an assumption Boyd seemed to share because he had not brought his gun up yet. He was inching to his right, ever so slowly, with the gun held behind his leg. I glanced over at Hippy John, who was inching to the left. His hands were still empty, but I knew that wouldn't matter much if Hippy John decided to go. He was the fastest draw I knew, and dead on balls accurate. Who do you think taught Boyd how to shoot?

Junior was pleading and protesting against the accusations, unconvincingly, it seemed. He claimed he didn't know what dog Otis was talking about. But he had an awful lot of knowledge about this booby-trapped yard to have never noticed the fucking dog before. Otis seemed to be of that same opinion, and raised the shotgun to his shoulder, training it on Junior.

"You goddam, no good, dog shootin' cock sucker!" he was yelling as he cocked the hammers.

Boyd and Hippy John each crow hopped two steps in opposite directions, guns bearing down on Otis. Junior

149

hopped two steps backward until he was directly in front of me, which I didn't appreciate as the shotgun seemed capable of blasting through him and into me.

"This is my sister Brenda's kid! He's never been down here to see you before! Otis, for fuck's sake let's talk about this!"

Otis lowered his shotgun, a grin spreading across his face.

"Brender's kid? Well shitfire, boys, why didn't you say so! I ain't seen you since you was knee high to a tadpole. Yore momma still running with that preacher man?"

Otis let the hammer off and leaned the shotgun against the door frame, bounding down the stairs, shoving Junior out of the way and pulling me in for a big bear hug. It was so gross and so relieving, all at once. I made a mental note to send him shirts for Christmas.

"Y'all still live in North Carolina?" he asked as he let me go.

"Kentucky, Otis," Junior stammered, holding his hand on his chest, trying to still his racing heart.

"Shut up, Junior, you dog shooting motherfucker. I'll deal with you later... y'all come on up to the house and check out my new batch!" and he bounced on up the stairs, pretty lithely for a fat fucker, grabbing his shotgun as he walked through the door. "You too, Junior..."

Boyd and I looked at each other, shrugged, and followed him into the house. Hippy John had a brief discussion with Junior about bringing him to places where people might shoot at him. I think he was explaining that Junior would be the one that ended up shot before it was all over if this type of thing should continue to happen.

I remember that the moonshine was really fucking good, and that Otis was really fucking funny once he wasn't pointing shotguns at you. At some point we stumbled the rest of the way to Junior's because I was in his living room floor when Hippy John woke me up the next morning.

He explained that it was nothing personal, he would never intentionally hurt me or any member of my family, but he couldn't stand idly by and get shot at, so he was sorry for last night. I wondered if Junior had made it, but then I saw him through the window. He was showing Boyd his compound bow and I figured nobody had ended up shot after all.

Hippy John already had the car packed, and after a quick breakfast from Mamaw's next door, we were on the way. As we pulled out of the dirt road back onto the blacktop, Hippy John said, "Jack, your family is crazy as fuck. But I like 'em," which meant something coming from him. 'cause Hippy John was crazy as fuck his own self.

That was the last time I had been in Clay County at the family dirt road, and I began to understand Boyd's point about not bringing Allison to this crazy place full of my crazy family. This would probably run her off for sure, I figured, unless we could somehow avoid everyone but Memaw and Papaw.

"Maybe Junior's working today," Boyd said, as if he was reading my mind again. "we could use a joint, though."

And I could use an Oscar worthy performance out of my kin I barely knew to help perpetuate this false narrative I was spinning about being a sane, normal person who Allison could love back, I thought.

But I knew that was asking a lot as we turned onto that old dirt road.

13 She Doesn't Speak Alabamian

When we pulled up to Mamaw's trailer, we realized Allison was fast asleep. She is so beautiful, I thought to myself, watching her sleep.

Hope we aren't fucking this up, I also thought, knowing I probably was.

"Probably for the best," I nodded toward Allison. "MeMaw sounded like she thought I was a prank caller on the phone earlier. Let's go smooth it over before we wake sleeping beauty there."

We had just climbed out of the car when Junior appeared out of nowhere. Must've had the day off again.

"Morning boys," he greeted us. "I was wondering when y'all would come back around. I seen turkeys yesterday over in the south pasture. But I see you brought other entertainment this time."

He grinned as he peered into the back of the car at Allison, letting out a low whistle. "Boy, you sure can pick 'em. What's her story? Come tell me all about it while we see if Memaw's got any biscuits left."

It took a while to get everyone to understand why we were in Alabama and who the girl sleeping in the car was. At about the time we had everyone on board, there was a light knocking at the door. Allison had awoken, and lucky for me, did not immediately flee upon seeing her surroundings.

I guess college chicks in horror movies do usually walk up to the house.

When she breezed through the doorway, smiling brightly, it took my breath away. Even Papaw was speechless, which was its own miracle. Memaw called from the kitchen where she was whipping up biscuits per Junior's request,

"Oh my goodness, she's beautiful, Jack! Don't be rude -- introduce us," she said as she bustled around the counter out of the kitchen, wiping her hands on her apron.

"Junior, you stay out of my bacon!" she called behind her, watching Junior with those eyes in the back of her head.

I made the introductions, but that was as far as I got, because Papaw launched into an explanation of the one time he had been to Rhode Island in the army, just a bump on the way to Boston he said.

I looked at Allison, to see if she was offended at his 'littlest state' dig, but she just stared at him with a pleasant, but blank, look on her face. She hadn't understood what he said at all.

After a few more questions and comments from Memaw and Papaw, met with equally pleasant, but blank, stares, we realized she didn't speak Alabamian. She had been able to understand the few words I had spoken to her in Kentuckyanese, so I assumed she was bilingual, speaking both Southern English and Yankee Proper.

I hadn't realized the difficulty of a non-native Southern speaker in understanding all the dialects. But she had no idea what my grandparents were saying, they may as well have been speaking Cantonese.

Luckily, Boyd sprang into action and translated. He was, after all, a true Southern gentleman, fluent in numerous dialects. I had even seen him converse in Creole pidgin while we were in the bayou. Allison didn't bat an eye, recognizing the necessity of translation and going with it.

It turned into a pleasant visit after that, with Boyd translating between my love and my kin. Papaw showed us his homemade turkey calls, and Memaw gave us the gossip on all the cousins. There was always plenty of gossip on all the cousins, us being white trashy and all.

Junior got bored and left, which meant Memaw could spill the juicy stuff about his kid, and Papaw fell asleep in his chair. He had heard all this nonsense before, and what the whole lot of 'em needed was Jesus, or so he said. When he compared them and all their problems to him and how good he was, (which is the oldest and most sacred of all Christian traditions), he made a compelling argument. He did have his shit together slightly better than his heathen brothers.

Boyd wandered off to find Junior and smoke a joint, and Memaw did what Memaw's always do, she kept feeding us until we were about to burst. Despite eating too much, I was happier than I'd been in a long time, sitting with Allison in hillbilly heaven, eating too much squirrel.

But like all good things, it had to end, which happened when we realized we were supposed to be picking Karen up at some point.

Shit. Karen.

None of us knew her aunt's number. So, we just had to head back to Sylacauga to pick her up, approximately 5 hours later than we had said we would be back. She might have been annoyed that we were gone so long, but I think she understood once we explained that we had been visiting my extended family too. Small world and all.

I had neglected to tell Allison it was Memaw's famous squirrel brain gravy on them biscuits, so she wasn't able to tell Karen, who would have bemoaned the violent nature in which the squirrels had died for the gravy.

I figured some things were better left unsaid.

14 She's Playing Creedence

We were in high spirits when we hit the brother's college in downtown Birmingham. We were also exhausted. Karen's brother Bill pointed to his roommate's bed when I asked where to crash, and I woke up the next morning with Allison cuddled up next to me.

Two nights in a row, sleeping together but not *sleeping together.* I thought about how weird this was starting to seem, although I knew there was no hope for anything to have happened the previous night. Sex hadn't even entered my mind. I barely remembered getting into Birmingham, I had been so tired. Alabama kin can do that to you. They are an exhausting bunch.

I felt that stupid humongous smile spread across my face as I lay next to her. I couldn't believe I had introduced her to my family, and it actually went well. And she still wanted to sleep next to me.

And I hadn't been high in a couple of days.

It didn't last long, though, not being high. We got some pot later that day from Bill's people. Bill's people were a bunch of weirdo punk rock kids living in a tenement house in the ghetto of Birmingham, Alabama.

Being from Bell County where our ghettos were tiny trailer parks and rural moonshine hollers, any urban area felt like a ghetto to me.

"Just like on TV," I wanted to tell Boyd. But I thought expressing my true fear of urban America would make me look like a hick.

We had to hang out for way too long to suit Boyd and me. We preferred a quick and easy business transaction for our drugs. Mel being the lone exception to that rule.

Although, increasingly, we didn't want to hang out over there either.

A lot of people start out using drugs socially, we're all just getting high together. It starts as a communal activity. For junkies, that communal shit goes out the window. You form a smaller and smaller group, until eventually it's just you. You and the dope.

You say it's just gonna be for fun, sometimes, and only if everybody's going in on the party.

But it never lasts. As the addiction boils inside you, steeping into your being, becoming a vital part of the concoction, it cooks off all the parts of you not integrating, not homogenizing with the new addictive compound you are becoming.

Your love of literature, or music, or art, goes away, because that doesn't contribute to your new compound.

158

Hobbies, interests, dreams... all casualties to the new plan of the day, the new goal set every morning. The new necessity of your life; the only thing that matters is your drug.

It doesn't always have to be a specific drug. We all have a favorite; we all have a ranking system. But for me, it was more important to have some sort of buzz on, rather than a particular one. I would jones for certain shit, of course, but I was a creature of convenience.

So, whatever I was around, booze, pot, pills, coke, acid, or whatever, I wanted as much of it as I could get, as fast as I could get it.

And Boyd and I had gotten good at scrounging and scheming and staying in dope of one kind or another for years. Every day. Fucked up high and drunk, every fucking day. Rarely, if ever, did we have a day we weren't at least able to come up with some pot and some booze. At least enough to get blasted and pass out.

I could tell from watching Boyd we were pretty far off of our typical regimen. He looked rough. He must have run out of all the pills. And having no pot either had put a'hurtin' on him.

I realized I should probably feel the way he looked, a couple days into a detox, but I was walking on sunshine and Allison was my sun.

Just when I thought things couldn't get any better, Allison found an old acoustic guitar in the corner, one that the spikey haired freaks hadn't smashed with the rest of the house. It appeared that getting hammered and hammering on the house with various musical instruments and farm implements was a favorite pastime of these punk rock kids.

That, and giving each other piercings and bad tattoos.

Anyway, Allison picked that guitar up, sat down in the corner and strummed it softly. I sat down a couple of feet from her, in awe at my good fortune. This amazing girl who was still putting up with me could also play guitar! She played a few bars and started to sing.

Motherfucking Creedence, how goddam cool is that? She's playing fucking Creedence Clearwater Revival and nailing it. Followed by Bob Dylan, followed by Janis, followed by the Grateful fucking Dead. This girl was perfect, a hot ass folk singer hippy chick, are you kidding me?!

There was no going back for me, this girl was everything I would have ever picked, if I was trying to design the perfect girl. And she was kind, so kind to everyone, and gentle and sweet and empathetic, attributes my shallow ass would have never thought to include in the mix of my dream girl.

But after listening to her and Karen talk about social justice, and the environment, and civil rights, and all the other tree hugging hippy dippy shit they were constantly talking about, I realized how much Allison's ability to put herself in others' shoes and see their viewpoint formed and shaped the beautiful person she was.

She was a beautiful soul. In a smoking hot body. And she could play guitar. and she had the voice of an angel. My angel.

I was getting nervous, because when shit is too good to be true, it usually is. I couldn't talk to Boyd about it. He was struggling with his detox and wouldn't understand anyway. So, I did the only thing I knew to do, shut the fuck up and keep on riding the train till the end.

When the mohawk kid with all the face tattoos finally returned with the pot, we smoked several blunts with the whole punk rock community in the type of social interaction setting that Boyd and I abhorred. Finally, after what felt like days, we were able get the fuck out of there. Allison's guitar playing was the only saving grace of the entire enterprise.

I realized after the second hit off one of the blunts that I didn't even care about the pot. I was content just being around her.

When we got back to Bill's dorm, he and Karen both left; her to do some random guy down the hall, and him to do some random girl somewhere. Boyd went outside to smoke copious amounts of pot by himself and try to ease his withdrawal pains.

Allison and I stayed in and watched a movie. Best date night ever. *SLC Punk*, 'cause we hadn't seen enough green hair that day. It was the best movie I had ever seen. Until I saw another movie with Allison, and then that was the best movie I had ever seen. Until we saw another movie. And so forth. Part of it was that we had pot for the first time in days. Part of it was that we were both movie buffs. Part of it was that she was absolutely amazing in every way.

We didn't "go all the way," that night, as I imagined my father would have said if we had ever had "the talk." My father and I never had "the talk." But I figured that's what he would call intercourse.

Allison and I made out, and felt each other up, and induced some orgasms, which she said hadn't happened to her before. I knew from previous experience that I had a knack for foreplay, and I also knew from previous experience that most twenty-year-old women hadn't had an orgasm of any kind, besides ones they gave themselves.

I had been lucky enough to have a couple of periods of instruction over the years, mostly before the drugs of course. But it's like riding a bike, you never forget.

And I had it bad, all the way crazy, crazy in love.

I knew this whole affair had to end, though. Allison's spring break was almost over, as was Karen's, and Bill's, and all the other people with a plan for their life.

I was so sad as we drove out of Birmingham, bound for New Orleans and our impending departures.

We had one more night at Tulane before Allison's flight. Clint was happy to take Boyd off my hands, not that I had been paying much attention to him in the throes of his detox. Boyd did seem to liven up as we got close to New Orleans. He could see the end of his reduced drug intake on the horizon. Probably figured on scoring a little dope down in the crowds.

He had wanted to keep moving toward home, but I insisted we stay the last night and hang out with Clint. I wanted to see Allison to the airport in the morning, and then head out.

Boyd did like Clint, so he consented to one more night.

We all went out together, back to the Boot. Mardi Gras might have been over, but the city was still partying. We went to the Boot, trying to find a nice quiet drink. We were all worn out from our road trip through scenic Alabama. I still wasn't talking too much, which was good, and I wasn't drinking too much, which was even better.

The Boot had a thing for Guns and Roses because every other song was GnR that night. Throughout the whole road trip, every time we flipped through the radio, we came across one Guns and Roses track after another. We thought Axl must've died or something, but upon questioning, the bartender revealed that the DJ was just a fan.

Allison and I joked that they must be our new jam too because they were providing the soundtrack of our courtship. I hadn't been into Guns and Roses since junior high, which is probably the last time I believed in all this lovey dovey stuff too.

I guess Slash and the boys were operating as a form of auditory conditioning for my emotional awakening, remembering how to love through Axl's piercing screams. Sounds like a dissertation.

All I knew was I was having the time of my life despite the musical selections. Midway through this evening, our first real date with wining and dining, I realized that it could be our last real date. Allison was leaving on an early flight the next morning, signaling the traditional end to a spring break fling.

I realized I didn't want this fling to be over, I didn't want this to be a fling. I thought about looking for wedding chapels, but I realized we weren't in Vegas. And also, I realized that it was a crazy idea.

Instead of proposing, I said, "What if you missed your flight?"

We were sitting back in Karen's dorm on the roommate's bed. Allison had her legs draped over my lap as she leaned back on her elbows. She looked up at me, a sly smile creeping up from the corners of her lips.

"I could look for a later flight. But I do have to get back to school at some point," she said. "I can't just stay on spring break forever."

"What if I drove you?" I answered. I could think of a thousand good reasons why that was a dumb idea, including gas, mileage, time and distance, and Boyd.

But I hoped she wouldn't think of any of them.

Her smile had widened until it was a full-on sunbeam. "You're serious? To Baltimore? Really?"

I hadn't been to Baltimore in ages, and the last time didn't go well. But yeah, to Baltimore, I thought.

"Absolutely! I would love another road trip with you!" I exclaimed, probably too loudly and too excitedly. I really would love to spend the rest of my life with you, I wanted to say. Luckily, she jumped into my arms and cut me off.

"You're crazy!" she said.

You don't know the half, I thought.

She continued, "But let's do it. It'll be fun!"

I fell asleep holding her that night, content I had put off the inevitable for at least a few more days. And relieved that she hadn't figured out my crazy yet. Although agreeing to traverse half the continent with some guy you just met a few days ago might be an indication of her crazy. But I decided that if she was gonna include me in her crazy, then it must be the good kind.

15 She Hates Fleetwood Mac

Boyd was less excited when I told him about the plan. We were loading the car.

"Jesus, man, the point of banging some broad on vacation is that you get to go home. Without them. You are fucking this up. Following her home? It's bad enough you brought her to meet your grandparents. Who does that? That, my friend, is some fucked around, 'I'm desperate and please marry me' shit, and now you are giving her a ride across the country? Not a ride to the store, or down the street, or into town. A ride across the fucking country. You're fucking up."

He was right. The point of having a fling on your vacation was that you could go back to your normal life and only have to put up with the memories. Conventional wisdom said that if you were trying to shack up with some chick, you didn't have to leave the holler to do it.

But I didn't want to shack up with some chick in the holler. More and more, I wasn't sure if I wanted to be in the holler at all. I knew I would live in squalor in the holler if that's what Allison wanted to do, but I was sure she had other ideas for her future. And if she was amenable to bringing me along with her, then shit, it wasn't even really a question of if I would go. I'd go at the drop of a hat.

The drive to Kentucky to drop Boyd off went by quickly, with Boyd and Allison sleeping most of the way.

I had been a little nervous that shit could go south during the layover. But Boyd had popped in to Memaw's and Aunt Lindsey's for some Xanax first thing, and it chilled him right the fuck out. They were in a good spot with their self-medicating that day, and since Kentucky is closer to the Mason Dixon, Allison could even understand them.

We hung out in the trailer for a bit, without incident. Boyd had retired early, happy to be back in comfortable environs, and happy to have a pill buzz. I thought it was weird that he didn't even offer me a Xanax, but I figured I could have asked Memaw for one had I wanted it. I thought it might be even weirder that I hadn't wanted one.

Allison and I watched TV for a little while, sitting among Memaw's knickknacks. She did not seem the least bit concerned that I lived in my friend's grandmother's trailer and that everyone seemed high on pills.

I counted it as a blessing that none of our junky acquaintances stopped by, and frankly, I was glad Boyd had gone to bed. He had been sullen the entire ride from New Orleans, but I figured he would cheer up when we got home. Quite the opposite, though, he had disappeared into his room when he got his Xanax from Memaw. I figured he had a secret stash of oxy or something in there. He was always bad to bogart the dope a little bit.

I didn't know how to explain to Allison, without sounding like a lunatic, that I didn't sleep in Uncle Mat's haunted room. I think she just assumed it was my room, 'cause obviously, I would have a room. Only a weirdo would sleep on the couch when there was a perfectly good bedroom available right there.

So we slept in Uncle Mat's room. There was no red light, no spinning cuckoo church thingy, no excessive heat.

Only love can kill the demon, I thought as I pulled the blankets down on the bed. But even in death, the demon can kill a libido. Luckily, Allison seemed just as tired as me and just as content to fall asleep without anything more. I was a little unnerved that we were developing this relationship without sex, it seemed so different than any other relationship I had been in. I laughed myself to sleep thinking that maybe this road trip was just preparing me for married life, which I had heard didn't include sex either.

I found the gym bag, shoved down beside the bed next to the wall, full of railroad spikes. I was wondering what Randy had done with the rest of it and trailed off to sleep.

We set out the next morning, Allison and me, on the way to Baltimore. We stopped for gas at the Happy Mart, which I figured would be safe since it was so early. I didn't want to run into anyone, better to just slip out of town undetected.

Fucking Stevie3fingers spotted me right away.

"Hey man, how's it going?" he had approached me at the gas pump.

"I haven't said anything about that shit from the other day." Until now, I thought.

"Good, Stevie, good. Let's keep that between us."

I should have held out for gas until at least Barbourville.

"Where's Boyd? You two are always together."

He had a puzzled look on his face. I didn't want him doing too much thinking, or trying too hard to figure anything out, or talking with anyone else to ascertain the status of my relationship with Boyd or anyone else. Better to keep him from straining his brain too much.

So, I told him, "He's home. This here is my girlfriend from out of town. Chicago. Gonna drive her back up there, maybe stay a couple of days, then come back. I think Boyd might be staying down at his parents."

I knew I had just told him Boyd was at home, and now I was telling hm Boyd was at his parents. But I figured life was best the less Stevie knew about your personal business. He would fold under questioning if it came to that.

"Chicago? Damn, she must be fire in the bedroom. That's a long trip."

"You got it, Stevie, you got it. So we gotta hit the road, and we'll catch up when I get back."

I was walking in to pay for the gas, Stevie3fingers trailing behind me.

"You think she's hot, Stevie?" I asked out of nowhere, glancing back at him over my shoulder. I wasn't sure why I asked him that. I knew she was hot, and his opinion didn't mean much.

He stopped and turned back to look at the car again. Allison's face was beautifully framed by the car window, her tan arm on the sill, smiling her big, beautiful smile at us. She lifted her hand in a wave, then brushed her hair back behind her ear.

"Son, she's hotter'n a two-dollar pistol, a full-on four-alarm fire. You done good."

And with that he slapped me on the back and wandered off in the general direction of Long John's. I don't know why, but it made my day to hear him say how hot Allison was, must be some innate sensibility you want others to acknowledge how pretty your mate is. Or something.

When I got back to the car, I leaned in, pecked Allison on the cheek, and said, "He's right, you are a four-alarm fire for sure."

171

Allison smiled, gave my hand a squeeze, and said, "You're not so bad yourself, mister. Not so bad yourself." We laughed and headed out onto the highway.

The best companion for a road trip knows good music and is willing to deejay. One who knows to watch for cops and directional landmarks. One who knows when to keep the conversation going so you don't fall asleep. And one who knows when to change the subject if it gets too uncomfortable. Allison was all of these things, plus easy on the eyes.

I knew she was the one when Fleetwood Mac came on the radio. Fleetwood Mac had long been a litmus test for the sustainability of my relationships. Between Fleetwood Mac and spooning, you could tell if a relationship had any chance.

I thought I had found "the one" once before, only to have the whole thing fall apart over Fleetwood Mac.

Boyd, Randy, and I always had a lot of traffic through our apartment back in the day. We didn't mind. As long as you brought some pot, or some other party favor, you could hang out. We had plenty of takers for pot, a couple of alcoholics that would bring a bottle over occasionally, several pill heads that would bring over some dope, and one chick we knew from the bowling alley always bringing gifts of women.

Our dope peddler, Bubbles, would stop by sometimes, plying his wares. Once he brought this junky from down the street with him, Barry. We didn't know Barry, although Randy said he had seen him around.

Barry was wearing these weird 'ninja shoes,' form- fitting around his toes. Looked ridiculous. And he seemed to know everything there was to know about the Red-Hot Chili Peppers, at least that's what he kept talking about.

Anyway, Bubbles was just trying to kill time until Barry's friend, named Laura, got free from her family obligation and could meet up with them. According to both Bubbles and Barry, this Laura was smoking hot.

Barry was trying to play it off like he had been friends with her for so long that he couldn't date her. Typical tactic taken by guys rejected by someone clearly out of their league. They still want to hang around until they can catch her on some rebound or drunken sexual rampage.

Anyway, it was clear he was completely in love with this girl by the way he talked about her. And if there was any doubt, it was cleared up when she showed up at our apartment and we got to see him interact with her. Ridiculous fawning.

I always questioned Bubbles' logic in inviting this girl he wanted to hook up with to our apartment. That was a stupid move. Boyd was a whore from way back, and Bubbles knew this. Pavo, who played fourth wheel with us, fancied himself a ladies' man. And Randy would cock block you just because. It was Randy's nature, to be a dick.

I know I would never invite a girl I liked over to an apartment like that. But that is exactly what Bubbles did.

Oh, he made it clear that this girl was off limits, he called dibs and all the rest of it. But I knew it wouldn't matter because nobody respected Bubbles. He wanted to be respected and admired, he wanted to be impressive with his business acumen for peddling small amounts of various pills and pot, and the very occasional baggy of coke.

But nobody was impressed. He was a clown, the butt of many a joke. Once he sold you whatever you were buying from him, his utility was ended. And it was back to being the one everybody was laughing at. It was sad, really, so generally speaking we would try to be nice to him.

But I knew if this girl was as hot as they said, she wouldn't be leaving with Bubbs.

She was, in fact, as hot as they said. Barry tripped all over himself getting the door and ushering her into the living room and trying to introduce everyone. He was gaga for this girl, and I couldn't say I blamed him.

She had long brown hair, pulled loosely in a ponytail down the middle of her back. She wore a loose linen button up shirt with embroidery running up the sleeves, roses I think it was supposed to be. She had a long brown skirt, but you could tell by the way she filled it out that her body was rockin under that thing. She had a tattoo peeking out of the bottom of the skirt, wrapping its way around her foot, obscured by her sandal. She wore toe rings, earrings, bracelets, and a hemp necklace with one of those stones that probably means something in the middle of it.

She had a nice smile, and quick brown eyes that seemed to be laughing at something all the time. If eyes can laugh, I guess, at the shit that only they can see.

Boyd spun his usual web of bullshit he always tried to ply strange women with. She was too smart for his nonsense, though. His game is tailored to strung out drug hoes, mostly. Gotta play to your base, I guess.

And Bubbs did just as poorly, sputtering about, trying to one up Boyd throughout the conversation, not realizing that Laura wasn't impressed with Boyd and she wasn't going to be impressed with him. Even if he succeeded in seeming smarter than Boyd, which he clearly was not. It was still well below the threshold she apparently maintained.

I figured Barry had a shot, he seemed to play the doting lackey well. Sometimes chicks are into that. Might get a pity fuck out of it.

175

She chose me halfway through the night, much to my surprise, since I rarely walked away with the girl. She came over, sat down on the couch next to me, where I was rolling a joint and smoking a cigarette. It took Boyd and Bubbles a couple of minutes to realize she was not still sitting across the room hanging on their every word anymore.

Barry saw it right away, of course. He was bringing her a drink from the kitchen, when he saw us there, chatting about how this pot Bubbles had brought wasn't really as good as he said. I saw Randy out of the corner of my eye intercept Barry and lead him back to the kitchen to smoke a joint with him. I figured he was probably recruiting Barry to help him carry out one of his regular cockblocking enterprises.

Or he was finding out where to get a pair of ninja shoes. Either way, I knew I had to act fast.

"You wanna get out of here?" I asked, much too quickly I'm sure, but the situation was tenuous.

"Like you wouldn't believe!" she said.

We bailed on them, probably just in time. We drove around a while. She was from somewhere in Indiana and was visiting her grandmother, so we took the grand tour of Middlesboro and Bell County.

She was really into classic rock, which was fine with me. I couldn't take another country girl. Jesus. She was a pretty cool chick and smokin' hot. So when she invited me inside her grandmother's house, I went.

It turned out to be one of the most miserable and memorable nights of my life. If I hadn't been a horny teenager, I would have got the fuck out of there. But teenage boys are ruled by their loins.

Turns out, Laura is a huge Fleetwood Mac fan. Has all their albums, and live shows, and interviews, and books, and everything related to Fleetwood Mac.

Except good cocaine. Their one redeeming characteristic and she's not even into it. I felt genuinely cheated on this front.

We must have listened to eight or ten Fleetwood Mac full albums that night, plus all the individual tracks she just had to play for me from this anthology and that box set.

I've never been so mad at my dick in all my life. I hate Fleetwood Mac.

I tried to move in on her and ignore the awfulness emanating from the stereo, but she would have none of it. She seemed to think I was a kindred music loving spirit, and she just had to bare her soul, musically.

I wished she'd bare a couple of other things, but damn it all if she didn't get all juiced up on Fleetwood Mac and ramble on and on until I finally fell asleep. Maybe if she had some of that good Fleetwood cocaine, I could have managed. But under those circumstances, I was lucky I didn't kill myself.

"Serves you right," I silently told my dick as we fell asleep still in our pants. Selfish motherfucker.

If I didn't already have a healthy hatred for Fleetwood Mac, I had one after that night. I left early the next morning and was glad she was shipping out back to Indiana later that day. Jesus Christ, I couldn't take hanging out with her again. There is no possible way any pussy could ever be worth enduring that much Fleetwood Mac.

Allison was in the middle of telling me about one of her favorite books, *Drifters,* and I was in the middle of lapping up every word she said. I was also fawning over her exquisite beauty as we cruised down the highway. We had been talking about movies, which turned into books that were made into a movie, and which version was better. Always the book. And then we were taking about favorite books.

For a nerd, I didn't read much for fun, but she had read quite a bit. Apparently, she had grown up in a bookstore on this island she kept talking about. It sounded wonderful, sitting at a beach resort, surrounded by books, with a view of the ocean in front of you. Even I would have read more books in that environment.

We had several favorite movies in common, and we both knew way too much movie trivia. We laughed and laughed as we traveled mile after mile up the interstate. This was my favorite road trip, and I was a big fan of road trips.

I was thinking of how I would make her laugh next, which is my favorite thing, to make Allison laugh, when Fleetwood Mac came on the radio.

I felt my heart go cold, and the color drain from my face. I thought of Laura, and how I had been duped into liking a Fleetwood Mac fan once before. I slowly turned my head toward Allison, to gauge her reaction. I was hoping there would be no real recognition. I could work with someone who didn't care about Fleetwood Mac one way or another.

Her face said it all.

It was at this point I realized she did wear her emotions right out there on her sleeve. Her lips were curled back from her teeth, as if she were snarling, her nostrils flared, eyes narrowing in concentration. It was the most beautiful murderous rage I had ever seen. Beautiful. And dangerous. Then she spoke.

"Motherfucking Fleetwood Mac! I fucking hate Fleetwood Mac!" she barked as she jabbed the seek button on the radio. The radio stopped on the next station, which was in commercial. "Thank God," she continued. "Anything but that Fleetwood Mac shit. Fucking hell."

She turned her head to look more squarely at me. She smiled, though I could tell it was a little forced. "I'm sorry, do you mind? You're not a fan, are you?"

I almost said yes, just to see what would happen, but I figured she would probably throw me out of my own car and make me walk the rest of the way to Baltimore.

I almost said I love you because I knew that I did. But instead, I smiled, shook my head no, and said, "Me? No, I can't stand that whiny shit."

She was definitely the one.

But I had to ask. All day in the car will do that to you.

"Why haven't we slept together yet?" I asked as we sat in a rest stop in Virginia, watching the cars whiz by. We had stopped to stretch our legs and were enjoying the sunny day by the picnic tables.

"Does it bother you?" she answered my question with a question, knowing there was no right answer. Women.

"Not particularly," I said nonchalantly. I realized as I was saying it that it didn't really bother me. We were still fooling around quite a bit. And I wasn't used to getting laid anyway. And I really felt like my time with Allison was about so much more than sex.

"I'm a born-again virgin," she said. "I figure if the Evangelicals can be born again in their stony hearts, I can be born again in my exquisite coochie. I just am tired of the same old thing. You fuck somebody, then you're dating for a while, then you break up. And you always wonder if it was all just a ploy to get in your pants."

She took a drag from her cigarette and turned her head to look at me.

"So I am going to date someone before I fuck them. Do the get together and break up shit without the sex. See if that makes a difference," she said, with an inquisitive look on her face, gauging my response.

I thought for a moment, then said,

"Well, I'm a born-again virgin too. Gonna save myself for marriage because true love waits and all that other shit they sell at Vacation Bible School. Plus, I would rather date you and be with you than fuck you anyway. I'm having the best time of my life right now, so whether we have sex or not, I want to keep hanging out with you."

She looked at me incredulously with those big beautiful blue eyes.

"You've been to Vacation Bible School?" she asked, an impish grin starting to turn the corners of her mouth upward. "Usually church boys can't keep their hands off me..."

181

"Oh, darlin, you just let this son of a preacher man show you a thing or two, and you won't be able to keep your hands off of him!" I replied, laughing. She giggled and started humming the Dusty Springfield classic as she hopped off the picnic table and headed for the car.

"Shake a leg, Mister Man, I don't know how long I can hold out after all!" she called over her shoulder as she skipped across the grass.

I knew deep down, sex or no, I was gonna follow her wherever she led me.

16 Charm City

Baltimore was a trippy place. Parts, like Loyola College where Allison was enrolled, were nice. Most of it was a cesspool though. Ghetto neighborhoods, like you only see on TV when you live in the sticks like I did. The sheer numbers of people cause their ghettos to dwarf ours.

We have the same boarded-up buildings, trashy streets full of trashy people doing trashy shit; I was living it. But we just didn't have the numbers the way they had it in Baltimore. Block after block of abandoned rowhouses, corner after corner with a bodega and a drug dealer on it. The human misery was palpable.

And then you'd hit Roland Park, cruise on down to Johns Hopkins, and back up to Loyola, and think you were in a lily-white suburban paradise. The contrasts were startling.

We had to park on the street at her dorm, but it was cool because Loyola is in the nice part.

The Loyola dorms in those days were refurbished apartments. Allison was in a two-person room, which was actually a big efficiency apartment. Full kitchen, full bath, and giant walk-in closet they were renting to this weird guy Stan. He worked for the airline and was the source of Allison's free tickets. I didn't meet him right away, as he was out. That was fine, because I am a jealous asshole, so it most likely would have been a dick swinging competition from the get-go.

Instead, I met her adorable roommate, Sarah. When Allison introduced us, Sarah walked right up to me, declared, "Bring it in!" and pulled me in for a giant bear hug. Smiling warmly, she explained that if I was with Allison then I was family.

Sarah was without a doubt the coolest girl I had ever met, second only to Allison. You could tell Sarah really lived by what she said, and she really did have nothing but love for every person she met.

You come across a lot of these hippy dippy people that preach peace and love, but you can usually tell they are full of shit. As soon as they let their hair down the bad mouthing begins. Not so with Sarah, she was the genuine article and I could see why Allison liked her so much. She was a true flower child, and welcomed me into their room as if I truly belonged there.

Sarah played guitar too and some of the best times I have ever had in my life was listening to the two of them play and sing one hippy folk song after another.

It wasn't my kind of music, but I could tell right away it would be. And the top shelf marijuana didn't hurt.

I wasn't used to pot like these girls smoked. Down home, only Hippy John grew pot this good, but it was all grown outdoors. He had good seeds, and babied his plants a great deal, but there are limits to growing outside, I suppose. His dope was as good as this indoor shit Allison and her friends were smoking, but it wasn't as dense. And he wasn't nearly so free with it as they were.

I was in a major detox from opioids and barbiturates, but I didn't even notice. I was so fucked up on their premium pot. And the beer. It was college, after all.

Two weeks went by in a blur. Allison would head off to class early and I would have coffee with Sarah when she woke up. We'd smoke some pot so she could get her mind right for class, and then I'd hang out in their room until Allison got back after lunch.

I'd usually have a beer or two while I waited for her, and smoke more pot, and watch movies. They had quite a collection of classic cinematography. As soon as Allison got there we would smoke up, and again when Sarah got back from class a little later. Then we'd wander down the hall to see the boys.

The boys were an odd collection of rich kids, but I tried not to hold it against them. There was Nick, whose dad owned an engineering firm, a big one apparently. Nick would run the place someday. Nice guy, but a solid silver spooner and he wanted you to know it.

There was Billy, with a story to outdo any story you had. Always one up you. He had this weird shifty eye thing he did when he'd lie, so you could immediately tell that the next twelve things he was gonna say were gonna be bullshit. I couldn't see why the rest of them let it slide, but they put up with it.

There was Lenny, who was skeptical of my intentions with Allison, and had a giant rabbit he had been keeping since high school as a science project. I offered to fry the fat bastard up, which didn't help Lenny's opinion of my intentions. I had just never seen a rabbit so big in all my life, and they taste so good.

I had eaten a lot of rabbit over the years, since Hippy John raised beagles. We went hunting with him and his dogs all the time. Although what I was doing was mostly drinking beer early in the morning and walking around with a gun. Hippy John and Boyd were a tough crew to hunt with.

They were in constant competition with each other, to see who could get the shot off first. I never stood a chance. By the time I could realize where the dog would flush out the rabbit from, and figure out where the rabbit was headed, and see that the blur was a rabbit and not the dog, Boyd or his father had shot it.

Plus, I was a little nervous about the whole ordeal of rabbit hunting with the beagles, because Hippy John loved his dogs. And he had told me on our first rabbit hunting excursion that if I accidentally shot his dog, he was gonna accidentally shoot me.

And Boyd quietly told me Hippy John wasn't bullshittin'.

"He won't kill you, Jack, 'cause he won't want to dig the hole, and since you're my friend he knows I won't want to do it. But he'll pepper you up with his shotgun. Seen him do Marvelle's cousin that way one time."

I saw from the get-go I was better off not firing my shotgun, than risking shooting Hippy John's dog. So rabbit hunting, for me, became one of my favorite wake and bake activities. You got to get up early, smoke a joint, drink, and wander around the wilderness with a gun. And at the end of it all, there'd be plenty of rabbit for everyone.

In my experience, the one who killed the rabbit got the backstraps to eat, and those of us who had been along on the hunt, mostly got legs. I killed only one rabbit in all that time, and it was on the ill-fated Christmas Day hunting trip, where Boyd refused to go, and Hippy John didn't bring the dogs or even his gun.

It had just snowed, so Hippy John drove us way up on top of Coldstone Mountain while we smoked a big fat joint in his Chevy pickup. He'd drive that little piece of shit anywhere, demonstrating that with four-wheel drive, nature couldn't stop you.

We left the truck and continued on foot, following the rabbit tracks in the snow. We found one set that broke off from the others and terminated in a big bush. Hippy John crept up to the bush, brandishing a big stick he found half buried in the snow. As he poked and beat around the bush, the rabbit suddenly bolted out from under and took off across the snow, heading directly down the hill away from me.

"Shoot, shoot, shoot motherfucker!" Hippy John yelled, and I obliged. Hit it on my second shot with my little 22 rifle. The second shot was always spot on.

Hippy John whooped and hollered and ran down to retrieve the little fucker. He was definitely as excited as me about bagging my first rabbit.

Since it was Hippy John, and shit did always go wrong with all his endeavors, when we arrived back at the truck it wouldn't start. We had to walk down the mountain, almost all the way home, before Coslin finally picked us up. He gave us a ride the rest of the way and was really proud of himself that he had aided us in our time of need.

As he pulled out of the driveway, I asked Hippy John what was up with Coslin.

"He's an old weirdo from way back. Some people say he's a queer, but I think he's alright. Shot his own mirror off trying to pull a drive-by one time though. Kind of a dumbass, I guess. Anyway, let's get Boyd and go fix this starter."

After we finally got the truck's starter fixed, which entailed me laying in the snow on Christmas day under a piece of shit truck on top of a mountain teaching myself automobile mechanics while Boyd and Hippy John quarreled over how to do it properly, I finally got to eat my rabbit's backstrap.

It was amazingly good. Big Carolyn could cook, like all them true mountain women can. It wasn't good enough to make me wanna try to shoot one and risk hitting Hippy John's dogs, so that was the only rabbit I ever killed with them.

I tried to explain all this to Lenny and the boys, but these city kids couldn't understand. As I told my rabbit hunting story, they looked at me more and more incredulously. They didn't realize you could eat rabbit, I guess, and that beagles were actually hunting dogs.

"Why do you think Snoopy is so smart?" I had asked them.

Crickets.

Some of the boys were a little fucked up.

There was Chester, who had tried to climb into bed with Allison one night freshman year, when he thought she was passed out. She was not, and promptly and loudly ran him out of there. This initiated countless references and snide jokes from then on about Chester's molester proclivities.

But he still came around, I presume because he had no other friends. And was probably still hopeful somebody with tits would have too much to drink.

It's possible I might have gotten drunk one night and threatened him with castration, should he ever come near Allison again. Probably unnecessary, but I was a prick when I got drunk.

New York Pete was from New York, obviously, and was probably the coolest guy in the whole place. He looked like he'd be a computer dweeb Dungeons and Dragons kind of nerd, but it turned out he rode a skateboard and surfed and was a huge Beastie Boys fan. I liked him immediately. Beastie Boys gotta stick together.

New York Pete would come down to Allison and Sarah's room pretty regularly for card night, while all the rest of the crew went out to the bars. We had a lot more fun staying in to drink and play cards, sitting around and toking a bunch of pot and chain-smoking cigarettes. Their card games were not like the card games I was used to.

Hippy John used to make Boyd and me bring him to the poker game up at Marvelle's cousin's barn, way up the holler in Brownie's Creek. Cousin Ray ran a straight game which made it popular on payday Friday.

Hippy John was an alright card player, usually coming out with a couple of hundred bucks in winnings, most of the time. I didn't know shit about poker, but he seemed to fold a lot, stay out of the big pots, and take a few hands here and there. He usually made out okay, so we made out okay.

We'd get a pill to spike, after, and everybody was okay. Hippy John always said how glad he was we were there to watch his back, although I didn't see too many people around who would actually try to jack Hippy John. He had a nasty reputation.

I only got into the Brownie's Creek poker game once. Hippy John rarely went up there if he was getting high, but he got ahold of some cocaine one time that was out of this world. And he wanted to play cards. Since he was getting us high too, Boyd and I agreed to go there with him despite our better judgement. It seems cocaine can cloud your judgement a little bit.

Hippy John was hanging in there pretty good, playing his usual game of nickel and diming the pots. Despite being blasted on coke, he was keeping it together. I was unduly paranoid, but I figured that was okay since I was supposed to be watching his back. And since he still had a shitload of cocaine left to share with us, we were watching his back extra hard.

About an hour in, Hippy John decides he needs to top off. So, he calls me over and tells me to sit in a few hands while he and Boyd run out to the truck. The other players looked like they were excited to have new blood at the table, especially a young kid like me who probably didn't know how to play anyway.

They were right, I don't know how to play poker very well at all. But cocaine is a hell of a drug, and that night I could see all the moves. I knew how to play all the angles, and I played the fuck out of them.

By the time Hippy John and Boyd dragged themselves away from their binge, I was up $250. I had no idea what I was doing, but it all made perfect sense in the moment. Some of the other players were getting pissed, though.

One old bastard kept talking about Yankee card sharks, and he didn't give a fuck who Hippy John was. I'm not sure why he assumed I was a Yankee just 'cause I wasn't from the holler, but I guess sometimes that is all it takes.

I had noticed another player who seemed to get upset and red in the face every time I won a hand, a great big bear of a mountain man with overalls and muddy boots and a Mack truck hat and the whole bit. I saw what could only have been the fruit of his loins, an equally hulking mountain man who looked just like him, sidling around the room.

I figured he was working his way around to get behind me, either to give signals to his dad as to what I was holding, or to hold me down while his dad beat my brains out.

Either way I figured I would jump up on the table like a wild thing, start rapid firing my pistol into the old bastard's face who kept calling me a Yankee, and make a break for it.

I knew I could run like the wind when I was on cocaine.

I was trying to decide if I should grab the money when I ran or leave it for them to fight over as a distraction. Before I could make a move, though, Boyd and Hippy John burst back through the door and Hippy John announced he was back in the game.

"How much of my money did you lose, Jacko?" he asked.

"This motherfucker is up about two bills since you left. Yankee card shark," the grumpy old man grumbled. Hippy John raised his eyebrows at me and let out a low whistle.

"Damn, Jack!" Boyd exclaimed. "You play cards?"

"Apparently," the bearded mountain man said. As I relinquished the seat to Hippy John, the mountain man's son had worked his way back over to his daddy's side of the room.

"Y'all motherfuckers better stop talking shit about my proxy. He's with me and that's all you need to know. Deal the fuckin cards." Hippy John laid it out there for them, and the grumpy old man shut up and dealt the cards.

193

"He yore kin?" I heard one of them ask as I headed out to the truck to do my rails Boyd had left for me.

"He's a Johnson family outlaw," I heard Hippy John say as the door closed behind me.

Johnson family outlaw, I thought, as I found the coke already lined out for me on the cd case in the console. I guess that's what I am for now.

I had been all in on that outlaw lifestyle, all in on the family. They had taken me in and treated me like one of their own when I had nowhere else to go. They had been my family. They were definitely outlaws, but they were family.

There was always a tinge of guilt, every time we sat down in Allison's dorm all the way off in Baltimore, to play cards in a safe environment where nobody would kill you if shit went sideways. A little remorse that I didn't miss my adoptive family more.

I felt a little sad, wondering if they were up there right now, getting jumped at the card game. I figured probably not, 'cause Hippy John did have that reputation and all, and Boyd's was growing into a pretty tough rep as well.

I did still feel a little guilty that I seemed to be in a much better place surrounded by much better people. Unlike the crowds I generally was around in Bell County, these college kids weren't thieves or felons, killers or convicts. They were just people, with plans for the future beyond

194

the next fix. It took some getting used to, but I realized these law-abiding citizens might be on to something.

My favorite Loyola pair were Jimmy and Sandra. They were from bumfuck Pennsylvania. Redneck for sure. Jimmy was rich, like all these pricks, but it was a country type of rich I was used to. He always said he was from Pennsyltucky, and when they talked about their hometown, they could have been describing my hometown.

Plus, Sandra was squatting in the dorm. Like me, she wasn't even a student. She taught me a lot about how to get in and out of the buildings without a student keycard or ID. She had been there for years, came with Jimmy after high school; she kept a job down the street at the convenience store, and picked up waitressing shifts, and as far as I was concerned was the only one of these kids earning her way in life.

I was mostly jealous of these college assholes because I had squandered my college opportunity, partying away my scholarship and getting booted from two schools in two semesters. So, I had a little bit of a chip on my shoulder for higher education, and Sandra was an inspirational figure for me, living the college life without having to pay the tuition and put up with the dumb shit. I figured, worst case scenario, I could copy her lifestyle until Allison graduated and then we'd figure something else out. There was a lot to be said for the college lifestyle.

195

It had so much more promise than the backwoods redneck criminal lifestyle.

For all the shit I talked about them, these kids could party, and did, every night. Which was right up my alley. Because of Sandra and Jimmy, me living in Allison's room didn't seem weird to anyone. And nobody in this crowd was concerned with my drinking, and everybody smoked the shit out of some pot. I don't know how they got any schoolwork done. And aside from the immediate group who knew the score, everyone else just assumed I was a student anyway.

It was a great two weeks. Weird Stan seemed to move out, which seemed fine with everyone. I had a blast living with Allison and Sarah, although they didn't keep enough food around. There were several days I didn't eat, but that shit was just as likely to happen back home anyway.

And rather than tiring of each other, Allison and I got more and more into each other. We would sit for hours, watching TV, playing cards, drinking, smoking, just hanging out. It was all so comfortable. The only bit of discomfort we encountered during the two weeks wasn't our fault.

We had gone to the local underage bar up on York Road, with all the other college kids. Despite being in the ghetto, this bar near Loyola was generally accepted as safe for all these honkies. And I suppose, in the end, it mostly was. But I was nervous the whole walk over there.

I had borrowed Boyd's little 22 for the trip. I didn't actually own a gun, myself. I had a couple of different hot ones that we'd use for different shit, but I hadn't wanted to travel so far with a stolen gun. So, Boyd had lent me the Colt .22. It was an alright piece, as reliable as .22s ever are. They don't call them jammies for nothing. I knew how to clear a jam in it pretty quickly though.

To be honest, a .22 was only for self-defense anyway, even then just to get away. You couldn't engage in a serious gunfight with a 22. Send rounds down range and escape was the plan of the day for that caliber.

So, I was nervous walking around Baltimore at night, even in a big group. I knew if the shit hit the fan, I would get away, and probably Allison if I dragged her with me. But I didn't hold out much hope for the rest of these fuckers.

When we got close to the bar, we could see the lights flashing from the ambulance and police cars. There was a crowd blocking the street as the ambulance worked toward pulling away and the police officers worked toward establishing their timeline from the witnesses.

Apparently, a Loyola student had been shot in the face in the bar, shortly before we arrived on the scene.

He was a basketball player, and apparently had gotten into an altercation with a couple of underage hood rats from the neighborhood. Lucky for him, they were only packing a .25 caliber, so the bullet glanced off his skull. Lot of blood, but no permanent damage.

My reasoning for preferring a .22 over a .25 was that at least with a .22, you had the possibility of the bullet penetrating the skull and rattling around in there. But at the very least, with either round, you could shoot 'em in the face and get away like these hood rats had done. Send rounds down range and escape.

We didn't stay at the bar, electing instead to go back to the dorm and party since everybody felt a little put off by the whole shooting thing. I agreed with the sentiment, since clearly you would need a higher caliber firearm than I had to safely hang out there.

That was true of Baltimore in general, so with mixed emotions I planned my return to Kentucky. I needed a bigger gun.

The emotions weren't mixed, I was hopelessly in love with Allison and wanted to stay despite the dangers inherent to the city. I didn't like that I felt in danger if I was outside after dark. That Loyola shooting was not the only one that happened during the two weeks I was there; it was just the only one in the neighborhood that involved a student. These locals were shooting each other all the time, four or five a night according to the evening news.

I didn't like it, but I knew it was where I wanted to be because that's where Allison was. I was over the moon for her, and rather than our fling cooling off, it was heating up. I didn't know much, but I knew I wanted to be with her; for me that was all that seemed to still matter. I knew I had to return to Kentucky, but that it would only be a temporary layover. My heart was staying with my love in Charm City.

17 Wallins is Full of Dope Fiends

The only real reason I left was to renew my driver's license. I didn't have sense enough to realize I could have just changed my license to Maryland. I also didn't have sense enough to know that I was two weeks clean from hard dope and pills and that was a good start. And I didn't have sense enough to know that being off drugs was due to being away from Bell County.

My limited plan was to pull a Sandra and live with Allison in her dorm if she was cool with it. I knew I would need a job to do it right, like Sandra did. But if she and Jimmy had been pulling it off for years, I figured me and Allison could too.

Besides, it was a good system these kids had going. Smoke pot all day, go to some classes, go to wherever the party was each night, or make your own party in your own room. Rinse, repeat. It was a very good system.

The damn DMV was throwing a kink into the whole thing, which is the point of the DMV and the reason for its damned existence.

The idea was to stay in Bell County for only a couple of days. A week at the most. I had to get a little money together for the license, and gas money to get back, but I didn't figure on staying long.

Boyd had other plans. My first night back, he broke me in with some pot and Xanax.

"Papaw said to come by tomorrow to work on getting a couple of patches going," Boyd said as I came up off a line of Xanax. So much for the two weeks.

We had hatched a plan with his grandfather over the winter whereby we would help him out with his pot farming in the spring and summer, and he would let us keep the proceeds from a couple of patches in the fall. It was time to work on this seasonal plan.

I decided I better say something about the DMV.

"I have to renew my license tomorrow, but we could go after that." I wondered when I should say something about going back to Baltimore.

Boyd agreed we could go by the DMV first thing in the morning, but then we would head straight to Papaw's. He also wanted to hear all about college life, all about the debauchery.

He was a little disapproving of my time there, since I hadn't been to any toga parties and hadn't had sex with six sorority girls at once yet. He kept saying I was lame every time I mentioned Allison. It was a little annoying, and I was tired. I had stopped at the Blood centers on the

201

way home from Baltimore. I had overdone it, hitting two in one day, but I needed the money.

Between blood loss and the Xanax, I didn't have the energy to party with Boyd that first night. After a few more digs about me being lame and in love with someone out of my league, he finally let me sleep.

The next morning, I hit the DMV early and got my renewal from that damn Elvis impersonator clerk they got down there. Then I picked up Boyd and headed to Pathfork. Boyd pissed and moaned that my trip to the DMV was making us late, but I felt his decision to track down his wily cousin Willie to score some Xanax before we went to Papaw's took longer than the license renewal.

By the time we finally made it to Papaw's, he was gone.

"Well, fuck," Boyd said. "Told you we didn't have time for the DMfuckingV. Well, as long as we're this close, let's ride over to Wallins and see if Jerry or somebody's around."

Wallins was a little dried up coal town frozen in time. They had no businesses left. They had no stop lights left. They had no working streetlights left come to think of it. Yet somehow it hung on for no reason. There was an elementary school, somewhat in defiance of the consolidated school shenanigans, and about ten streets laid out in a grid with houses and yards and a few people. There weren't nearly as many abandoned houses as you would have thought. Most all the little shotgun clapboard houses were occupied, in one way or another.

I don't know how legal the whole thing was, 'cause there was no law in Wallins. No police force. No sheriff's department. No local governing of any kind. The state police were technically in charge, it was under their jurisdiction. There hadn't been a Statie drive through there since Hippy John shot out all the streetlights in the 80's. And that time they hadn't even stopped to do any investigating.

It was a cute little town, and you could get away with just about anything. Which was why it was a great spot to party. We found Jerry and ole Half a Heart waiting on Earl. Earl was Jerry's brother, freshly released from the pen. Did three years, this time, on a weapons charge. He was banging one out with Totsy behind the blue abandoned shack on the second street.

Most of the street signs were gone, so I just kept track of which number they were in my head. Second Street had the blue abandoned house. The third street had a green one and a pale white one, but the pale white one they used for a whorehouse sometimes. So it was best to avoid it. Unless you were looking for that sort of thing.

It appeared Totsy was moving the industry onto second street. She always was an industry leader.

Half a Heart had been born with an undersized heart muscle, which they discovered when he was in sixth grade for the second time and overdosed for the first time. He had never been to a real doctor before, until the ambulance brought him to the hospital in Harlan after the overdose. Nobody knew about his heart defect, they all just figured he had asthma bad. He was a heavy smoker.

He didn't let his small heart lead to a small life, however. He did everything all the rest of us did, and he and Jerry were constantly in trouble. Larceny mostly. Earl was always in and out of prison, and we figured Jerry would end up there too, but so far, he had been lucky.

"What do you know, what do you say?" Boyd greeted them as we pulled up. "How's about we go in together on a pill, boys, Jack's been up in Yankee land and is fully detoxed!"

Half a Heart let out a whistle, "What the fuck you doing in Michigan? They got dope up there too, you know."

Michigan was about as far north as anyone ever went for any length of time.

"Not Michigan, Maryland," I said. "I been staying with this college girl. They are all a little square up there, they don't really party the way we do."

"Maryland?" Jerry asked. "I was up near there, in Delaware, for this coke thing one time. Beautiful country, but the people suck. Especially the cops up there. Must be some good pussy if you stayed up there with no dope."

I decided this was not the time to come clean about not having actually had sex with Allison yet. I would never hear the end of it, as males judge each other heavily based on sexual conquest. I just nodded and lit a smoke.

"What's that about good pussy? Totsy here is the primo delectus," Earl declared as he and Totsy emerged from behind the shanty.

"Y'all know my rates. Who's up?" Totsy was all business, as usual; she was a captain of industry and a leader of men.

"Now Totsy, you better watch it. Jack's been up in Yankee Maryland, and he says he's had the actual primo pussy off some college chick up there. He said you can't hold a candle to what them poindexter girls got," Boyd said, ever the shit starter.

Totsy stepped in front of me and placed her hand on my crotch. "Son, them Einstein bitches can't do half the shit I can do with this thang. C'mon, I'll show you, half off 'cause I like you."

Now this was a predicament. I wouldn't fuck Totsy with Boyd's dick, STD storage facility that she was. I couldn't say any shit like that 'cause Earl had just been fucking her. And I didn't want to be insulting, since he was fresh from jail and would want to fight. Plus I always liked Totsy and wouldn't want to say anything like that to her face.

And I couldn't say the other reason was because I was in love. I would never hear the end of that shit either. My street cred was tenuous especially in Wallins with actual hard cases. So, I made a joke out of it.

"Now Totsy, preacherman said on Sunday that true love waits. So I reckon I'm gonna keep on waiting on true love," I said with a big smile.

Totsy laughed, and said," You ain't even ever been to church you little shit! But you just keep on talking sweet to me, and maybe you'll be *my* true love someday, ya fuckin smartass."

She leaned in, gave me a peck on the cheek, and released my crotch from her grasp. Whirling around on her stiletto high heel shoe, she strutted down the sidewalk, in the general direction of the whoring quarter over on third street.

"What did she charge you?" Half a Heart quizzed Earl when she was out of earshot.

"Half off, "cause I was just out of the joint."

Half a Heart looked puzzled. "She gave me half off 'cause I got half a heart."

"And half a brain!" Jerry punched him in the shoulder. "That's just what she charges everybody, you morons.

206

She tells everybody half off, so you think you are getting a deal, but really that's just the price."

Jerry spat on the ground and shook his head, seemingly upset about the duplicitous pricing scale utilized by the local prostitution contingency.

"Oldest trick in retail." I offered, bolstering Jerry's point.

"Fuck all that," Earl said dismissively. "I got a line on some morphine. Who's in?"

Boyd let out a holler, clearly excited that, hookers aside, we had come to the right place.

Earl got the morphine from some chick he was living with before he went away the last time. We had to wait until her new man went to work, though. We all figured the new man was a sucker for going to work while Earl snuck in and fucked his old lady. But such is life for the workin' man, sometimes.

Earl emerged from the ex's house with a 100 mg morphine pill and an oxy 80.

"This is not nearly enough, but it will have to do," Earl was wearing a shit-eating grin despite our narcotic shortfall. Must've been a good time in there. And so soon after Totsy, I thought; he must be making up for lost time.

"Don't worry," he continued, "Half a Heart can't have a big shot anyway."

Half a Heart protested that he could have just as big a shot as anybody else, he just had to plunge slowly, but it fell on deaf ears. Earl was already divvying up the pills in his mind as I drove us back over to the abandoned house on second street.

He figured he and I should share the morphine pill because of he just got out of jail and I just escaped Yankeeland. Jerry and Boyd should share the oxy pill, and Half a Heart would have a little from each one. He was only fifteen anyway, and he had no money. But this being America and all, Earl said the little feller ought to get something.

"Everybody gets to eat in America," he said emphatically.

So we all shot up together inside the abandoned house on second street, the sight of Earl's earlier sexual escapade.

The sun shone through the crusty, dirt caked window onto the yellowed and ripped linoleum in what used to be the kitchen. Probably was a nice kitchen at one time. Plenty of counter space.

I was against one of the few remaining walls that hadn't been torn open to retrieve the copper. I was sitting cross legged on the floor, eyes half closed. There was an electric outlet in my back, and I wondered why they hadn't stolen its wire with the rest. Seemed strange to miss this one, I thought as I drifted off, the morphine taking control of my ability to remain coherent.

At some point I climbed up the unbroken wall, followed it to its conclusion at the doorway to the hall, and stepped through to the other side to take a piss. Seemed rude to do it in the kitchen where Boyd was still passed out.

As I stood there relieving myself into a pile of what I hoped was puke, I realized one of the great truths in this life. The copper had been torn out of that outlet from this side of the wall, and I realized junkies will leave no stone unturned, no copper wire unstolen, no bridge unburned. I realized that a junky is a lot like this old broken-down house. It used to be beautiful, and with a shit ton of work, it could be again. But meanwhile, we keep tearing it apart, one needle prick at a time, one line at a time, one copper wire at a time. We slowly destroy ourselves, causing immense damage, damage that is not commensurate with the payoff we receive.

Much like destroying a whole wall to get 25 cents worth of copper. And we'll try for as long as possible to leave that one side of the kitchen wall intact, one side we can show the world, one side that says everything is still okay. Not all the wiring is gone yet, there is still hope.

But that intact wall is only a façade. And behind it we're pissing in a pile of puke.

It was only Boyd and I left in the house. I lit a cigarette while he came to. Half a Heart had wandered home for lunch, he had said, but it was probably just to sleep before his dad got home. The dad was a well-known terror, and for his own safety, Half a Heart hadn't spent the night there in a couple of years. Sneak in and out while the dad was working the last remnant of the coal mine. A miserable man eking out a miserable living. I didn't figure coal mining was that much different than stripping wire. Lot of work and trouble for little payoff. And it was only a onetime thing and then it was gone. Mighty short sighted, I'll admit, but I had stolen my share of copper like any junky.

Earl and Jerry had gone off in search of another pill, claiming they would be back if they found one. We knew better than to believe they were coming back, especially if they found one.

"Let's bounce, Motherfucker," I mumbled to Boyd as he stumbled to the door. As we climbed in the car, we heard the roar of a diesel engine, the squealing of tires, and the blaring of country music growing louder and louder until it was pulsing through our bodies. The vocals were something about the singer being a redneck girl. Jesus, here we go, I thought.

As the dust settled, both in the street and in my foggy brain, the familiar outline of Linda Lou Buchanan's 4x4 Dodge coalesced. She had screeched to a stop, inches from my bumper. The diesel growled as she left it idling, killed the music, and hopped down from that giant rig. She leaned sexily up against the fender, dressed as always like an even hotter Daisy Duke. If that were even possible, 'cause Daisy Duke is pretty damn sexy.

"Hey Boys," she purred, "thought that was you. Listen, my friend Trina is coming into to town today. Y'all wanna party?"

This was a silly question. Linda Lou was hotter than a two-dollar pistol, just like the song says, so of course we wanted to party. Stunning redhead, wearing a plaid shirt halfway unbuttoned and tied at the waist, low rise cut off shorts and cowgirl boots. Her bra strap and thong seemed to be a set, like always. Today's version was fiery red, like her hair.

She always had a thing for Boyd, so I figured the friend must be for me. That would be fine, I thought. I can fend off the friend pretty easily, let her down gently. I could pull one of Randy's classic self-cockblocking maneuvers or something. Because I only had eyes for Allison.

I realized I was telling myself this through inner monologue, while simultaneously checking out Linda Lou and wondering if her friend would be half as hot as she was.

I was glad Linda Lou was into Boyd, and not me. She would have been hard to resist, even being in love with Allison as I was. I figured the friend couldn't possibly be as hot as Linda Lou.

Linda Lou's dad was Hippy John's best friend, which made it a little weird for her and Boyd. They had this heavy sexual tension, that to my knowledge had gone nowhere yet. I figured Boyd feared her dad, but he always said it was because he feared her.

She did have a crazy streak, especially regarding ex boyfriends. Several vehicles had lost their lives because of dating Linda Lou, and she had cut the shit out of one old boy who thought he was gonna manhandle her. He was lucky to be alive; it took 22 staples and a shitload of stitches to sew him back up.

I figured she was so crazy to make up for her father. He had made it publicly known that anyone who he caught with Linda Lou would die a horrible death. I thought it was sweet she would burn their car or cut them up to keep her dad from actually killing them.

Sorta touching, in a psycho kind of way.

So Boyd said yes, they should come by when Trina got into town. We would want to have a sexy psycho evening with two sexy psycho girls. Get your popcorn ready and all that.

"Super!" Linda Lou smiled, blew a kiss, and hopped her tight little ass up into that giant fucking truck. She roared off like a firecracker, and we headed back to the trailer, still numb from opioids.

"I hope she brings some dope, 'cause I don't know if I can manage," I said tiredly.

"She always does, my friend. She always does." Boyd assured me.

I hoped it would be downers. I realized I could use the sleep.

18 The Wisdom of Linda Lou

Linda Lou did not disappoint. She showed up that evening with her friend Trina, a handful of Xanax, two Oxy 40's, and an 8 ball. She said she had raided her dad's stash he hid two weeks ago and forgot about. I figured nobody just forgot about an 8 ball, no matter how big a coke head they were. But I hoped that would be her problem, not mine.

"So, I hear you shacked up with a Yankee woman. What's that like?" Linda Lou asked me first thing as she lined out some coke. I had not realized that my love life was common knowledge among the dopeheads of the county, but I took a hit of cocaine anyway and told them all about it.

I talked about Allison, and how beautiful she was, how sweet, and cute, and funny. How musically gifted she was, with guitar and her lovely singing. I told them about her a Capella group she sang with through the college, and how wonderful it was to sit and listen to her.

I talked about the odd cast of characters I had met, how Sarah's brother was half of a traveling bluegrass duo, how most kids seemed alright despite being the heirs of runaway capitalism. I told them about the rednecks pretending not to be, Sandra and Jimmy. And I told them how Sandra was squatting in the dorms too, which is where I got the idea.

Trina was rolling her eyes a lot. "Sounds awful," she finally said. "Are you glad you're back?"

"I guess," I answered, "but I am headed back up in a couple of days." Boyd shot me a look. We had not discussed this yet, but it would have to wait. The phone rang, giving me a stay of execution.

I hit a line of coke and picked up the receiver.

"Hi Jacky! It's Allison. How's it going?"

Oh. Shit. What was happening? My mind was racing as the cocaine coursed through my body. I was getting that hollow ringing in the ears you get sometimes.

Oh fuck, I thought. What can I say? I had been so quiet with Allison, and also so sober, comparatively. It's easy to be chilled out when your smoking copious amounts of Marijuana. Less so when your banging rails of cocaine. If I started in on mile a minute cocaine-speak she would know something was up.

I froze, which is hard to do on good coke, and this was very good coke.

"Hello?" she said again.

"Oh, hey man," I croaked out. It didn't make sense as a greeting in this context and I'm sure it couldn't have made sense to her either. She started telling me

215

something, or asking me something, but I was concentrating on using telepathy to make Boyd, Linda Lou, and Trina keep it down. They were cooking up one of the Oxy's and laughing about something. I hoped Linda Lou had brought fresh rigs, 'cause I didn't want to use the one I had left here before I went to Baltimore. Who knows who Boyd might have loaned it to? Hep-C is real.

"What are you up to?" I heard through my mind's chaos.

I didn't know what to say. I'm here with two horny girls and a pile of cocaine? We're about to shoot some Oxy and these girls didn't both come here to fuck Boyd, so I am gonna have to fend one of them off because I am in love with you? At least I think I am even though I haven't said it to you yet, but I do know for sure that I don't want to be with anyone else but you, even though these girls are fucking hot? I'm gonna try to get so fucked up I pass out, but not so fucked up I accidently screw one or both? I wanna come home? I want your home to be my home. Help?

What I came out with was, "Chillin, man, just chillin. What's up with you?"

She told me I was being weird and said she was gonna go. I said okay and we hung up. Not the phone call I had hoped to have. In retrospect, I should have jerked the phone out of the wall and claimed the lines were temporarily down, rather than talk to her like she didn't matter.

I realized she might be the only thing that did matter. At least she didn't know the truth about my lifestyle choices, I thought, as I grabbed my smokes and walked out onto the porch to clear my head.

I was sitting on the steps when Linda Lou came out.

"You really in love with this Yankee?" she said as she sat down next to me and stole the cigarette out of my mouth.

"I think I might be. That was her on the phone."

"And that's how you talk to her? What the fuck is your problem? When you love somebody, you have to be able to express yourself to them. You have to be able to tell them how you really feel. You have to be able to be honest with them, always. If you really love this girl, get your head out of your ass and show it!" She took a drag off the cigarette.

"Boyd know how you feel?" she asked as she exhaled.

"We haven't exactly talked about it. You're kind of the only person I've talked to about it. She doesn't even really know. I think I want to move up there to be with her."

"Jesus." Linda Lou squinted her eyes as she looked at me. "You got it bad. She must be great in the sack." She took another cigarette out of my pack, saw it was also a Camel, like the pack said it would be, and made a little face. Pretentious cigarette borrower, I suppose. She lit it up off the butt she was finishing.

"We haven't slept together yet. Sorta taking it slow I guess."

"Jesus," Linda Lou's eyebrows were raised in surprise, green eyes staring at me with a mix of incredulousness and admiration. She turned her head and stared across the highway at the mountain. The spring flowers had mostly all gone away, and the lush green was overtaking the whole thing. I always thought the best part was when the leaves covered up all the decrepit trailers and shanties that dotted the sides of the mountains. Wild and beautiful was so much more pleasant than poor and hopeless.

"You got it really fucking bad," she finally said. "Holy fucking shit. I wish somebody would come along and fall in love with me without fucking me first. You better not fuck this fairytale shit up. It's shit like this that gives me hope for this world! Love without fuckin. Wow!" She seemed amazed at the circumstances I found myself in. I had not thought about it like that before. I guess it was different than most of my other relationships.

"Anyway," she continued, "I'm sure Trina has jumped Boyd by now. When they're done you ought to tell him how you feel and what you're planning. He's gonna be upset, you're like his best friend. But he'll understand, I know he will. And besides, if you do it tonight, Trina can cheer him back up!"

"Thanks," I said, "you're right. I gotta get my shit together a little bit around here. And also, I thought you were coming over here 'cause you were interested in Boyd? I thought I would have to fend Trina off of me?"

Linda Lou leaned over and gave me a peck on the cheek.

"She called dibs on Boyd when we got here. No hard feelings, sugar. And now you're in love anyway, so I'm not gonna jump your shit. That wouldn't be right to this mystery Yankee woman. Besides, Daddy says I'm not supposed to fool with either one of you bastards. He says you're a bad influence on my virtue." She tilted her head back and laughed, red hair flowing down her back and gently swaying as she chuckled. "Imagine that, me listening to my daddy about anything!"

I laughed too and put my arm around her.

"Don't worry, Linda Lou, you'll find a way to disrespect, disobey, and dishonor your father soon enough, with or without my help."

"It will have to be without your help, Lover Boy, because your heart belongs to another. And besides, we both know I would be a bad influence on *your* virtue, not the other way around. You hide it well, but you're a sweetheart in there." She flicked me in the chest.

"Now I hope those two love monkeys are done, or at least on a break, 'cause I could use another hit!"

And with that, she hopped up, took the stairs two at a time, and burst through the door, hollering, "Hope y'all are decent 'cause we're coming in you motherfuckers! And wait until you hear about Lover Boy out here. It's Disney Hallmark channel type of shit that will make your heart flutter!"

I smiled despite her ribbing. I knew she meant what she had said on the steps, and she was right. I needed to let Boyd know my plans, and more important, I needed to let Allison know how I felt.

But since I was already on this coke binge, I figured I should ride it out the rest of the way, and call Allison later. I might have been in love, but there was still an 8 ball in there on the table.

Linda Lou was in the midst of defending my honor when I got inside. Trina was threatening to fuck that crazy lovey dovey bullshit out of me. Boyd was giving me the high sign I should let Trina try. Ordinarily I would have, 'cause she looked like she'd be a wildcat in the sack.

But listening to Linda Lou talk about how much I clearly loved Allison, (she used her name instead of That Yankee Woman), and how wonderful it was that I was interested in more than sex, and how it was probably a sign that we were soulmates, made my heart swell to proportions hitherto unseen.

I was so happy talking about, and thinking about Allison and how wonderful she was, and how much I loved her.

Linda Lou was fucking right. I had it fucking bad.

220

19 Karma's Snakes

The next morning, after they were gone, Boyd and I discussed where things stood.

"We are supposed to grow a couple of patches with Pepaw this year," he began. "it'll be enough to set us up. Like we always talked about. Are you really gonna be around here to do that?"

We had agreed to do that. Actually, Pepaw had agreed to take us on to help him. And it would be a good deal for us. Help him with his season and keep the proceeds from some patches.

I don't know about setting us up, whatever that meant. Most likely, we would blow whatever money it was on whores and whiskey. But sure, we'll call that 'set up.'

"Look man, yesterday I was completely off my nut," I assured him. "it was the first real dope I've done in weeks, yesterday, man. I haven't even seen a pin since I been up there. We got to banging that morphine and I got weepy and lonely and talking crazy..." I trailed off.

"But that's fucked up if you leave man! We're partners man, brothers. That hurt me man, thinking about you leaving," Boyd said, looking wistfully out the window.

Usually these conversations were under the influence of a lot more alcohol. I never realized how it sounded sober.

We were brothers. That was true. We'd been through a lot, and I loved Boyd like a brother. And the thought of leaving him to move across the country would not have occurred to me, and had not occurred to me, until I met Allison.

To be fair, I put little time into pondering the future one way or another. Sorta just rolled with the punches, I guess. And Boyd and I made a good team, that much had been established. And he was an exceptional partner to have. Smart, decisive, clever. He was hell on wheels with a gun or a knife, and he could teach that shit in ways that even I could comprehend. We were a formidable pair, to be sure.

And we were brothers; at least I loved him as much and sometimes more than my biological brothers.

But the romantic in me believed in love, and in love at first sight, and I just knew that what was going on with me and Allison was precisely that. No one had ever fluttered my heart, to borrow Linda Lou's term for it. No one had ever made me feel that euphoric sensation of excitement and joy and anticipation and contentment all rolled up together, all around and through me.

The closest thing to that was real good dope. And it wasn't that close to it. And I thought that if Boyd could understand that, he could understand why I had to go to her.

But I knew he wouldn't understand that. I knew, or at least thought I knew, how he viewed love and relationships. For all his talk about me and him being partners and brothers, I knew he was forever a loner. In a cosmic, long range sense, he was alone on his journey. And he knew that.

Not to say he wasn't loyal; he was loyal to a fault. If Boyd was your friend, he was your friend forever. He would never stop having your back.

But if you were not his friend, if he thought you had turned on him, or had lost your sense of loyalty to him, he'd toss you aside.

It was an all or nothing approach, and I had seen him cast others out of our circle before. He would never turn on you for no reason, but sometimes the reasons were a mystery to everyone but him.

I knew I didn't want to have this conversation right now, so I continued to assure him I was in for whatever schemes and plans he had in mind.

"Good. 'cause in addition to this here gardening, we got the thing for Trey, and Mel and Derek are talking about Mexico again. Only this time they want to bring Derek, so he needs a fake ID," he concluded our conversation, thankfully.

I put everything on the back burner of my mind and smoked a joint on the way to Pathfork. We needed clear heads to deal with Pepaw. He was cool, but he did not suffer fools; you had to have your shit together a little bit when you dealt with him.

"Goddam, you boys missed a good grouse hunt yesterday, son of a bitch!" he shouted as we got out of the car in his driveway. He was under the carport, drinking warm Miller High Life and tinkering on his truck's engine. He was always tinkering on something.

"Shitfire, Einstein! You ever warsh that goddam car?"

He yelled at me. I just smiled. He always yelled, 'cause he was deaf and refused to wear hearing aids, and he always cussed and shit 'cause he didn't give a squirrel fuck what anybody thought about it. And he always called me Einstein, 'cause I had been to a semester or two of college. And I always smiled 'cause he was a funny motherfucker, and he could never understand me when I talked anyway. He was still shouting.

"Goddam bitch fucking dog almost lost one, but she finally found it. She's a good girl, ain't ya, buddy."

I didn't ever know if he was talking to Boyd or me or one of his dogs. He was already loading his cooler of beer and bologna sandwiches into his jeep.

He had built the jeep himself. Took a pickup truck frame, cut it down and welded it back together to his own personal specifications, built an engine out of a couple of old ones he had in his barn, threw seats in it, and called it a jeep. It would go absolutely anywhere.

"Ya'll get in. You bastards have made us behind schedule," he hollered as we climbed aboard.

From his rambling account of yesterday's events, he had gone grouse hunting 'cause we didn't show up, sorry bastards, and he wanted to take his brother Bucky, but Bucky wouldn't go that lazy one-legged prick, so he went by himself, shot three birds and the goddam dog nearly lost one but then she didn't, so all in all it was a successful day.

Especially since he had spied out a couple of good garden spots we could use.

"And poor old Bucky ain't never been the same since he lost his leg in that four-wheeler accident, bless his sorry little heart, but I know he's gonna snap out of it one of these days, goddammit," he lamented.

It had been forty years since Bucky lost that damn leg, and at some point, we just have to accept who people turn out to be, instead of who we wish they used to be. But I didn't bring that shit up. He wouldn't have heard or understood me anyway.

Pepaw had spied some good garden spots. though. We left the jeep up on an old logging road and walked about a hundred yards into the dense forest, until we came to a little clearing. A tiny clearing really, probably about 20 feet across of direct sunshine. Decent shot to the sky, I guess.

Pepaw's agricultural plan consisted of multiple small patches spread throughout the county. He planted pot all over the place, in little clearings and spaces in the trees. At this clearing, Boyd and I made two little rows with our garden hoes while Pepaw followed behind pressing seeds down into the earth. Took five minutes, and we were on to the next spot.

He'd lose some every year to the cops, and some to the thieves, but he had so many plots throughout the woods they never found them all. He supplied most of the pot dealers in the hollers, and had for years, using his system.

At our fourth stop, we had parked the jeep and hiked further up the mountain, working our way to a rocky outcropping to get back to the tree line. This was my favorite part about living in the Appalachians. Being out in the woods, on the side of a mountain, little valley spilling out below you, winding its way into the folds of the next mountain, ridges stretching our as far as you could see. I was daydreaming and admiring the view when I crashed into Boyd, who had stopped short in front of me.

"Snake," he hissed, slowly pointing out a copperhead coiled up on a rock.

"Now be still, goddammit, and look for others," Pepaw said in the quietest voice I had ever heard him use.

I wondered if he was thinking about the story he always told us of when he and his brothers used to sell copperheads to the Pentecostal church at the end of the holler.

It was all I could think about. How they had got drunk one time and his brother Larry had kept one snake for two days in a cage, poking it with a needle taped to a stick to make it sore and grumpy. And how the preacher had gotten bit that next Sunday by Larry's special snake. I couldn't remember what the preacher had done to piss them off, but I knew this could well be Karmic payback sixty years in the making.

As we looked around, we realized there were snakes all over these rocks, one here, one there, every couple of feet another one. I counted nine different ones and realized I had to stop counting them. I cursed my luck I was caught up in Karma's retribution against Pepaw. I never tried to kill a holy roller preacher with a sabotaged serpent, what the fuck?

"Now boys, let's get off these fucking rocks, nice and slow," Pepaw was still using his indoor voice I didn't know he had.

As we made our way back, he suddenly shouted, "Fuck you!" and brought the blade of his shovel down on the head of a copperhead at his feet, severing it.

"We gotta go!" he shouted and pulled out that big 44 magnum he carried. Boyd took his cue, pulled his nine and started blasting snakes, clearing a path through the snake infested rocks. I didn't want to miss out, so I started shooting at snakes too, although its questionable whether I actually hit any. Pepaw was blasting with that .44, boom, boom, boom. Gotta love the high-cal for dramatic effect.

When we got back to the jeep, Pepaw passed out the beer. "Somethings done claimed that spot, boys, and left sentinels. In these mountains, you let that type of shit have what it's claimed. We've already done too much to these hills, son of a bitch."

Pepaw had a sad look in his eyes but it cleared up and he gave us a stern lecture about the dangers of fucking around with fucking snakes as he drove to the next spot.

We planted six patches that day. Pepaw had fifty or sixty going at any given time, so we figured it was generous of him to let us in on ten percent like that. He always said you could make about fifteen thousand off of a good patch, but you lose about 2/3 of your crop to weather, lawman, and junky thieves. By that math, Boyd and I looked to make about 30k, which is a fortune to two white trash trailer park kids.

We partied it up that night, just the two of us, like old times. Dreaming big dreams about what we would do with all that pot and money in the fall.

But I woke up early the next morning, dreaming about a girl I knew I had to see again. A girl I hoped I hadn't blown it with. A girl I knew I had to call back.

20 There's Always a Problem at the DMV

To my relief, Allison answered the phone when I called. She didn't give me too much shit about our last phone call either. I said I had been on pills and didn't remember.

She officially told me she was not cool with pills. I felt that glow starting when she told me about not wanting to date anyone that was a pill head. That meant she still wanted to date me, if that is what we were doing, and *if* I was not a pill head. The jury was still out on that point.

I sort of already knew from various context clues and what kind of person she was that she was not down with dating a dopehead. But I was excited that she cared what I did. I was floating on cloud nine as I assured her I was not that into them either, and that I would stay away from them like any sensible person would from now on.

I told her I wanted to come back to visit, and she seemed happy about that too. I was elated, and immediately planned my next road trip to Baltimore.

I knew I needed gas money to make it to Baltimore, so I went to see Mel and Derek about some work. They always had something going, and this day was no different.

"Hey brother, we was just talking about you," Derek greeted me at the door. "Mel says you're shacked up with some Yankee woman and never coming back."

I answered when Mel called from the kitchen, "Jack, is that you? I thought you had escaped this place, and without even saying goodbye, you asshole!"

Mel grinned at me as she stuck her head around the corner.

"What happened? Throw you out already? Come give me a hug, I haven't seen you since Mexico!"

"Yeah, yeah, that's right. Last I heard you was playing the Cisco Kid at the cabins," Derek said with a wink. "You crazy bastard. Where's your boy Boyd at? He ain't been around neither, but he don't have a good excuse like you!"

I figured Boyd was a little unnerved by the whole love triangle thing, but I kept that to myself.

"He was helping his aunt bring Memaw down to get her pills. You know they take pill day serious over there."

Derek laughed, but Mel made a face like I was calling the kettle black with my charcoal ass.

"So, tell me about this girl," Mel said as she brought me a cup of coffee and a Xanax, held discreetly so Derek couldn't see. He didn't like overt drug sharing in the mornings, but Mel would always hook me up. "What's she like?"

So, I got high and told them the story of Allison up to that point. How I had seen her on the balcony that night in the moonlight, how beautiful she was, how blown away I was. I told them about all the long conversations we had, about mostly nothing, just life and stuff, but about how time seemed to stand still when we were talking. How we would sit for hours and just hold each other, enjoying the quiet stillness and the beating of each other's hearts.

I told them about how great her singing and guitar were, how she had the most beautiful voice I had ever heard. I told them about how I thought I was head over heels in love and it was kind of scary. Once I started talking about her, I couldn't stop.

Derek laughed a little at me but nodded approvingly at the right moments. Mel stared at me, eyes wide, smiling a sweet smile, perhaps the most honest looking smile I had ever seen on her face. There was usually a little mischief in her smile, a little private joke she was debating whether to let you in on or not. But this smile she had while I was talking about Allison seemed genuine, and happy.

Happy for me, I guess. Happy that at least one of us had found love.

"Well, well, my little Jacky," she said. "you've turned out to be a pure romantic after all. She's a lucky girl."

I didn't know how lucky it was to have a dopehead stalker following you across the country. I said as much, which elicited a laugh out of Derek.

"Not to change the subject, Mr. Romance, but I do need to talk a little business with you," Derek smiled, shaking his head. "You've got the love bug bad, by the way, but I do need your help."

"And I need gas money to continue this little romance I've got going," I answered, feeling glad they didn't seem to think it was too crazy to be in love like this so soon. "What have you got in mind?"

What Derek had in mind was a simple job: transport an entity from point A to point B. Of course, it's never that easy, and this job would prove to be no different.

He wanted me to drive him over to Tennessee, bring him to the DMV in Tazewell to procure his fake ID, and then bring him back home. Simple. We settled on a hundred bucks plus gas and planned it for the next morning.

"Now that we have that settled, can we please do this pill?"

Mel had been methodically prepping an Oxy 80 while we had been talking. She always crushed them up and lined them out on coffee saucers. I guess since we were always drinking coffee, and all her mugs seemed to have saucers, she had plenty to spare. A white line on a white plate is not really the easiest thing to hit, but we always seemed to manage.

I thought, often, about getting her a mirror like normal junkies use. But then I'd hit the line and forget.

"Here you go, a welcome home present for the romantic," Derek said as he handed me the rolled-up bill.

He would not let me live this down, I could see that much at least.

"Don't worry about him, it's sweet," Mel smiled at me as she leaned back into her chair and brought her knees up to her chest, wrestling a cigarette out of her pack.

"It's sweet," she assured me again.

I just nodded, nodded thanks to them both, and then nodded off as the drugs made their way into my brain pan. Oxy *was* so sweet, she was right about that.

And she was right about Allison. The last thing I remember was her sweet voice, singing in my ear as she strummed her guitar and I drifted off into the ether.

I picked Derek up early the next morning. I had tried to get Boyd to come, but he was being weird, so I left him at the trailer. It was smoother with just Derek anyway, what with Boyd fucking his woman all the time. I felt awkward, even if they didn't.

234

Deep down, I liked Derek. He was an alright guy, and I would have given Boyd more shit about the whole thing under normal circumstances. But after seeing the ease with which Mel had made her move on Mike while we were in Mexico, I knew Boyd wasn't the problem. Mel just had a different sense of what being with someone meant. I liked her, but she was too free spirited with her nether regions for my taste.

I dropped Derek off in the parking lot and drove over to McDonald's to get a coffee. I pulled back over to the DMV and parked in the side lot across the street. It wasn't too busy in there, judging by the parking lot.

I was just trying to decide if I would have enough time to smoke a joint before Derek got back, when the Emergency Exit door burst open and Derek sprang through it. He ran across the parking lot, jumped the row of hedges between the DMV and the bank next door and disappeared around the corner of the building.

I glimpsed him ducking down an alley two streets down, about the time two fat sheriff's deputies emerged from the still open Emergency Exit. The emergency door alarm they always warn you about on those things was going off, giving the fat deputies an air of importance.

They split up, talking into their walkie talkies, and I put the car in gear and slowly pulled out of the parking lot. I circled back in the general direction I had seen Derek. I only made it three blocks before Derek jumped out from behind a dumpster and dove into the car. I made the next left and headed for Kentucky.

"Holy shit, man, I thought I was busted for sure! Thanks for coming back for me!"

He seemed genuinely surprised I had doubled back.

"What are friends for, bro?" I answered. "What the hell happened in there?"

"Ahhh, I got a bad feeling in there. They took my birth certificate and social security card and disappeared in the back. You know they never leave their little window unless there's a problem. Fuck, those docs cost me $200!"

"Well, nothing ventured, nothing gained," I said.

I started to say we were almost home free, when I saw the blue lights in the rearview.

"Shit, was I speeding?"

Derek looked forlorn as the cop came up to the window. I wanted to tell him to stop looking so guilty, but I guess that would have sounded like something a guilty person's accomplice would say. And since the cop was right there, I kept my mouth shut about it.

A second cop was waiting outside Derek's window, telling him to get out. He put him in the back of the cruiser while the other one grilled me through the open window about my knowledge of this identity theft we were engaged in.

I always kept it simple with cops, which was always the best policy. They were generally not Rhodes scholars, so the simple explanation was the one that always made the most sense to them. And the more complicated your story got, the harder it was to keep it straight.

I said I didn't know what they were talking about, I was just giving a guy a ride. I didn't know shit about his identity documents. I suggested they look at their tape to see what went on in their DMV, I was outside the whole time.

The cop ran my tags and shit anyway. Luckily, I was up to date, and there were apparently no warrants out for me, so they had to cut me loose. When he brought my license back to the window, the cop said, "Son, you seem like a smart kid. But you need to start making better choices about who you run around with and who you give rides to."

I assured him that was what my mother always said, and it was high time I listened to her. I thanked him for his understanding and began my solo trip back to Mel's house.

When I explained what happened, she cried, and made me go pick Boyd up so we could figure out what to do. I thought she was moving on from Derek pretty quickly, but I figured if he was on parole, he might already be headed back to the big house.

I told Boyd on the ride back over to Mel's that I was planning to go back to Baltimore to visit Allison. His impending sexual encounter softened the blow.

"Uh-huh," he mumbled. "Of course you are. Visit for how long?"

He was being calm, which with him was sometimes worrisome. But maybe he was just coming around to the idea.

"Couple of weeks, I think. I'll be back in time to help out with the field work this summer."

Fuck, it was already April.

I continued, "She goes back to Rhode Island in the summer anyway. Some tourist trap island off the coast. She's probably fucking surfers and rich tourists all summer."

I didn't believe that, but it seemed like the right thing to say, sound like I didn't care about her too much.

"Doubtful," Boyd answered. "She's not that type, bro. She's too straight edge to be out there truly playing the field. Still, it sounds terrible. You going all the way up there too?"

I shook my head. "No, I don't know. Maybe to visit. She says housing is real fucked up, she has three sisters and her parents all crowded in together so they can rent the house out. Or something like that. So maybe for a little bit, but I can't see myself staying in there with her whole fucking family for too long."

"When are you leaving?" he asked, watching the trees whiz by on the wooded mountainside.

Tomorrow, I thought, unless I come into some coke somehow and can pull an all-nighter.

"Soon," I said, as we pulled into Mel's driveway. When we got inside, I mentioned my cocaine desires, and Mel was all over it. Desperate to get Boyd alone, I guess. She made a call, got about a gram delivered and told me it was on the house. Plus $50 gas, she said.

She must've been horny as fuck. Poor ole Derek must not be stroking it right, I thought to myself.

Boyd seemed torn and moody about the whole thing, no doubt a little happy about the prospect of having a night alone with Mel and a fuckload of drugs, and also a little unnerved about being stranded in a house all night alone with Mel and a fuckload of drugs. No matter what else happened, he was gonna be sore and hungover when Mel dropped him off in the morning on the way to Derek's bail hearing.

But that was *his* problem. I had my cocaine, and I was ready to hit the road to go to the woman I loved. If there was one thing I had figured out on this short trip to the county, it was that life with Allison was way more sane than life in the mountains.

239

I needed to get back there, I needed to be with Allison.

21 Starring in the Dope Show

I bid them farewell, after doing a line with Boyd, the greedy fucker. Fucking a drug dealer, house full of drugs, and he wants in on my free cocaine. What a dick.

I hadn't pulled an all-night drive to the Beltway region since my Marine Corps days. I had been stationed at the Barracks at 8th and I in Washington D.C., where the Silent Drill platoon was housed. I didn't do any cool shit like that though; I was a paper pusher. And I spent quite a few weekends driving back to Kentucky to party.

I would leave Friday night, drive the eleven hours back to Lexington, and crash for a couple hours once I got there. I knew a guy from the county, Darnell, who we used to run around with before he moved to Lexington. He knew a guy with a great cocaine hookup. So, I would drive in Friday night, hang out all day Saturday, score a couple of 8 Balls, and head back to D.C. on Sunday.

It was a convoluted way to get high but, at first anyway, I knew no one at the barracks. And I was too scared to just ask random black dudes in the streets. I had the high and tight haircut and looked like a cop.

So, I brought my own coke from home to one of the biggest drug cities in the country. It made sense in a solo junky kind of way.

It all changed when I got a new roommate, however.

Charley was in trouble when they assigned him to my room. I had been living alone for a couple of months when they put him in there. It was punishment for him for some kind of paperwork bullshit, lying on his timecard or something. He was married and could live outside the barracks. So to punish him, they made him live in my room for thirty days.

He didn't miss his wife because the marriage was a sham. Charley was gay, and his wife was a lesbian. They had gotten married so they could each move out of the barracks and get a normal house. They split the house in half, with him having the downstairs and her having the upstairs.

So, Charley wasn't missing his wife during his stay with me. But he was missing his freedoms a little bit. Charley was a dopehead like me. Well, not exactly like me. He preferred ecstasy to all the rest and went on and on about how I had to try it, and how this barracks life was bullshit, and how we had to get the fuck out of there.

I didn't disagree with him on any particular point, except that I didn't think ecstasy could be better than cocaine. I knew I would have to take him up on it though, if only to put the debate to bed.

"You're not gonna try to fuck me while we're on it are you?" I asked, jokingly.

I didn't have any openly gay friends, just ones we always suspected in high school. I never cared who anybody was fuckin' though. All sex is weird when you think about other people doing it, so who the fuck am I to judge?

"Honey, you're not my type. And with that attitude you'll be lucky to ever get laid again, gay or straight," he said with a laugh. "Especially with that haircut. Jesus, we gotta get you a normal barber. You look like a cop."

Charley and I had hit it off almost immediately. We had the same sense of humor and had enjoyed talking shit about all our fellow Marines who took this shit way too seriously.

"We gotta go out tomorrow night," Charley had said. "We'll get some E from my friend Suki, and then we'll go to this rave party downtown I heard about. You're gonna love Suki, his E is the best!"

I took his word for it, and we set out for the rave party the next night. I mean really, what the fuck else was I gonna do? *Not* go to the drug party?

Suki lived on the nice side of D.C., in a high-rise apartment building. I had no idea there was a nice side of D.C., having only been to the shitty sides.

The trouble began as soon as we walked up to the building.

"Oh my God, Suki! What's happened?" Charley exclaimed as he rushed up to a guy laying in a heap on the sidewalk, crying.

Charley stroked Suki's beautifully cared for hair. It had obviously been perfectly in place before whatever tragedy had befallen him. Charley was cradling him in his arms by this point and trying furiously to smooth the hair back into place.

"It's awful! I am locked out, and the landlady is unreachable.

"And the homophobe maintenance man says he won't open the door unless the police are here to protect him because of that time Phillip tried to attack him with the life board at the pool last summer."

Charley was meticulously providing background material for me as Suki was speaking, explaining that Phillip was Suki's ex, and was a bit abusive, and had assaulted the janitor at the rooftop pool last summer. It had particularly traumatized the maintenance man because Phillip wasn't wearing any clothes at the time, and Suki was wearing his Brazilian thong.

244

You know how homophobes are, I suppose, and the maintenance man had never been the same after that.

"Suki, Suki, this is Jack," Charley interrupted him, trying to calm him down. "He's here to help."

Suki's face brightened. "Of course! This handsome police officer can make the janitor let us in! And then we can see what else you can help me with..."

I held up my hand to interrupt.

"I'm straight. And I'm not a fucking cop. I get it, I need a new barber," I said.

Gay dudes always want to talk shit about your fucking hair.

"He's straight, but he's fag friendly!" Charley said brightly. "He's my new roommate."

Suki looked confused at the roommate bit, but he seemed okay with my designation as fag friendly and shook my hand.

"Now, which condo is yours?" I asked him, looking up at the building.

"It's all the way on the third floor, that one second from the end. But we need a ladder, and a big one at that," Suki pointed up at the side of the building.

"Charley tells me you're always looking for a big one," I said with a wink. "Now y'all wait right here, and I'll see about your apartment. Is the balcony door open?"

Suki was still trying to decide if it was okay for me to make dick jokes at his expense, but he answered, "Yes, it should be. But we need a really long ladder to get up there."

"Yeah we do," Charley said smiling. "A big, long one."

Suki laughed and punched him in the shoulder.

"What are you trying to do?" I heard them call from behind me as I walked over to look up at Suki's balcony.

All the balconies were over each other, with metal railings across the front of each one. So, I stood on the railing of the first floor and pulled myself up to the second floor by the second-floor railing. Then, as Charley and Suki nervously shouted encouraging euphemisms, mostly about dicks, I stood on the second-floor railing and pulled myself up to Suki's balcony. In theory, I could have done that all the way up the building, but I was glad he was only on the third floor.

"Come open the door for us!" Suki called as he and Charley ran into the building.

I entered the apartment and immediately saw why Suki didn't want any cops over there. His kitchen looked like a mad scientist's laboratory.

It appeared he was making, or at least packaging, vast amounts of Ecstasy for distribution. There were thousands and thousands of pills, some already bagged up, some in little vials, some just loose in boxes.

I felt like if I had all that going on, I would have locked the balcony door. He was only on the third floor for fuck's sake.

I opened the door for the boys, and Suki threw his arms around my neck and gave me a big kiss on the cheek.

"You're welcome," I said, reaching up to pull his hands down from my head.

"See," Charley said. "Nothing. Now leave him alone, he's not gay. He's just my friend."

"Fine. He's just your straight friend with awful hair who saved the day, and now he is gonna party with us! Let's get out of here!"

Suki ran through the house, gathering up various containers of ecstasy, shoving two pills into my hand and saying, "take one now and one later."

He also threw two obscenely flamboyant hats at me with the encouragement to just pick whichever one matched my outfit.

I took both pills right then and left the hats alone. Charley's face said I couldn't pull off either of them, so I went with the cop look.

247

By the time we hit the rave, I was lit.

Charley seemed to know everybody in the whole place. He kept introducing me as his new roommate, straight but fag friendly. Everybody was on ecstasy and having a great time. Suki disappeared right away, and Charley was running around like a nut.

I found a wall to melt into where I could see the dance floor and watch all the beautiful people do their beautiful dancing. The place was packed, plenty of hot girls in varying stages of clothing and varying levels of sobriety. I realized I was one of only a handful of straight dudes in the place, but I was frozen in my wall and couldn't take advantage of the numbers.

As I stood there feeling the music pumping through my body, I saw a familiar face. Then I saw another, and then another. I slowly realized several bouncers were Marines I'd seen around the base. None made eye contact, I assume because they knew they were not supposed to have outside jobs, and I was not supposed to be at a rave with a bunch of gay dudes.

Charley and I finally made it out of there. Suki had disappeared much earlier, after gathering a large group of guys together to thank me for breaking into his apartment for him. I guess I saved the rave scene for at least that night.

I hadn't thought about that night in years, but I replayed the whole thing in my head as I drove to see Allison, coked out of my mind.

I realized I didn't have many memories that were not drug induced. It had been a haze for the past several years.

Aside from cleaning up during basic training, and the couple of weeks I had spent with Allison, I had basically been high every day for about six years. I had no real reason not to be, I decided. I wasn't ready to admit I was an addict.

In my mind, I was just having fun, living life in the moment, not worrying about tomorrow.

But Allison was changing my worldview a little bit.

By the time the sun was rising, I was getting close to Baltimore. And I felt like I was getting close to a decision. I knew I wanted to be with Allison. And I knew I was still pulled to Bell County. Or at least to the dope that Bell County entailed, the rush and excitement of living on the edge, the thrill of knowing each day really could be your last so you better go all out.

Allison's life seemed so much more tame than that, so much more sustainable.

I never put much thought into the future. In the mountains it seemed kind of pointless to ponder on such a thing. I had a chance, after high school, a chance to get out and make something of my life. But I had blown it, I had partied instead of going to class, I had been too distracted to focus on school. I lost my scholarship and came back to the mountains.

The mountains would always take you back, the hills would always swallow you back up if you were willing. Sometimes even if you weren't willing.

I had tried the military as an escape mechanism. Washed out there too, failed drug test. I always figured one of those bouncers had turned me in. When I had to come stand before the Master Sergeant, one of those gay bar bouncers was busily stuffing files into a filing cabinet in the outer office.

He wouldn't even look at me. Fuckin' rat. Probably thought he better do me before I turned them in for being gay bar bouncers in the evenings. Like I give a fuck about his part time job.

But truth be told, I would have eventually failed a drug test anyway. You could take the junky out of the dope den, but most junkies will bring a little dope with them when they go.

Again, I had returned to the mountains and the familiar lifestyle.

Allison's lifestyle wasn't all that different, I suppose. My time with her had still been focused on getting wasted.

But they all seemed to live with meaning, they all had a purpose driven life.

Down in the mountains, life doesn't always have much purpose. We just sort of exist sometimes, especially in the circles I ran in. But those college kids lived with a sense of purpose, they had a plan.

That dumbass cop's words of wisdom kept coming back to me. Making better choices about your friends; and it sounded so much like what my mother used to always say about birds flocking together.

I knew I was a wild bird, and I liked running with the other wild birds.

It was so much fucking fun, starring in the dope show.

But I had an inkling they were right, my mother and that dumbass cop. That I was hanging around some wild-ass people, because I was a wild-ass person, but that maybe I should make some better choices about that.

I thought about the short time I'd spent with Allison; most people we encountered had been semi-model citizens. There was no jail time in these people's futures, except maybe some white-collar country club jail for stealing the pension fund. Maybe some tax evasion, or divorce court.

Then I thought about the short time I had been in Bell County, between my Baltimore visits. Everyone I encountered during the past few days already had an extensive criminal record or was on the way to one. Larceny, armed robbery, assault, narcotics, B and E, prostitution, several unsolved murders, and that was just the stuff I knew about.

Shit, I thought, I could qualify for most of those, guilty but never charged.

I thought of the role drugs played in my life, and the times I had tried to walk away from them. Okay, I had never tried hard to walk away. It was always with a specific time frame in mind, like getting' clean for this drug test so I could try for this job for the summer.

Never had I ever wanted to quit getting high. It was too much fun. And I had never had a reason to quit before. But I knew when I told Allison I would lay off hard drugs, I meant it.

I resolved to at least try.

I was doing the last of my coke at a rest stop in Delaware, aware of the hypocrisy within my inner monologue. Lay off hard drugs? I'm high right now.

But really, what kind of asshole would I be if I wasted the last of this good cocaine?

I was thinking of how things had been with these college kids during my last visit. There was partying, but it was booze and pot partying. Nobody was doing anything heavy, besides the Ecstasy kick some were on. But it was easy to just stick with Allison and stick with booze and pot.

I wondered if we were on the verge of a breakthrough on the opioid addiction crisis. Maybe instead of methadone they could give a bottle of booze and a bag of pot to the junkies.

I figured AA would never go for it, but it seemed to work for me the last time.

My last visit I had made it two solid weeks, more than that really, because Boyd and I had run out of good drugs while we were still in Louisiana. They always said the first few days are the hardest anyway. I guess if I had been smart, I would have abstained while I was back home.

But I was never that smart. Fuck it, I knew I could detox again. It would be even easier this time. And Allison was worth it. She was so fucking worth it.

22 Sarah's Our Leader 'cuz She Has the Helmet

I was admiring the beautiful rantings of my coke filled mind as I arrived at the campus for my second stint in Loyola dormitory detox. This session got off with a bang because Allison's drug ban apparently did not include opium.

Sarah had scored some opium from somewhere back home over the weekend. That was a fun few days, turning their room into an opium den, just laying around high as fuck. Mushrooms were also on the menu during this detox. We went on a little weekend getaway with them once the opium ran out.

Sarah brought us to a place called Accokeek, some wildlife reserve or preserve or some shit. Whatever it was, it was beautiful, and that's not just the drugs talking. It was on the Potomac River, serene and peaceful. There were little docks and walkways along the marshes, lush vegetation for acres and acres, flowers and birds, and animals; they even claimed there were wild horses running around somewhere.

But that last part could have been the mushrooms talking.

I had never done any mushrooms, only read about them in High Times. I had done some acid, whenever we could find it, and generally it had been a good time. Mushrooms were a more mellow high than my acid trips had been. Less visuals and more giggles. Still intense, though.

It was Sarah, Allison, and me, the three amigos on the trip. We were staying with some of Sarah's friends whose overly rich parents owned a house on the edge of the preserve. Some were tripping too, but the three of us banded together and went on our own trip.

Sarah was our leader, because she had been there before, and she had the bike helmet. She knew with her helmet on, she would be safe. And we knew if she was safe, then we would be safe following her.

We tromped all over the woods that night, laughing and playing, marveling at the moonlit beauty all around us, climbing trees and swinging from the branches. At one point we broke into some gymnasium and ran around, although I don't know why there would be a gymnasium in a nature preserve.

So maybe we imagined that whole part. I added mushrooms to my list of treatments for opioid detox.

By the end of the second two weeks I was firmly entrenched in my desire to stay with Allison forever. But the semester was ending. They were all getting serious about their final exams and the partying had abated somewhat. Allison was preparing to return to her island for the summer.

"Tell me again about your island," I asked her one night as we lay in bed watching a movie.

Sarah had gone out drinking with the boys, but we stayed in. it was a school night.

"It's the best," she said simply. "Beautiful sandy beaches, hiking and biking trails, beach fires and parties every night. There is a lot of hard work, but you make a lot of money and have a lot of fun. You should come get a job for the summer. You can probably stay with us; my dad lets employees live there sometimes. Maybe you could get some hours in our gift shop. But there's plenty of other jobs if you don't like that. You just have to make sure you have housing, 'cause sometimes that's a bitch."

She had her head on my chest as she spoke, and then she squeezed me tighter, whispering, "I don't want to spend the summer away from you. You should come to Block Island, it will be fun."

I was putty in her hands. I was just lucky she had no nefarious plans for world domination because I would have done that shit too. All I wanted was to be with her and make her smile; when she smiled it was the most beautiful thing in the world.

I held her tight and said I wanted to come to her island, wanted to spend the summer with her too. I wanted to spend my life with her, but I was trying desperately not to freak her out. So, I hadn't proposed yet. We had only known each other a couple of months, but I knew she was my everything.

I felt like I had always known her, that my soul had always been searching for her. Restlessly searching, until the fates brought us together.

I knew if I was going to Rhode Island for the summer, I needed to square things away back in the County. I needed to tell Boyd face to face, and I needed to get the rest of my clothes from the trailer. I figured I needed any shorts I had if I was going to spend the summer at a beach resort.

Allison had mentioned the laundry facility crisis on the island, so I figured I better bring all the undies I could lay my hands on, too.

So, with only a few days left in the semester, I headed back to Kentucky to sort things out. I wanted to wrap things up in case things continued to go well with Allison and I never came back to the Bluegrass. I wanted to feel like I wasn't just running out on Boyd and the rest of my life in the mountains.

Had I known how this final trip would turn out, I would have just sent a postcard explaining things from the island.

23 What a Way to Dump a Broad

Boyd was not as excited to see me as I had expected him to be. Or maybe it was the dope. Being away from the daily scrounge for a pill had made me realize how fucked up it is. I found myself annoyed with him and his jonesin' and his bitching.

Annoyed with typical drug addict behavior I had been a full participant in just a few short weeks ago. Jesus, I'm a dick, I thought.

Fuck, did I act like that, I wondered, knowing full well that I did. It felt like a million miles away though.

Boyd had been spending a lot of time at Mel's during Derek's absence. He was still being held, awaiting trial they said, on that stolen identity thing.

"You been over to see him?" I asked, figuring the answer would be no.

"Sure, sure. Mel goes in and I wait in the car."

"That's kind of fucked up, isn't it?"

"It is what it is," he replied. "He got locked up, not me. And Mel won't leave me at her house by myself. And she don't like leaving me here either."

I glanced around Memaw's trailer, where we were waiting while Boyd worked on rolling a joint out of all the

258

roaches. His nerves, which were never good appeared to be shot.

"Why not here?" I asked.

"She knows I can escape her grasp from here. She's crazy you know," he said as he glanced up from his work. Almost done, it looked like. Appeared to be a fine spliff. Now to get him to light it.

"She's always been crazy," I said, sipping my breakfast beer.

I had rolled into town at 8:30 am and surprised Boyd with a 12-pack. "And you are the one who perpetuates this saga. You could stay away from her.

"Why did she leave you here today?"

"She was here last night, but one of the kids had to go to the doctor. I think that boy eats too much diaper cheese."

It was true, the diaper cheese was definitely a dietary concern.

Boyd lit the joint, finally, and continued, "And what would I do, exactly? You're gone all the time. I have no other real friends. She keeps me in dope and the pussy is not bad. Those older women know tricks them young girls never even dreamed of."

I had heard this line of reasoning before, Boyd always wanted to justify banging old broads. I felt there was nothing wrong with milf hunting, but Boyd always had to overcompensate his justifications..

I never cared who he was fucking, just glad he was enjoying it.

"Then what's the problem?" I asked as I hit the joint. "Enjoy it while it lasts."

"But I told you, she's fucking crazy, man. Like chain me up to the bed and break my legs, *Misery* crazy. Makes me nervous."

He did look nervous as he explained it. But he always looked a little nervous. And he read too much Stephen King. And all his relationships make him nervous, he always says the women are too clingy, too possessive. He always feels caged.

"Well, don't worry. She'll kick you to the curb as soon as Derek gets back out." I thought this was solid advice, based on experience.

"That's just it, if this thing ends up going against him, Derek will violate parole and be back in for six more years. Six Years! I can't do six more years with Mel!"

I could see the fear in his eyes, the desperation. I laughed a little on the inside, thinking about Derek worrying over going to jail while Boyd was worrying over having to fuck Derek's wife while he was in there.

"Guess he needs a lawyer?" I asked, knowing there was no way to afford a good lawyer, even if one existed in that neck of the woods. Boyd nodded. They needed a lawyer.

"There's a way," Boyd said. "You aren't gonna like it, but there's a way."

He paused and fished a cigarette out of his shirt pocket. "Mexico."

I looked at him like he was an idiot.

"We are not fleeing to Mexico so you can get away from your crazy girlfriend! I am not fleeing to Mexico, regardless, but surely you can just break up with her. Hide out a few weeks, avoid Frakes Holler, and find some other piece of tail. Mexico is too extreme. Don't be stupid."

"No, dingus. Mexico like last time Mexico. With Tracey and Mel. Only instead of that other prick, it will be the four of us. Same deal, go in, get out, make some money. Make a lot of money actually, and Mel hires a lawyer, gets Derek off, he comes home, and I am finally free."

He finished, looking proud of himself. I could feel the look of disbelief all over my face.

"That might be the stupidest shit I've ever heard. Jesus, man," I finally said, shaking my head. "But what a way to dump a broad."

I had to hand it to him. It was a convoluted, ridiculous mess of a plan to break up with his girlfriend, but it could just work. No hard feelings for Mel, which meant he could swoop in the next time Derek got arrested.

And meanwhile, Boyd was just doing the right thing, stepping back once the Baby Daddy was home. And everybody makes money. I knew I could use some travel cash anyway.

"Well, when do we start?' I asked with a smile.

I always loved this part.

24 Giant, Fuckoff, Shiny Knife

We spent all night over at Mel's, planning the caper. We would follow the same basic outline as before, two couples on a trip to party it up south of the border. Mike was gonna help us out and contact his guys at the border. Mel would run it just like last time: same payoffs to guards, inspectors, doctors, etc.

Mel said Mike was not going with us because we weren't going through his boss, Wolf. He was, however, going to help grease the border and keep shit quiet because of Mel's winning personality.

"Plus," she said, "I've kept him on the line with a little lovin' now and then, especially since Derek's been away."

Boyd had left this part of the love story out in his description earlier.

Mel continued, "But don't say anything to Derek, he don't know about Mike. In fact, he don't know we're even going down there. We need the money, though, to pay the lawyer and try to keep him from going back to prison. I was just getting him cured and back to normal. You know how prison fucks people up. I don't want to have to start all over with him."

"You think we can trust Mike?" Boyd asked. "Why is he sticking his neck out, going behind Wolf's back?"

"Because he don't know it's for Derek. He thinks I am trying to start over since Derek's gone, and I need money to move out of this house. And he thinks I'll keep seeing him."

Mel leaned back on the sofa, walking her fingers down the back toward Boyd.

"And who knows, I might keep seeing him a little on the side. He's got the connections in Mexico, and we could make our own runs whenever we want."

Her walking fingers had made it to Boyd's shoulder, where he playfully swatted them away.

He was right, she was crazy. As fuck.

But her dedication to the life was admirable. Hustler to the end.

"Allison's coming here after she gets out of school in a few days. I need to be back before she gets here. She don't need to know anything about this shit here."

I felt I should say that, even though obviously the fewer people who knew about your drug smuggling, the better.

I was a little worried they would ask how long she was staying for, what my summer plans were, but they both just nodded. Allison couldn't know about this shit.

264

Besides, they were making lusty eyes at each other by this point. Boyd was right. She was crazy.

But he always did love crazy.

"Don't worry, Jacky, we'll have you back before your lover gets here," Mel said encouragingly.

She was nodding her head slightly toward the bedroom, looking intently at Boyd. He was right there with her, it appeared. I knew this meeting was almost over.

"So, let's set it for Wednesday next week. Allison should be flying in on Saturday or Sunday, so that should give us plenty of time to get down there and back before she gets here."

I had to get it in fast before they lost interest altogether.

"Yes, yes, Wednesday," Mel said as she stood up and pulled Boyd toward the back of the house. "There's some oxy already lined out on the saucer by the coffee pot, and you know where I keep the joints. Help yourself and lock up if you leave.

"It's great to see you!" Mel called as the two of them disappeared into the bedroom, slamming the door behind them.

I shook my head, grabbed two joints, skipped the oxy, and headed back to Memaw's trailer. I could use some rest anyway. And I was a couple weeks in with my detox.

Why fuck it up just to sit in the trailer, fucked up by myself?

And Boyd was full of shit about trying to get away from her. He loved that intense sex shit as much as anyone. And she always had dope. Mel was just about perfect for him, truth be told.

I woke up the next morning feeling good about the situation. Boyd had called early for me to come pick him up from Mel's house, and he seemed a little peeved that I had not slept over there.

But we smoked a joint on the ride back to the trailer, and overall, things were looking good.

By the time Allison got to Kentucky, I would be ready to leave with her for Block Island, a little money in my pocket. Just one last job to help my peeps out and leave everybody feeling like I was going out on a high note.

Yep, things were looking good that Monday morning, that fateful Monday morning, when the phone rang. I picked up the receiver, "Hello?"

The sultry voice on the other end of the line said, "I'll be there tomorrow! I can't believe I get to come see you early, isn't that great!?!"

She was so sexy. Even on the phone, which is sometimes not the case. Not a guarantee, at least, by any means.

Sometimes that shit didn't match, and a sexy phone presence was not translated to the earthly plane.

And, sometimes, a hot girl sounded like your grandmother on the phone.

Lucky for me, the hotness matched all the way around.

But it was not great news, her coming early. I was supposed to be leaving for Mexico. Back in a couple of days, before she got here. Now she was coming early.

"That sounds great,"

I didn't believe myself when I said it; not very convincing, not a very good performance.

"Can't wait to see you," I continued.

I knew this part was the truth, and it came out much better. I couldn't wait to see her, I could not get her out of my mind, actually. I had just been wistfully contemplating how great it would be to see her again, to reunite with this amazing woman. We'd been apart for what felt like ages but was in reality only a few days.

I heard myself go on. "But right now I gotta run. Gotta take care of a few things, I will tell you all about it when you get here."

I wasn't sure if this was true or not. There was no good way to explain this shit.

A couple of crazy ideas swirled around in my head. She might just come with me. That might not be so bad... or better still, maybe I just don't go.

I might just skip the trip altogether because there was no way Allison would think this was a good idea. I realized I didn't know everything about her, but I knew that much.

A sense of relief washed over me. I realized her coming early was just in time to save me from going on this Mexico run. I thought about how our whole relationship had been an exercise in perfect timing, being in the right place at the right time, placed there through the confluence of numerous seemingly unrelated events that resulted in me being in New Orleans with a car and no plans, and her being in need of a ride.

I thought about how life with Allison was so different than the life I had built in Bell County, so much cleaner and safer, so much less violent, so much less dangerous, so much more law abiding, so much more...better.

I realized that I wanted to be with her, because she was her and I loved her, and all these ancillary benefits were just icing on the cake. I wanted to be with her no matter what, but it was nice that her life, the one I was attempting to join, was a definite upgrade from mine.

I was in the middle of picturing a little house with a picket fence in a nice little neighborhood with some rug rats underfoot and a steady 9:00 to 5:00 with Allison by my side, when Boyd interrupted.

He brought me screeching back to the reality of the dope show. Which is his way.

"When is she coming in?"

He was sitting at the kitchen table, cleaning his nails with his knife. He seemed to have heard my phone conversation pretty well for a deaf guy.

I noticed he was using his giant Knifemaker's fixed blade to clean his nails.

Boyd always cleaned his nails with a knife, and the size of the knife usually corresponded to the level of intimidation he was trying to impart on whoever was in the room.

Usually, at home, he used a little three-inch pocketknife. This giant fuckoff shiny one was his favorite intimidation knife.

"Where's your little ColdSteel blade?" I asked, ignoring his question.

"Couldn't find it," he responded, looking at the knife edge as he held it up to the light. I looked past the light glinting off the razor sharp 9-inch blade as he studied its edge and saw the little bowl over on the counter where Boyd kept his keys and wallet and things when he was

269

home. I noticed the little ColdSteel three-inch pocketknife, right where it always was.

"Is that it over there on the counter?" I tried not to sound like my mother, but maybe he had just overlooked it.

He paused, looked over at the bowl on the counter with the knife in it.

"So it is," he said. "When is Allison getting here?"

He slowly and deliberately went back to cleaning his nails with the scary knife.

"Tomorrow," I said, wondering if I should be concerned about Boyd's mental state. I mean, more concerned than usual.

"Good. We need her for the trip, anyway. What better cover for a guy pretending to be on a romantic getaway with his girlfriend than to bring his actual girlfriend?"

He had grabbed his knife sharpening gear from out of the cabinet above the microwave and was honing the blade of his intimidation knife. Like it needed it.

Had I been unsure of his intentions with the nail cleaning, I knew damn well what his intentions were in sharpening an overly large and already sharp knife during a negotiation.

If that was what we were having, a negotiation.

"What about Tracey?" I asked, knowing he and his knife would shoot it down. "You could bring Stevie or Glenn or Dante or somebody else. And Allison wouldn't even have to know about this at all."

"Tracey apparently broke her femur and can't ride in the car that long. And I am not going down there with Stevie3Fingers or any other junky motherfucker for my backup. It has to be you. And Mel and I worked it all out to where Allison doesn't even have to do anything. We only have enough for three sets of scripts anyway, so she really is just for the cover story. She's really only going to be walking over the border and back, emptyhanded."

He had been pulling the blade across the sharpening sticks in rhythm with his cadence as he explained the new reality.

He paused and pointed the blade at me. Punctuating each word with the tip of the knife, he said emphatically, "We need her. She has to come."

And then he went back to cleaning his nails, apparently satisfied with the sharpness of the blade.

"She'll never go for it," I offered, distractedly, as I tried to remember if Boyd had ever pointed a knife at me in such a fashion. He was using it to talk with, the way some Italians talk with their hands.

I had seen him use that move plenty of times over the years. Just never seen him use it on me before.

271

"You'll talk her into it," he said without looking up.

I could tell he was done with the conversation, and I went out on the porch to smoke a cigarette and calm my nerves.

Did that just happen? Did I just get lightweight intimidated by my friend, threatened into coercing my girlfriend into participating in a drug smuggling operation?

Also, if she was my girlfriend, and I really wanted her to be my girlfriend, could our love withstand this ridiculous proposition?

It was not possible, in any realm of possibilities, Allison would go to Mexico. But I did think it was possible that Boyd had been insinuating what I thought he was insinuating. So, I knew I had to ask her, but I hoped when she said no, we could call Boyd's bluff. He and Mel could just figure out two other people to bring.

Allison had made mention, during one conversation, of the fact that Boyd would be sad he and I were breaking up. I had not thought about it in those terms, but I could see the parallels.

It was a little like a breakup, or a separation. We are going to see other people.

The first time I had met Boyd was at a concert. I was in a little garage band in high school, and we put on a show at the old theater downtown. There were a few notable people who came, but none so memorable as Boyd. He was by far our loudest and our drunkest fan.

I remember wondering, who brought this idiot? He was obviously too fucked up to be in public. I didn't know Hippy John had turned him on to a half pint of Jim Beam, two joints, and a rail of coke before he dropped him off.

Hippy John knew how you were supposed to prep for a concert, I guess.

We were 16.

The first time I hung out with Boyd was with Randy. Randy's dad went to the Bible college where my dad worked, so Randy and I hung out some. Mostly, he would come up to the college rec center where I had a job after school. Randy would always have his little brother, Jess, in tow.

"Dad said we had to come up here and play basketball so he could have some alone time with my mom," Randy would say every time.

"They're gonna fuck in all the rooms and it's gonna be nasty," Jess, eight-years-old, would always say.

I would just nod, 'cause it probably was nasty. Randy's dad was a big, fat, sloppy looking motherfucker, and probably smelled like old cheese feet all the time.

I felt bad for the mom, she was a sweet lady.

She ended up sucking on a garden hose duck taped to the tailpipe of her Chrysler, parked in her cousin's garage.

This just confirmed my old cheese feet theory.

Right around her death was when we all started hanging out. Boyd and Randy hung out at school a lot. I was in a different school, so I only saw them after. I think when Randy's mom passed, Boyd made it a point to always be there for his friend. He would bring Randy everywhere; he wouldn't just let him sit in his room and be fucked up. I think Boyd saved Randy in that way.

I was all for saving Randy too, but I am a lazy fuck. Boyd really drove us to stick together and check up on Randy and be there for him. Boyd *is* a really good friend and loyal beyond measure. The three of us became inseparable, and once Randy ended up staying in the Marines without us, Boyd and I became inseparable.

Boyd and I had been heterosexual life mates for about four years at this point. We lived together, ate together, scored dope together, survived together. We had seen other members of our tribe come and go, but it had always been us at the core. We had been through a lot together.

And for me, I didn't feel so much like I was losing Boyd, more like I was gaining Allison.

Of course, I had no idea how he felt because dudes don't talk about our feelings. But I was starting to wander just how crazy he really was, and whether he had turned on me or thought I had turned on him. I knew it was going to take all my skill to keep this Allison situation from coming to a head.

25 Plinkin'

I realized just how testy things had become with Boyd later that day.

We had gone plinkin'. Plinkin' is probably just about the best way to spend a Sunday. We sometimes pretended it was Sunday just so we could go plinkin''.

We would take an old coal road up to what used to be the top of a mountain. I guess it was still the top, just flatter now. Mountain top removal would create these weird little plateaus. I had never seen a real plateau, only ones in pictures.

But the plinkin' spot was what I figured a plateau would be like. Up and up and up on a little switchback coal road, which is a damn sight better than a switch back logging road. You would run the car off the side of one of those old logging roads if you didn't have your shit wired tight.

Or if you were too fucked up.

Up on the former mountain top you could get some great plinkin' spots, though. You could line out a 500 yarder here and there if you were of a mind to. Which was a hard thing to find, living in the woods the way we were.

Everything around the county that wasn't town, a house, or a road was fucking forest. Hard to work on your sniper fire in the forest. You need open spaces to hone your long-range skills.

Boyd was an expert. Sure, he would do trick shots and quick draw stuff and fuck with those cheating bastards at the shooting match. But when we were out plinkin' was when Boyd would scare you with a firearm.

That motherfucker could reach out and touch you with a firearm from serious distance. We would set up milk jugs full of water, do two and three hundred yarders, and work our way back to 500. I couldn't see a milk jug at 500 yards without the scope, but I could see them explode when Boyd would hit them, first shot almost every time.

I was a two or three shot kind of guy, myself, on a good day. But Boyd didn't miss.

After we'd exhausted the milk jugs at distance, we'd have created enough empty beer cans for the real fun to begin. We'd set up beer can target ranges and work our way through them with pistols, then hip shoot the shotgun a while, until all the cans were obliterated.

Then we'd bounce freshly created beer cans down the road with the .22 rifle, then play some quick draw games on unsuspecting consumer goods remnants. There was always plenty of trash and shit to shoot at.

"Probably from assholes like us bringing shit out here to shoot at all these years," I mused to myself under my breath.

"What's that, man?" Boyd asked through a cloud of gun smoke. We'd just waylaid an old hubcap with Boyd's favorite shotgun, an 870 he'd taken the plug out of so he could jack a couple more rounds into it.

"Huh?" I said, "I didn't say anything."

That shit about the garbage is what Allison would say, I thought. And she was right. Yes, these hillbillies had been swindled, in collusion by some, I'm sure. They had been swindled out of their lands and the coal companies had come in and blown the top off their mountain to get to the coal. Turns out it wasn't all that much coal because many mines were already abandoned.

But who the fuck was I to shoot up trash all over the place? I guess if you're going to litter you should have fun with it, but the real solution is to not litter. Boyd and I contributed an awful lot to the trash problem in the mountains through our plinkin'.

And I knew Allison was right about littering, I'd listened to her and Karen bemoan the state of the natural world while on our road trip. It had annoyed the piss out of Boyd, but I sort of found it endearing. She had such a passion about the environment.

I had stopped throwing my cigarette butts out the window that first day in the car. She had said, "Aww, man!" when I flicked my butt out the window and into the wild.

Boyd had looked over with raised eyebrows, and I sort of shrugged and rolled my eyes.

That was all she said, "Awwww, man." She didn't bring it up or say anything every time Boyd threw one out the window, but that "Awwww, man," had gotten me. I didn't throw another cigarette butt out the window. I figured she didn't notice, but I secretly hoped she did. I wanted to do any little thing I could that would make her happy, even if she didn't notice.

It was harder to hide it from Boyd. I had a pocket full of cigarette butts. We had been plinkin' all day. I had purposely flicked one onto the ground in front of him early on, to throw off suspicion. But I had saved the rest to dispose of later.

I was explaining, again, to myself that she was never going to even know, when Boyd asked, "You got any more shells for the Smoke Pole?"

The Smoke Pole was an old, old, single-shot .410 shotgun we always brought plinkin'. It was one of his favorites, full of nostalgic memories of being a young kid blasting squirrels out of trees and rabbits out of the bushes. I did have a couple of 410 shells left, down in my cargo pocket with all my cigarette butts.

"Yeah, here you go," I said, pulling one out and tossing it to him as he reached into the trunk to retrieve the shotgun.

The Corsica didn't have the same trunk space to which we'd grown accustomed with the Beast. We were still able to fit all the firearms in there, though.

"Bodies will be a different story," Boyd remarked that morning as we stood over it, fully loaded with enough firepower to subdue Paris. He was right, bodies were always harder to fit in a trunk than they made it look on TV.

As I tossed that .410 shell to Boyd, I realized I had a cigarette butt from my pocket caught somehow in my hand, and I watched in horror as it flew from my hand toward Boyd, following the shotgun shell, although at a much slower and weaker pace. The cigarette butt seemed to move in slow motion as it ran out of steam well before the shotgun shell did and fell to the earth 4 or 5 feet in front of Boyd. He caught the 410 shell as his eyes followed the slow arc of the cigarette butt.

"What the fuck is that?" he asked, a frown on his face. "You saving butts now?"

I didn't know what to say to save myself the most ridicule. I knew I was pussy whipped hard by this girl, albeit without the actual pussy. I was anticipating his jokes coming in droves, ready to burst through my lovey dovey bubble and slap me upside the head. Maybe it is what I needed to snap out of it, but I didn't want to be out of it. I was in love with this girl and my inner monologue went into high gear, preparing to defend myself from Boyd's inevitable onslaught of insults.

"Don't answer that," Boyd said, thrusting the shotgun back into the trunk. He silently strode over to the cigarette butt, plucked it off the ground while shaking his head, and marched ten or twelve steps down the road, still shaking his head.

He set the shotgun shell I had tossed him on the ground standing straight up, and then balanced the cigarette butt on the end. He then turned and walked back toward me. I prayed for wind, or a minor earthquake, or a stampede of wild buffalo, anything to cause the butt to topple off the end of the shotgun shell and disrupt whatever the fuck was happening

When he was just about back to the spot where the cigarette butt had fallen to the ground, he stopped shaking his head, looked me straight in the eye, and suddenly wheeled around drew his pistol and fired, all in one swift, fluid motion. The cigarette butt disintegrated from the top of the shotgun shell, which itself remained still. Boyd looked over his shoulder at me, grinning that sick grin he sometimes got when he was plinkin' and pulled off a great shot.

"If you're gonna save garbage, at least do something creative with it," he said with a smirk.

I smiled weakly, happy that he apparently would not make fun of me over saving cigarette butts out of some sense of environmental courtship. My smile hid that Boyd sometimes scared the shit out of me with his firearm proficiency, and I was glad we were on the same side. I knew it would be a major problem, for me, should this not be the case. I wondered if he would think we were still on the same side if he knew how I felt about Allison.

I decided that delving into that conversation was probably not advisable while we were out plinkin', half drunk and armed to the teeth as we were. It was a conversation Boyd and I needed to have, but it would have to wait.

26 Just Like Old Times

As I picked Allison up from the airport, I was glad she was so sensible. She was so sensible that I knew she would get us out of this Mexico shit. I was worried about having to tell her about it. At least there was a two-hour drive back to Bell County to figure out how to do it.

I was also worried, since she was so sensible and would obviously say no, that we would then have to find out if I was imagining that shit with Boyd or not. How mad was he going to be? How was he going to take it?

I was shocked by her reply.

"Of course, Sweetie, whatever you want to do is fine with me. I'm not doing anything wrong, just going to Mexico with my boyfriend. Why not? It will be fun!"

I was speechless. She called me her boyfriend. I was so elated I didn't even worry she had not saved us from this drug smuggling fiasco. The idea that she would go along with such a thing sent me into a long running criminal fantasy about being a real-life Bonnie and Clyde.

Every criminal's romantic fantasy.

And she called me her *boyfriend*.

I was on cloud 9 when we pulled up to the trailer. Boyd was waiting outside on the steps to bring me back down to earth.

"Don't get out of the car. They just called me and we gotta go do that thing for Trey. Right now."

Allison looked confused so I stammered out an explanation of needing to go meet a guy for our buddy Trey. It was not a good explanation, but she probably just figured we would pick up some pot or something.

She squeezed my arm and said, "No worries, my dear. Let's go meet your friends. I'm happy to be here with you."

She always knew just what to say to put me at ease. I just smiled and nodded.

Boyd demanded shotgun, which Allison was kind enough to give up. She hopped over the front console and into the backseat.

It made more sense, from a tactical standpoint. Sometimes shit went sideways and you needed your best shot riding shotgun.

Once we were all rearranged in the car, we set off for the address Boyd provided.

"Have to hurry," he said. "Not sure how long he'll be there." We headed toward Harlan, and took the Page bridge, driving by the Clampett establishments.

Several of the Clampett brothers built a little empire along the riverside, now abandoned. But besides the pot dealing and pimping the daughters, which all the brothers were involved in, one brother was carrying on an incestuous relationship with Memaw Clampett.

When the other brother found out, he went to shoot the memaw-fucker. But as you'd expect in these tales from the holler, he missed and killed Memaw Clampett. The third brother tried to kill the memaw-murderer, and the cops took the whole bunch of 'em to jail. All the kids went in to foster care, never to be heard from again, which was probably the best thing for them, especially the ones getting raped by their uncles and grandmother.

Boyd and I had figured the Clampett saga would end in this fashion, after that time we went over to buy some pot and the whole family, four generations of Clampetts it looked like, were all piled into the living room watching gonzo porn in complete silence.

"He's really giving it to her," Memaw Clampett had said, commenting on the film, when we had stepped through the door. They even had their pack of chihuahuas all lined up watching it with them. We knew them people wasn't right.

I wanted to ask Boyd more about the intel, partly to get my mind off the fucked up Clampett clan. I wanted to know who had given the bastard up, who else was in on it, how many pedestrians would be there.

But I didn't want to ask too much in front of Allison, so I just kept quiet and drove. There is a certain level of excitement to flying blind.

When we got to the house, I asked Allison to wait in the car while we went to see if our friend was home. A familiar face opened the door to Boyd's soft knock. I saw Chuck and realized we were probably alright.

Chuck was a couple of years behind us in school, but we knew him from the local music scene. He played guitar a little bit, Boyd played bass a little bit, I played drums a little bit, and we had spent a few evenings jamming out at various parties.

I never knew him to be involved in anything like this, but I had heard he was bad into dope these days. Skinnier than I remembered, he closed the door behind us and retreated up the staircase, pointing us down the hall toward the living room.

Boyd pulled two pistols. His 1911 model .45, and then my favorite, the Smith &Wesson .357 Magnum with the 6-inch barrel. He handed me the Magnum.

"Let's get it, you soft Yankee fuck," he gave me an evil grin and a wink and set off down the hallway toward the living room, 1911 leading the way.

We burst into the living room, surprising our quarry, who jumped up off the couch and pushed the young half naked girl at us as he bolted for the garage door. Boyd leaped past the screaming girl and shoulder checked Romeo, who tumbled through the door and into the garage. He fell down the stairs and crashed, spread eagle on the concrete floor, with Boyd in hot pursuit.

I followed them into the garage and covered the door as Boyd beat the statutory rapist about the head and face with his pistol. All the while, he's explaining about how this has been a long time coming and this prick is just getting what he deserves.

I was laughing a little bit at Boyd's commentary, and wondering how much Romeo was actually comprehending, when the door burst open. An enormous motherfucker rushed through, possibly the biggest human I had ever seen in real life.

He stopped short when I pointed my gun at him. The magnum is the great social equalizer of our time.

"Hi," I said.

"What the fuck is going on?" he said as he placed one foot down the first step.

"Retribution, Old Testament style," I said. "Have a seat. This don't concern you."

I knew the .357 could stop him, but it might take a couple. This fucker was huge! I thought about head shots.

"But that's my nephew. Ahhhh, come on. Man!"

He took another step down. There were only three steps.

287

"This doesn't concern you," I said again, this time cocking the hammer on that old .357. "Don't make it concern me."

Click always works well as punctuation, even when it's not at the end of the sentence.

The giant sat down on the bottom step and put his giant head in his giant hands.

"He's just a kid," he mumbled, "leave him alone."

"Well, that kid is twenty years old and likes to fuck fourteen-year-olds and take pictures of it. So, we are gonna let nature take its course, you, and I, and then we will part ways. And we'll never cross paths again."

I spied Chuck peeking around the hallway corner, looking through the garage door completely off its hinges after the big man's grand entrance. I wondered if this is how he thought it would go?

"Hey Bud?" I called out. "Anybody else here I should know about?"

Chuck shook his head weakly. He was as white as his t-shirt and might have been crying. He winced every time Boyd landed a blow, thunk, thunk, ca chunk. Chuck shook his head again and disappeared out of view. I heard the front door slam behind him.

Boyd kicked Romeo one more time for good measure, number 1000 I think it was, and said, "We're all done. Let's go."

"Don't let me see you again," I told the fat man as we walked back through the house.

Boyd was tracking bloody footprints across the living room carpet. That beige color they always use soaks up blood, and it is a bitch to clean up.

Boyd turned around to grin at me as he wiped blood off the barrel of his 45 with what appeared to be the girl's blouse from the couch.

"Just like old times," he said with a wink.

I just stared at him, realizing how easily it had all just seemed to happen, how easily I had pulled a gun on a potentially innocent fat man, how easily I followed Boyd's lead.

"Don't look at me that way, Jack," he said as we made our way through the house.

"He fucked my sister last year, and she made me promise not to do anything. So this job for Trey was a little personal as well."

I understood. I had a sister too. I was still a little unsettled, though. This random violence rarely came up in what I had seen of Allison's world. That peaceful, college world seemed a million miles and years away, and I realized I desperately wanted to go back there.

"He wasn't in there, and we got tired of waiting," I explained to Allison as we got back in the car.

She shrugged. "Well what else can you show me of your beloved Bell County?"

I shook my head, knowing there was nothing I wanted to show her in Bell County. The sooner we could get out of here the better. The past 10 minutes had clearly illustrated that my life here was out of control and I didn't need to let Allison become an accessory to any more felonies.

She had a good life and a bright future, and I didn't need to screw it up. The longer we were here, the more chance there was for that to happen. Shit, she'd only been here an hour and we had beaten one man and threatened to shoot another.

And we were enroute to Mel's to finish prepping for some narcotics smuggling. Things were pretty fucked up and the only thing I knew for sure was that I needed to get her as far away from this place as possible. Soon.

Just one more job, I thought, just one more job and we'll be clear.

I grinned despite myself, a sick grin found its way across my face, as I sped us through the twists and turns of the holler's one lane road. It had been like old times. And deep down, I knew I fucking loved it.

27   The Cartel's Man

I woke up early the next morning, on the couch with Allison. She was so cute while she was sleeping, all curled up and smiling. I don't know what she was dreaming about, but it was making her smile.

I knew she must not be thinking about the same shit as me, 'cause I was feeling pretty nervous about the whole Mexico plan.

Boyd was already awake, which was weird. I almost always woke up first. He had the coffee already made, which was even weirder.

"You ready for today, motherfucker?" he greeted me as I poured a cup of coffee.

"Ready as I'll ever be, I guess," I mumbled in return.

"Well, it's up to us to hold this thing together. Mel is a basket case, as you know, and Allison is a newbie. So we have to have our shit wired tight 'cause they probably won't be any help at all if shit goes sideways."

He was right. All valid points, and probably sufficient reason to call the whole thing off. But I knew that would never happen.

"Better wake Allison, Mel will be here soon," Boyd instructed.

I figured I better bring her a cup of coffee, to soften the blow of such an early morning wake up call. She opened her eyes, still smiling, and smiled even brighter when she saw the coffee.

"For me?" she said softly. "How sweet."

I knew right then I would bring her coffee every morning for the rest of our lives…if she'd let me.

We dressed and smoked some weed and waited for Mel. She was picking us up in the car we would use for the trip. I had been a little worried they would try to use my car and was relieved when Mel said she had the transportation covered. No way I wanted it to be my car full of illicit drugs.

I rethought my position when she pulled up in her borrowed shitbox. Maroon Oldsmobile Cutlass Calais, circa 1991. I immediately missed the Saturn we had taken on the first trip. Roomy and a real smooth ride.

And it had been quieter than I remembered Saturns being. My high school sweetheart's mother had driven a Saturn. She had been the sort of lady an adolescent teenage boy imagines his mother-in-law will be once he gets hitched. She doesn't like you; she thinks you're an idiot, and she makes sure you know it.

Shits on any good idea you ever have and generally works to undermine you in front of your wife at every turn. She spends her days sowing the seeds of discord all over your unfortunate marriage where they will eventually take root and sprout an unfulfilling life.

Your mother-in-law would drive a Saturn and work in a gas station and know everything. And you would always want to say, "if you know so goddam much, why do you work in a gas station and drive a fucking Saturn?" but you never would, because your wife would flip the fuck out if you talked that way to her momma.

So you'd hold it together for years and years, until it eventually worked its way to the surface at the most inopportune time. Probably while there was still time to write you out of the will.

The wife would divorce you. You'd be broke and miserable, having worked in a shit job for fifteen years to keep your wife and her mother off your back. A job you've hated every day for fifteen years.

It would feel like it was too late to start over, so you would resign yourself to being a sad little man. A sad little man in a sad little apartment, who stood up for himself just once and lost everything.

Yep, marriage sounded like it sucked, and my ex-girlfriend's mother-in-law in her Saturn had illustrated this long ago.

Although, come to think of it, I never rode in her Saturn. I think since she was so loud, I remembered the car as loud.

While riding to Mexico in a 91 Cutlass Calais, I missed the Saturn we rode in last time. And I wondered what Allison's mother would be like. Probably think I was an idiot. I decided that she might not be that far off, given the circumstances.

I missed the professionalism we traveled under last time too. Mel was passing out Valium and Xanax and passing joints around the car. Boyd and I were pounding beers. Allison had taken a valium, the first recreational pill of her life, she said, and it knocked her on her ass. She slept almost the whole way, which was good because she didn't see us being so stupid.

We were headed to Mexico to smuggle narcotics across the border. We had a fairly large sum of cash for narcotics and bribes. We had several guns in the car, several types of pills, a little pot, a comatose girl, and a case of beer dwindling at a rapid rate.

The empty beer cans were being slung out the windows at road signs by two drunk idiots, and it was only 10 am. And there was a distinct possibility this was a stolen car. Mel didn't own a damn car, that's why they were always asking me for rides.

We were operating with a complete lack of professionalism, which was unlike Boyd and me. Normally, we held it together better than this.

But shit was far from normal. I had brought my girlfriend, who I was in love with, for one thing. A girl not from, or of, this lifestyle. And I had brought her on a massive drug run with a couple of junkies using a junkie plan.

The more I thought about it, the more concerned I became, so I quit thinking about it. Allison's mom would be right. I am an idiot.

Allison woke up when we got to that same shitty motel where we had stopped on the first trip. Once again, I smoked dope on a picnic table while Mel got her groove on.

I shook my head at my bringing Allison to all my usual hangouts, and these were the hangouts. What the fuck kind of people were we?

We got into Mexico, no problem. Which is, of course, the easy part. Mexico didn't give a flying fuck what you smuggled into their side.

We tried to go to the same doctor as before, but his office had moved. So, we had to go deeper into the town to find his new spot. We finally found him, the little gold-toothed doctor, in the second-floor space of a Pharmacia.

Seemed like they were helping you save time by having the doctor and the pharmacy in the same building. It was a definite model of efficiency in healthcare.

We took the exterior staircase up to the doctor's office where the fire door was propped open to allow some airflow into the stuffy waiting room. Mexico is hot as fuck. We sat in the waiting room while a young assistant in a white lab coat scurried back and forth, to and fro, getting everyone's information and trying to keep the line moving.

He was very dedicated to making this the most efficient experience one could have in a Mexican doctor's office.

We still had plenty of time to enjoy the waiting room, such as it was. Green plastic chairs lined one wall, about half of them occupied by patients in various stages of illness and injury. Seemed to be a general practitioner's office.

There was a little desk where a pretty young secretary-looking lady talked on the phone, absently watching the telenovela on the old TV suspended in the corner of the room. The young assistant kept coming and going through the single door, back into the confines of the examination room. There seemed to only be the one exam room, and I assumed the doctor was in there somewhere. It seemed odd there was a window in the exam room door. So much for privacy, I suppose.

The assistant finally came for us, bypassing several patients who looked like they probably needed medical care more urgently than we did. But the doctor needed our dollars more urgently than he needed their pesos. I discovered why when we got back into the exam room.

The exam room was larger than the outside waiting area would have indicated. A door in the back led further into the building from the exam room. The doctor sat at a little metal desk, similar to what a teacher in a poor rural school district would use. My mother probably had that same desk in her classroom, I thought.

The doctor took our id's and set about filling his prescription pad. He and Mel haggled over price since she wasn't buying as much as last time. He said he thought Mike would be here. Mel stood her ground fairly well though and seemed pleased with her price.

Once an agreement was reached, the doctor paused in his writing long enough to knock on the wall behind him. Two men emerged from the door that led to the hallway that led to somewhere and counted the money Mel had placed on the table.

Boyd and I were in opposite corners of the room. I didn't move from my spot, because I could see through the window in the door to the waiting room, but Boyd moved over a little closer to the door the men had come out of.

Boyd wanted to get into a better position to block the door, in case we were being robbed, but one of the men quickly stepped directly between Boyd and the door.

Now he was blocking the door in case we were being robbed.

I was watching the waiting room, and watching them count the money, and glancing over at Allison periodically who was in the far corner of the room, sitting on a little couch and looking beautiful. I couldn't help myself. She was so hot.

I saw the man step through the doorway from the world outside before the scurrying assistant did. The man paused for a second in the doorway, letting his eyes adjust to the dim glow of the waiting room's fluorescent overhead lights.

This gave the assistant time to notice him, and when he did notice, the assistant immediately rushed over to greet him. The man walked right past the assistant in the lab coat, raising his hand as if to say 'halt' as he passed him, clearly on his way over to the receptionist's desk.

Or maybe it was a high five attempt.

Either way, the assistant, stopped dead in his tracks. He waited until the man was past him, spun on his heels, and made a beeline for the exam room door, a look of consternation enveloping his face.

This was the cartel's man.

He wore a silk shirt; top two buttons open at the collar to reveal a shiny gold crucifix. His custom suit seemed to shimmer in the glow of the lighting and probably was magnificent in the sunlight. His shiny black cowboy boots set off an outfit in stark contrast to the attire of everyone else in the building. Even the doctor was wearing jeans and ratty sneakers, hole in the elbow of his stained sweater. The cartel's man's dress code starkly contrasted with the entire building, and was probably in stark contrast to the entire country.

He smiled easily as he flirted with the receptionist, revealing pearly white teeth, neat and straight. He placed his hand on her arm as he sat on the edge of her desk and said something that made her blush. The assistant in the lab coat suddenly obscured my view of the proceedings, filling the window in the door with his panicked face before promptly bursting into the exam room. He closed the door behind him and stood in front of it.

He motioned for me to move out of the line of sight of the cartel representative and talked a mile a minute to the doctor in nervous sounding Spanish.

The doctor grabbed about a third of the stack of Mel's money, stuck it in a white prescription bag and gave it to the assistant. The assistant promptly stuck the bag in the pocket of his lab coat.

The doctor sent the other two men away, gesturing toward the back door and gathering up the remaining money to send with them, speaking quickly and quietly to them. Mel protested, and Boyd stepped toward the desk.

The doctor raised his hands, and said in perfect English, "Friends, please, we are almost done. But this is how it must be. I will have your prescriptions ready soon and they will fill it downstairs. But please, just stay quietly in here for a few more minutes. And away from the window, please."

The assistant quickly left the room, and I stepped to the side of the door, where I could flank anyone who came in from the waiting room. I peeked through the window in time to see the assistant pull the prescription bag of money from the pocket of his lab coat and hand it to the man.

The man took it, looked inside, and flashed that toothy smile at the assistant. He patted the assistant on the shoulder and stood up from his perch on the receptionist's desk. He made one more flirtatious comment to her, based on the creepy smile he flashed her, and strode back out of the waiting room and into the bright Mexican sun where his suit could really shine.

It felt like the entire building breathed a sigh of relief. I know the doctor did. That was probably the last thing he needed was the cartel's man spotting the gringos in his office. Much easier to just make the payoffs and carry on about your business.

After a few minutes he handed the scripts over to Mel and we headed down to the pharmacy to fill them. I saw no sign of anybody that looked out of place as we made our way back toward the border. Although, to be truthful about it, we were the junky gringos who looked out of place with our duffel bag of pharmaceuticals.

28 I Was on Oxy

I Don't Know Why Anyone Else Thought This was a Good Plan

T hings began to unravel at the bridge. Although, to be frank, things weren't wrapped too tight to begin with.

Mike's guy was nowhere to be seen. The guy we got wouldn't stamp the prescriptions; he didn't confiscate them, but he wouldn't stamp 'em either.

The plan for the vehicle checkpoint wouldn't work now. No way to get past the drug dogs. And without the stamped batch on top to give Mike's other guy something to verify, they'd have to toss the whole car. And that's assuming Mike's other guy was gonna even be where we thought he was supposed to be.

No stamp equals no modicum of legality to perpetuate the cover. Just some dopeheads with several thousand dollars' worth of narcotics in their luggage.

At this point our best option might have been to bring the dope across the river and hike it through the wilderness like the coyotes do. I wanted to nominate Boyd to bring the bag of dope across and meet us in Texas somewhere. I suppose I could have gone too and made an adventure out of it, like the old days.

But those days were gone, I guess, because I was thrilled with Mel's idea to mail the drugs back to her house. I thought it was a dumb idea, truthfully. I knew that if it was that easy to mail dope to yourself, everybody would do it, but I didn't even care about the money anymore.

Two thoughts occurred to me while we were waiting in the customs line trying to get our stamps. One, I had no idea how many people had been killed trying to buy drugs, or deal in drugs, or fool with drugs down in Mexico. But I knew it had to be a whole hell of a lot. Especially if you included Mexicans in the equation. Throw the cartel into the mix and God only knows how many deaths over this stupid shit.

And here I was bringing Allison into this environment. What the ever-living fuck?

My second thought was, I had no idea how many people had gone to prison, Mexican or American prison. I had no idea how many had gotten serious prison time trying to bring dope across the border. It had to be a whole shitload.

And again, here I was, bringing the woman I loved into this shit. What the fuck?

So, when Mel suggested getting the dope as far away from us as we could via the postal service, I was all for it. I knew we'd never see it again, but it wasn't my dope anyway. And even if it did work, and Mel pulled this off, I'd probably see nothing out of it, anyway.

But Allison had shown me a way of life that didn't involve death or the penal system.

I had never worried about such things before. I knew that mine and Boyd's way of life had only two possible endings. You got killed or you went to prison and then got killed.

At least how that's how my mother always put it, and from what I had seen, she was right.

But I had never let it bother me. I was having too much fun. Drugs are fucking fun. And danger is fucking fun. And partying is fucking fun. And you don't worry about consequences, not for you or anyone else, because when you are in it for real, no one else matters.

Until one day someone does.

Mel rented a pay by the hour type of motel room, and we spent our hour popping pills out of blister packs and dumping pill bottles out into the ice bucket. I would have preferred that we wash the ice bucket first, but I guess then we'd have to worry about moisture. At least whatever crusty germs were in the ice bucket were dried on. I had never seen a hotel room with no towels before.

Mel took the ice bucket full of pills to Mailboxes, etc. and mailed it.

Minus the last oxy I ever did, which I palmed during the packing process. I wasn't all the way reformed.

We drove through the checkpoint without incident since we didn't have anything on us anyway. My oxy was starting to hit, and I was just settling into the thought of snuggling up with Allison for the long car ride home.

We had no drugs. We weren't gonna make any money. But fuck it, I thought, I was with Allison and we were on a road trip. Road trips with Allison were a good time.

And then the piece of shit Oldsmobile shit the bed. It just made a clank, then a pow, then a lot of smoke, and then nothing. Mel coasted into the shoulder and called AAA. I think everyone was more shocked that she had an active AAA account than that the car had died.

The car was a piece of shit, and the mechanic basically told us that. He could fix it, but it would take a while to order parts, and it would be expensive. It turns out the car belonged to Mel's uncle, and so it had to make its way back to Kentucky somehow.

Allison was tired. She had her head leaned on my shoulder as we sat outside the garage, waiting on Mel and Boyd. They were at the payphone, thinking up a new plan.

"I could buy us a couple of bus or train tickets, and we could leave them to deal with the car," she suggested.

That sounded so wonderful. But I didn't want to ditch them down here in the middle of nowhere.

They were saying they were out of money, which I was used to hearing from Boyd. He never had any money. I had expected more out of Mel, though.

We came up with a plan.

I was on oxy. I don't know why anyone else thought this was a good plan.

The plan we came up with was to rent a U-Haul truck with the tow package and drive the whole rig all the way back to Bell County.

Four people can't ride in the front seat of a U-Haul truck from the Mexico border all the way to Kentucky without getting pulled over. And people can't ride in a car being towed by a U-Haul truck all the way to Kentucky without getting pulled over.

But at least two people can ride in the back of a U-Haul truck as it pulls a car from nearly Mexico all the way to Kentucky without getting pulled over.

I assume you could haul more than two people in the back of your U-Haul, but that would require more bathroom and oxygen breaks. And those were already gonna be sparse, I feared, as Allison and I climbed aboard what I could only imagine would be the last ride we took together.

If we got into an accident on the freeway, we would die.

And if we didn't get into an accident, she would surely leave me after this shit.

Either way, I knew this was the end.

29 Choices

We had a couple of blankets, some cigarettes, and a little water. Not nearly enough water. We had not anticipated how hot it would be and how dehydrated we would get. It was so hot and stuffy, mile after bouncy mile.

Sometimes we laughed because that was the only way to keep from crying. We laughed at the irony of traveling from Mexico in the back of a U-Haul, like thousands of immigrants had done.

Not because we were illegals, but because we were making poor choices. We laughed at how stupid we must be to end up in such a predicament.

But as the hours dragged on, and the oxygen grew thin, our patience slipped away. I knew it was only a matter of time until she decided these poor choices were my fault. I knew that despite my attempts to seem like a normal, alright kind of guy, I was exposed as a very small-time hood with very limited resources and prospects. And her mother would be right, I am an idiot.

When riding in the back of a U-Haul with your boyfriend, there is no way not to know he is a loser.

I figured she was being nice by not outright blaming me and giving me shit about the situation. I knew she had to realize that being involved with me was a bad idea. A terrible, horrible idea that could only end in disappointment and disaster. Our predicament had proven just how badly things could go.

At one point we thought we were dying for sure. We had been knocking on the wall to the cab, to let them know we needed to stop. The air was so hot and heavy, and it was hard to breathe. We knocked and knocked, but to no avail. We both passed out, and when we came to, we continued to knock weakly on the wall.

Finally, after about another hour, they finally stopped the U-Haul.

But they didn't open the door. I had no idea where we were, and no idea why they weren't letting us out. We knocked and knocked and there was no reply. After about a half an hour, we heard the latch on the door.

As soon as the door slid open, Allison jumped to her feet and tore Boyd a new asshole. I don't know where she got the energy, I could barely sit up. She tore into him for not only refusing to stop as often as had been agreed upon, but also ignoring our knocking, and keeping us in there an extra half hour after we were stopped.

By the time the door had made it halfway up the track, Boyd had heard enough. His face had twisted into a murderous rage, the kind with the crazy eye, and he slammed the door back down, locking us inside once again.

I don't know what effect he thought it would have, but Allison went into a murderous rage of her own.

I tried to yell out, but I was drowned out by her. She had raised her decibel level to hitherto unseen heights, for such a petite little thing.

The door immediately raised back up, swiftly running up its track and coming to a crashing halt at the top. Boyd was storming off, but I would not let him get away so easily. I chased him down, screaming about how fucked up it was, and what kind of bullshit this shit was. When I caught up to him, he wheeled to face me.

The look on his face stopped me in my tracks. I had never seen a look like that. It was like you could see all the emotions and thought processes playing out in hyper speed on his face.

He loved me...He hated Allison ...He wanted to save me...He had to kill us both...he couldn't let a woman like Allison talk to him that way...he couldn't let me leave with her...he knew I wouldn't stay, probably no matter what he did.

It was over in the blink of an eye, and his face was back to the cold determination and furious anger I had been expecting. He grabbed me by the shoulder and screamed in my face, "I love you Jack, but get the fuck away from me! Right now! Get the fuck away from me!"

And with that, he wheeled around and stomped off into the trees. I looked around. We were at a rest stop, Tennessee flag flying from the welcome center.

The fucking Vols. Thank God, I thought. Getting close to the end.

Allison was standing on the sidewalk, smoking a cigarette, and shaking. She was so mad.

"Is he fucking crazy? We're the ones locked in the fucking U-Haul for hours and hours. We could have died back there!"

I looked around for Mel as Allison fumed. Fuck. Didn't see her anywhere.

"We should take a piss if you need to," I said quietly to Allison. "Don't worry, we are almost there."

I was worrying seriously about our safety, but not in the way Allison thought.

She continued, "What the hell is that? Locks us up and then acts like he's doing us a favor, like we should be grateful, like we should be sucking his dick for letting us out? You saw his face, how mad he got when we questioned him! He better watch who he's fucking with! He don't know me!"

She was a firecracker, that one. I smiled despite the situation, turning my head so Allison wouldn't see. I finally got her up to the bathrooms where Mel was just emerging, looking strung out.

But at least she was still alive. I had been worried about that.

The rest of the ride was done in silence. Allison slept, exhausted from the whole ordeal.

I sat in the dark, in the back of that U-Haul and figured things out. It had occurred to me that Boyd might be a little hurt I had ditched him for a girl. A sort of bros before hoes mentality he embraced.

It had also occurred to me that Boyd is a crazy person. And Allison's assessment of his facial expressions and attitude at the moment he raised the U-Haul door was accurate. He did look like he thought he was doing us a favor and that we should be grateful.

But the look he gave me when I caught up to him had been entirely accurate. I could see what he was thinking as crystal clear as he was thinking it.

I saw that he might not have been planning to let us out at all. I thought that one or both of us had been under consideration for being dumped on the side of the highway, just another unidentified drifter found dead in a ditch.

I had been nervous when I didn't see Mel right away because she would probably have to go too in this scenario.

Had his plan been to kill Allison, then kill Mel to keep her quiet, then kill me if I could not adjust to the new reality? How unhinged was Boyd, really?

Had his expression been the result of talking himself down from triple homicide, of talking himself into doing us this favor, giving us this gift as he saw it, giving us back our lives, even though he felt like our lives together were ruining his life?

When he opened that door and was greeted with anger instead of gratitude, his face told that story. That crazy fucked up story of how closely he had been considering stopping Allison and me from running away together.

I realized Boyd loved me, just like he always said he did. I realized we were brothers, just like he always said we were.

I realized I loved him too, we were brothers. But I realized I had to leave. And I realized he might kill me before I got the chance.

30 The Window

Everyone was calm when Mel dropped us all off at Memaw's trailer. We shuffled into the living room.

"Want a beer?" Boyd asked. I nodded and sat down in my customary spot on the couch. Allison sat down beside me, and Boyd took the seat in the recliner across from us. I turned on the TV, SNL reruns.

We watched a few sketches in silence. Nobody felt like laughing, and SNL had fallen off anyway.

Allison said she was tired, and that we should get some sleep. I agreed, although I knew I would get no sleep. I looked over at Boyd, trying to gauge his mood.

He was leaned back in the chair, not with the leg thing propped out, just leaned back comfortably. He always said he didn't like that leg thing, 'cause you couldn't get up fast in a firefight.

The shadow from the bookcase was obscuring his face, so I wasn't sure who he was looking at. But the light from the kitchen glinted off the barrel of his 9mm.

I wasn't sure who Boyd was looking at, but Mr. 9 mm was looking squarely at me.

My breath caught in my throat. How long had he been pointing a gun at me? A refrain from a Manson song pumped through my mind, "Shoot, shoot, shoot motherfucker!"

I had no gun on me, and at this range he'd get us both before I could even get off the couch. So fuck it, do what you gotta do motherfucker!

But I said none of that. I just stared at him, a little sad that it had come to this. But I knew I would change nothing. I would still have followed Allison home; I would still have fallen in love with her.

In hindsight, I would have just stayed in Baltimore with her, rather than returning to Bell County to get shot. But I would change nothing about my feelings for her.

I hoped Boyd knew that.

After what seemed like a long time, the two of us looking at each other in the semi-darkness, not speaking, him thinking I couldn't see the gun, me not acknowledging it, he finally moved.

He put the gun back in his holster, stood up, and said, "I'm gonna go to bed. I'll see you in the morning Old Buddy."

"Good night, Boyd," I said.

Allison was already asleep, her head resting on my shoulder. As Boyd walked down the hallway to his room,

315

I reorganized Allison on the couch and quietly packed my bag. It didn't take long to pack up my life, a few clothes was about all I still had in the trailer.

It took a little longer to come to terms with it all. In some ways it was easy. I had known from the moment I saw her I wanted to be with Allison. It had been love at first sight. And the more I was with her, the more I knew that my first instinct had been the right one.

Shit, she had just ridden in the back of a U-Haul from nearly Mexico with me because I brought her on a super sketchy drug deal with my junky friends and it had gone horribly awry.

And yet, she was still here. Still beside me. Still planning on bringing me with her to her home to meet her family. Going with her was the easy part.

The hard part was leaving Boyd. We had been through a lot of shit together, an awful lot of crazy shit. We'd lost our minds and found them again, together. We'd cheated death on numerous occasions, together. We'd pulled off some wickedly crazy shit, right under the noses of the cops, and gotten away with it, together.

We'd seen our lives crumble and our families fall apart and everybody turn against us, and we had pulled ourselves through it all, together.

But life around Boyd did not seem like a sure commodity anymore. There was always death around us, like there is

316

for anyone in the game, people died and got killed. But it was different now, somehow.

I had never once even considered that Boyd could hurt me. And now, twice in the same day, I thought he might have been planning to kill me.

See, the thing about having a crazy best friend is that they are crazy. And I thought his crazy had taken a turn.

I knew what I had to do. I knew that when God closes a door, he opens a window.

I waited for about two hours, lying on the couch with Allison, feeling her breathe in her sleep. I listened for Boyd's snoring, which finally came. When it did, I quietly woke up the love of my life, climbed through that window, and drove off into the night.

As the sun broke free of the horizon, as Allison slept peacefully in the passenger seat, I realized I was watching the dawning of my new life.

I put the pedal down, eager to move on, ready for whatever the road ahead offered. I knew that if I had Allison, I would be fine, no matter what follows.

It was finally time to leave that old life behind...and I never looked back.

Acknowledgments

Special thanks to Wade, who brought me into his world and showed me how to live.

Special thanks to Carol and Korus, the best kind of friends two crazy kids could have.

Special thanks to Hannah who fearlessly leads our adventures when called upon.

Special thanks to the llama who keeps this outfit running and puts up with me.

Special thanks to my mother who always gives good advice, whether I follow it or not.

Special thanks to police departments and customs officials across the land for their tireless and selfless service to the common good.

Shout out to UHAUL

About the Author

A naturalized citizen of the South, Mal Stevens now makes his home in New England with his lovely wife and family, trying very hard not to work too much.

About JEBWizard Publishing

JEBWizard Publishing offers a hybrid approach to publishing. By taking a vested interest in the success of your book, we put our reputation on the line to create and market a quality publication. We offer a customized solution based on your individual project needs.

Our catalog of authors spans the spectrum of fiction, non-fiction, Young Adult, True Crime, Self-help, and Children's books.

Contact us for submission guidelines at

https://www.jebwizardpublishing.com

Info@jebwizardpublishing.com

Or in writing at

JEBWizard Publishing

37 Park Forest Rd.

Cranston, RI 02920

CPSIA information can be obtained
at www.ICGtesting.com
Printed in the USA
LVHW080526280421
685801LV00015B/1073